BELIEVE ME NOW

BELIEVE ME NOW

S.M. GOVETT

NEW YORK

Books should be disposed of and recycled according to local requirements. All paper materials used are FSC compliant.

This is a work of fiction. All of the names, characters, organizations, places and events portrayed in this novel are either products of the author's imagination or are used fictitiously. Any resemblance to real or actual events, locales, or persons, living or dead, is entirely coincidental.

Copyright © 2025 by Sarah Govett

All rights reserved.

Published in the United States by Crooked Lane Books, an imprint of The Quick Brown Fox & Company LLC.

Crooked Lane Books and its logo are trademarks of The Quick Brown Fox & Company LLC.

Library of Congress Catalog-in-Publication data available upon request.

ISBN (hardcover): 979-8-89242-020-4
ISBN (paperback): 979-8-89242-244-4
ISBN (ebook): 979-8-89242-021-1

Cover design by Lila Selle

Printed in the United States.

www.crookedlanebooks.com

Crooked Lane Books
34 West 27th St., 10th Floor
New York, NY 10001

First Edition: June 2025

The authorized representative in the EU for product safety and compliance is eucomply OÜ Pärnu mnt 139b-14, 11317 Tallinn, Estonia, hello@eucompliancepartner.com, +33757690241

10 9 8 7 6 5 4 3 2 1

For Noa, Alba and Ned

MONDAY, 18 MARCH

Natalie

Tiger stripes of sunlight stream in through the shutters. Is it morning already? Eyes squinting myopically towards the clock, I decipher the digits: 6.30 a.m. Dawn always comes earlier than you expect in the spring. Ryan's dressed in running gear. He puts a mug of tea down on the bedside table next to me and kisses my forehead. It's delicate. Tentative. Like I'm a Fabergé egg; to be appreciated and valued rather than held.

"I'll be back in a couple of hours," he says. "I'm going to try the longer woods loop with Steve. Might grab a coffee and talk shop after."

I smile my encouragement. He needs it. After all, men are just boys expecting praise from their mothers. I wonder, as I often do, what sort of mother I might have been . . .

As he leaves, Ryan pauses momentarily to glance at himself in the full-length mirror by our bedroom door. He's still in good shape, but the slight sag in his shoulders suggests disappointment at his reflection. Late thirties can be a cruel age. Your twenty-something self is still visible, yet chipped away at: hair starting to recede, muscles weakened, cheeks beginning their descent into jowls. It's like looking at a weathered limestone statue and imagining how magnificent it must have been when first unveiled. And Ryan had been pretty magnificent. The sort of handsome that makes you catch your breath and marvel at how very lucky you are to be with him. To be chosen.

Once I hear the front door close I step into the shower, tilting my head so the water pummels my face. After five minutes, I turn down the temperature dial and gasp as the water comes out cold. I force myself to stand there, shivering. And I begin to feel alive.

Dressed in jeans and a faded pink sweatshirt, I pad downstairs in slippers for my second tea of the day. It's a ritual, and rituals are encouraged. Assam in bed to cut through the brain fog of sleep and then Earl Grey with breakfast. It's softer. Soothing. I step round the paint can that's currently being used as the kitchen doorstop, flick on the kettle and open the larder. You can still smell the paint fumes coming off the door. Charlotte's Locks is the colour. Bright orange. A "bold" choice. I'm trying to take risks again. Paint colour wasn't perhaps the best place to start.

I pour myself a bowl of Alpen and sit on a bench at the table, choosing, as always, the side that faces the window. I like being able to see the street and, besides, the living area through the arch behind needs tidying. Mess always increases my anxiety. At the end of the table to my left sits the green upholstered chair that's never been sat in. We felt there should be a chair there. A "head" of the table. *Should*—that ever-present guider of decisions.

I glance through a plant catalogue as I eat, admiring obelisks embroidered with tendrils of summer clematis. I never thought I'd be a plant person. My mother was a plant person. She prided herself on knowing the Latin names of everything that grew in her garden, finding it easier to bestow love on flowers than on family, and I'd resolved never to be like her. But it's true what they say about finding peace in nature. Plants rebuild themselves every year, coming back stronger, more vibrant. There's a lot to be learned from plants.

I've found that days are most manageable when divided into segments. Segment one is showering, dressing and breakfast. Segment two is pre-coffee writing. My desk is in the small office off the living area that overlooks the garden. It's my favourite room in the house. The walls are a deep, smoky green and entering the space feels like stumbling upon a forest clearing. Cocooned yet not claustrophobic. I open up my laptop, my view framed by candelabras of magnolia blossom. The left-hand border of the garden is my favourite:

semi-formal, edged with ilex and filled with roses. Gertrude Jeykll. Olivia Rose. Silas Marner. A painter's palette of pink hues and intoxicating scent. They're like friends to me. I started the spring prune last week and need to find time to finish the last few shrubs soon, as new foliage is already starting to emerge. Red, soon to fade to green. Reaching into the desk drawer for a Post-it note, I scribble on to the square: *prune roses*. I stick it to the bookshelf to the left of my desk. A neon reminder.

I have an article to finish for *Property Law Monthly* on the ownership of graffiti and welcome the feeling of immersion as I begin to concentrate. What happens if someone defaces a Banksy? It's interesting. But then I find most of the articles I'm commissioned to write interesting. Dry and impenetrable to many, law, with its statutes and labyrinth of precedents, has always held a fascination for me.

My phone rings just as I enter an almost meditative state of focus and I pick it up with an irritated sigh. Then I see who's calling. Rachel. The sigh turns into a smile.

"What's up?"

"Is this a good time?" Rachel asks. "I know I'm interrupting segment two."

I laugh. Some people don't know how to act around me. They tiptoe. They don't joke. But Rachel's always known how to make me laugh. Ever since we first met at law school. She might now have consciously ironed out all remaining traces of her Midlands accent, but the girl beneath hasn't changed. My surrogate sister. Every only child needs one.

"For you, it's always a good time."

Rachel explains that her firm's property team is looking for a professional support lawyer. Four days a week. Immediate start.

"You'd be the perfect fit, Nat."

I think of the job security. The salary. And the work would be interesting. Research-based rather than transactional. I want to speak but my mouth goes dry.

"Nat?"

"Could I work from home?" I ask, my heart already starting to race.

A pause. She'd been expecting this.

"Mainly, but you'd need to be in occasionally for the training element. No more than one or two days a week at most."

My fingers start to tingle. I can't go back to an office. It's impossible. Rachel should know that.

"It's all open-plan," she coaxes. "At least think about it, Nat, OK? Promise me you'll think about it. It'd be good for you."

I force a nod, forgetting that she can't see me.

"You're nodding, aren't you?"

"Yes," I say, smiling.

"And don't let Ryan talk you out of it," she adds. "You're stronger than he thinks you are." I ignore her. Ryan's the one thorn in our friendship. It used to really bother me that my two favourite people don't get on, but now I just don't engage.

"See you tomorrow," I say, hanging up.

The call has unsettled me. I can't get back into the article so, even though it's not yet ten, I fast-forward my timetable to segment three: my morning coffee break. I've just put the kettle on and selected the mug I want—the small grey one with the embossed bee detail—when there's a ring at the front door. I'm not expecting anything. Surprised, I head into the hall, turning off the star-shaped brass lantern that hangs from a hook in the ceiling there. Wasting energy is a bugbear of mine. I open the door to find Matt, our postman, standing there, in shorts in spite of the cold, wearing a smile and enveloped in the faint odour of weed. The contentment that comes with always being a little bit high. He hands me a small parcel balanced on top of a stack of envelopes.

I thank him and head back inside. The parcel's for Ryan. There's a "Cyclista" stamp on the back. No doubt something expensive for his new bike that he didn't want to tell me about. I stopped regularly checking our joint account after we had a particularly heated argument over one of his purchases. A £750 bike bag. Seven hundred and fifty pounds for a bike bag. He said he saves so much money cycling into work. Did I know how much a season ticket costs? The bag was even suitable for triathlons. I said he doesn't do triathlons. He said he might start.

I put the parcel down on the console table a little too forcefully then leaf through the envelopes. A phone bill . . . a magazine about specialist reading lamps—I'm shortsighted, not sixty . . . a fundraising circular . . . Then I reach the fourth envelope. It's an unusual size—A5, white, my name and address typed on a label stuck perfectly symmetrically to the front. My stomach rises, but I tell myself I'm being stupid. A Pavlovian response, nothing more. That was in the past.

A different house.

A different time.

I rip across the top and pull out the letter.

The paper is pale cream and heavy. Expensive. My heart-rate increases.

It's folded simply in two. I take a deep breath and start to open it, telling myself it'll be nothing. A letter from an insurer or estate agent. Someone using expensive paper to impress a potential client and solicit business.

Then I glimpse inside.

Instantly, my hands start to tremble and the world slows down.

Stuck on the paper are crudely cut-out letters arranged into words.

My eyes run across the page and the letters deliver their message.

LIAR.

WHORE.

My heartbeat accelerates and reverberates in my ears.

I can't believe it.

It's happening again.

After all these years, it's happening again.

I start shaking all over. Uncontrollably. I drop the letter and back away towards the kitchen. I can't touch it. I don't want to be near it.

I want to scream, to call for Ryan, to call for anyone, but the words lodge in my throat like glass shards.

Colours intensify, the hall rug spinning in a kaleidoscopic pattern of greys and blues as my vision pixellates.

Then, blackness.

Stratton

Someone's taken the last tea bag. It shouldn't be a big deal, but it is. There's a way we do things here. And one of those things is if you open the tin and it's down to the last fucking tea bag, you go out, buy yourself a packet of PG Tips and restock. I can feel my mood drop even further. I really need a caffeine hit if I'm going to get through the morning, but there's no bloody tea and the only coffee's instant. I don't go for poncy bread or loose-leaf tea or anything like that, but I need my coffee real and not some dissolve-in-the-cup crap. Mark used to say I must have some Italian in me. Mark used to say a lot of shit.

I need to vent so I kick the sink cupboard. Sandra, who's passing, laughs, but then remembers what day it is and shoots me a look of apology.

"Stratton's in a shit mood," Dev whispers to Sandra, mockscared. Sandra nudges him and flashes him a frown. It's not Dev's fault. He's new to our Murder Investigation Team. Only just made detective constable. He's one of the younger breed of coppers—like Sandra, he wants us to call him by his first name. Thinks the surname thing is archaic. He doesn't get that it's a form of affection as well as formality. He also doesn't know us all properly yet. Which means he doesn't know the significance of today. He probably also swiped the last tea bag. Dickhead.

I manage to calm myself down, make myself a pepper-mint tea—a pointless drink if there ever was one—no surprise that tin's still full—and then head to my desk. Cooper squeezes my arm as I skirt his desk, and it helps. We're a good team here. Got each other's backs.

Reynolds looks up from the opposite desk as I pull out my chair and switch on the monitor. The light from the LED ceiling spots bounces off the top of his smoothly shaved head, giving him the echoes of a halo as he adjusts his blackframed glasses. He started shaving it a couple of years ago. He'd gone so receding he was starting to look slightly Friar Tuck. He thinks he looks younger with it all off. He's probably right.

"You OK?" he asks. I don't want to meet his eye so I look down instead. A cup with the dregs of two-day-old tea sits at the edge of my desk. The top's started to congeal. I broke my one-cup-only rule. If you stick to one cup you have to rinse it between uses and it never gets to this stage.

"Stratton?"

"Sure," I reply. Reynolds nods. He doesn't believe me, but he knows to leave it at that. Then, in a moment of weakness, I allow myself a glance at the photo Blu-tacked to the bottom of my monitor and I can't keep it together any more. It's of Karen and me. Me thirteen, Karen sixteen, though she looks a lot older. There's a knowingness to her eyes and the tilt of her jaw. She stares out of the photo, from under a self-cut block fringe, challenging the world. There's a tattoo of a butterfly on her right shoulder. Mum nearly killed her when she got it done. She stormed down the tattoo parlour and yelled at them. "Mutilating a minor", she called it. Mum could put the fear of God in people back then. I never thought I'd miss her yelling. Next to Karen I look small, thin and bookish. I gaze up at her in awe. My big sister. She was everything I wasn't. Everything I wanted to be. She'd be forty-six today. Fuck.

My phone vibrates. It's a text. Angie from Mum's home. She wants to have a quick chat. Mum's had a bit of a "dip". "Dip" is nursing-home code for pissed herself or bit a nurse or attacked another resident or fell down the stairs. Mum always "dips" on Karen's birthday. She doesn't know what day of the week it is. What year it is, even. But some things are hard-wired, I guess. They mess you up even when you're not aware of anything else.

I imagine Mum, sat, hunched over, in the home, staring out the window. Eyes open but the lights out. They say burying your kid is the worst thing that can happen to a parent. That's bollocks. Not knowing what on earth happened to your kid is worse. Not knowing if they're still alive or not. Not being taken seriously when you say they didn't just leave home. Just because you don't speak with the right accent. Just because you live in the wrong block of flats, where most take off at sixteen anyway. At least if your kid dies, you've got something to bury. A chance to move on.

It was Mum who first said I should be a cop. It was two weeks after Karen disappeared, and she hadn't given up, not yet. She was angry. A pure, distilled rage. I thought it was a joke at first—Mum hated coppers. But she placed her hands on my shoulders, squeezed a little too hard, and then looked me straight in the eye. "No one ever changed anything from the outside. If you want a job done properly, do it yourself," she said. Then, a few days later, she marched me down the station to ask about the enrolment requirements. The sarge on duty laughed at us, and that sealed it. No one was going to tell me I couldn't do something. I joined aged seventeen to try and find Karen. I stayed to find all the others. To give them justice. Victims need someone in their corner. They can't protect themselves.

Especially if they're dead.

I stand to find somewhere quiet to call Angie back when Cooper's voice booms across the room.

"Briefing room now," he says. "New case just in."

I quickly text Angie that I'll call later. She'll be annoyed, but she knows what my job's like.

I take a couple of deep breaths, then head to the meeting room with everyone else. Dev's already there, notepad out, grey trousers pressed and hair neatly coiffed, like he's some bloody estate agent, not a copper. New recruits are always the keenest.

DCI Parker enters last and stands at the front, thumbs hooked through his belt strap. He thinks it makes his shoulders look broader, makes him look more authoritative, the idiot. He admitted it to me once—back when we were Helen and Mark rather than DI Stratton and DCI Parker. Back when he was going to leave his wife.

He throws me a look of sympathy—he more than anyone knows how this day messes with my head—but I refuse to acknowledge it. He doesn't get to do that any more. Offer support. Pretend he cares. He sees himself as a moral man. I think that's the main reason he stayed with Sally. He couldn't be the good guy if he was also the guy who walked out on his wife and kids. Screwing someone else he could somehow deal with. Just not the fall-out. Weak bastard.

Parker opens the folder he always brings to meetings and clears his throat. The bulb in the LED directly above his head flickers and temporarily distracts him. His eyes bulge a little as he looks up to take it in. It's not a good look. They're already slightly too big for his face. He's like a poor man's James Nesbitt. Same round face, large eyes, just less of the charm and none of the accent.

"A body has been found at the allotments behind the Academy. It was called in ten minutes ago. A Mr. Peter Harper—an allotment holder—discovered the body and identified it to be that of another allotment holder—a Mr. Brian Benton, thought to be in his seventies. An attending officer is already at the scene and a suspect has been apprehended on site. We're to take over. Reynolds, you're lead."

Reynolds runs a hand over the top of his smooth head in frustration.

"I'm still on the Williams case," he says. "Can someone else take this one?"

Parker looks round the room. I'm here. I'm sitting right in front of you, you prick.

"Stratton?" he says finally.

Natalie

" ... Nat? ... Nat?"

I'm being shaken. I'm damp. My side and my feet. Where the hell am I?

"Natalie?"

A voice. Ryan's voice.

Then birdsong. A breeze.

Above me a criss-cross lattice of branches dips in and out of focus.

"What are you doing out here?" His voice is gentler now. My eyes readjust and I see him, crouched down next to me, his forehead creased with concern.

My surroundings begin to make sense. I'm towards the bottom of the garden. By the last of the roses and under the old apple tree. The grass is wet with dew. It's soaked into my clothes and through my slippers. I'm lying on my side, facing the roses and the first of the tulips. I have no memory of leaving the hall. None at all.

"Nat?" Ryan calls me back to him.

I look at him and the creases deepen.

"Can you stand?" he asks.

I say that I don't know. It's only when he tries to help me up that I realize there's something in my hand. My pruning secateurs—the sharp yellow ones. I glance again to the left and my breath catches. The final rose bushes have been cut back—a third of the previous season's growth shorn. The trimmed stems and old leaves sit in an old plastic plant pot on the soil next to them. Fighting back waves of fear, I search my brain. Nothing. No memories. I was in the hall. Then I was here. I feel cold inside. It's like a small rodent is burying into my stomach.

I can't go back.

I'm better. I have my segments. I avoid triggers. I fixed myself.

I thought I'd fixed myself.

Wordlessly, I put down the secateurs and, very slowly, Ryan lifts me to standing, pausing every few seconds to check that he's not hurting me. I wince as I put my weight on my right leg; I've hurt my knee, but the pain is bearable. A bruise rather than anything more serious. My right arm is sensitive too, and I suppress a whimper as Ryan tries to steady me with it. I must have fallen on that side. Luckily, I'm left-handed. Focus on the small things.

Once I'm upright, Ryan picks me up ever so gently and carries me inside.

He lays me on the sofa and makes us both a cup of tea. I can tell questions are eating away at him, but he senses I need time before I can talk and he's trying to give it to me. He knows me. We know each other. We have, right from the moment we met. A meeting of minds, a symbiosis of sorts. I could ask him the most vaguely worded question and he'd know what I meant. Did you read it? Did you see it? Did you get it? And that would be enough. Whether "it" was an article in the paper, a flock of starlings or a packet of dishwasher tablets we needed to pick up. He'd understand. It's still there, the connection. Faded but present.

Only when the tea is steaming next to me does he ask again.

"What happened?"

I focus on my breathing. Inhale. Exhale. Inhale.

"There was another letter."

Ryan freezes and the colour drains from his face. "You mean . . ."

"Yes."

A muscle starts pulsing in his jaw. Fear and anger fighting for dominance.

"But it's been nearly ten years."

I nod.

"There's still a letter."

"Where is it?"

"In the hall."

Ryan storms into the hall and returns carrying the piece of paper. He's bristling with rage now. Anger's conquered fear. He examines the letter, turning it over, searching for clues.

"It's the same, isn't it?"

I nod. Everything is the same. The way the letters have been cut out in rough squares. How they've been stuck on at slight angles. The mix of capitals and lower case. Some from newspapers, some from glossy magazines. All in black.

Everything's the same.

Ryan slams the letter down on the table. "I'm calling the police."

"No," I say quietly. I can't face the police. Not now. I don't want them here. I don't want their questions. Their accusations dressed up as sympathy. *If you can just help us clarify . . . What we're having trouble understanding . . .* Every interaction with them has been the same. The smirk on the officer's face when I first reported the rape. His questions. *What was I wearing? Had I been drinking?* The boredom of another officer when I told him about the first set of letters and my fears I was being followed.

"They won't do anything. They didn't do anything last time."

"They put a restraining order on her," Ryan snaps back. "The letters stopped after that. I'll make the call." Ryan steps towards the landline phone that sits on the windowsill.

"No, Ryan!" My voice comes out louder and harsher than intended and he looks taken aback by my anger, but at least he puts the phone down.

He starts pacing the room. Up, down. Up, down. Taking out his aggression on the painted floorboards. Finally, he's calmed himself sufficiently and perches on the arm of the sofa next to me. It sinks under his weight. He takes my hand in his and, when he next speaks, his tone takes on a pleading quality.

"We should make an appointment with Dr. Browning."

I sigh. Dr. Browning again. We've had this conversation before.

"No," I say quietly. Ryan first suggested Dr. Browning a year ago. A friend of his from work had been to him with his wife. They'd been going through a "rough patch". He'd "worked wonders" for them. In recent months Ryan had stopped mentioning him. I thought the subject was closed. I thought he'd agreed that we'd find our own way back to how we were. That we didn't need a stranger to guide us. Force us. After all, a relationship is like a magic trick, a conjuring. You need to believe in the magic for it to work. Talking through the mechanisms, dissecting it, would be like the magician exposing the wires. Revealing the place he'd hidden the rabbit. It would break the spell and destroy everything that was special in the first place. I need Ryan. I need our marriage. I need to believe in us.

"I told you. Everyone I know who goes to couples therapy gets divorced."

"Not for couples therapy," Ryan says quickly. "Just for you." He runs his hands through his hair so that it stands up in tufts, elongating his forehead. "Fuck, Nat, you blacked out again. We can't ignore this. If it's returning, you need to speak to someone."

"I talked to someone the first time. It didn't help."

"The blackouts stopped, didn't they?" He throws up his arms in a caricature of frustration. I don't want to fight him on this. I need to know he's on my side.

"The letters stopped," I say, forcing my voice to stay neutral. "We moved house. I developed a way to cope. You helped. Rachel helped. Real people. People I trust. People I *love*. Not someone I'm paying to care. A stranger who wants to comb through every painful memory. Expose it. Dissect it. *How did it make you feel, Natalie? How did it make you feel?*" I realize I'm shouting, but I can't stop. Until I do. And then suddenly I'm crying. "I relived what happened weekly, Ryan. I sat opposite Dr. Thomas and relived what happened to me weekly for a whole year!"

Ryan wraps his hand round mine. Swallows it.

"Dr Browning might have different strategies."

Strategies. Tactics. Such a male approach to see everything in terms of war. I don't want to see Dr. Browning. I don't want to see anyone.

But Ryan's staring at me, his green-blue eyes burrowing into mine. They're the colour of the sea—they're eyes you can drown in. I relent. Maybe he's right. I can't go back to how I was before. I can't start regularly losing time again. And Ryan needs this. He needs to be able to help me.

"I'll go and see Dr. Browning," I say, and a weight seems to fall from his shoulders. He has provided a solution. He has acted.

"Good," he says. "That's really good, Nat. I'll make an appointment for tomorrow or whenever he can fit you in."

He puts his arms around me and I instinctively burrow in. I read an article once about the subconscious importance of smell to humans. And Ryan smells of home. He's my home. My rock. My constant. I lift my chin and his lips brush mine.

"I need to go into work in a minute, is that OK?" he says. "I hate to abandon you. Are you going to be all right here? I could try and move the meeting, if you'd like?"

I want to ask him to stay. To skip the meeting and sit here with me instead. To act as guard dog. Or exorcist. The house feels tainted now. Defiled. I want to ask him to stay here until it feels safe again. But I can't. Ryan's pitching a big new marketing campaign to a potential client at lunchtime. It has to be him; there's no one else who knows the material as well. Plus, they haven't promoted anyone for a while and Ryan's boss has been making encouraging comments. Now is not the time for him to look like he's shirking. Now is not the time for him to have a weak wife.

"No, go. I'll be fine," I say, pasting on my most convincing smile.

"You sure?"

"Absolutely."

Ryan smiles back, clearly relieved. I don't think he completely believes me, but I've been convincing enough to allow him to pretend to himself that he does. He goes to grab his coat.

The letter is still sat on the table. A white flag. Demanding rather than offering surrender.

"Ryan," I call, fighting the tremor in my voice.

He comes running back in.

"Yes?"

"Please can you get rid of the letter?"

Ryan picks it up, flustered. "Sorry, I shouldn't have left it in here. I wasn't thinking."

"Burn it."

"No, but I'll put it away. It's evidence, Nat. If there's another one, we're going to the police. No debate. OK?"

"OK," I reply.

Another one.

I don't want to think about it, but I know he's right.

She's still out there.

There'll be another one.

It's only a matter of time.

Stratton

Parker finishes the briefing and I tell Dev to come with me in my car. Sandra will take her own.

Parker corners me as I prepare to leave.

"A quick word, please, Inspector."

Clenching my teeth, I follow him into his office. I can feel everyone's eyes on my back. Our affair/thing/whatever you want to call it was supposed to be secret, but nothing's ever secret when you're part of a Murder Investigation Team, working all hours and living in each other's pockets.

I smile grimly at the photo of him with his wife and two boys that has pride of place on his wall. It's staged. Bleached-out background, coordinated clothes, brushed hair and fixed smiles. Taken by some fancy photographer in a studio and then displayed for all to see. The perfect, happy family. He never took it down. Even when he was fucking me every other night. It still sat there. A framed lie.

Parker shuts the door and offers me a seat. I remain standing.

"Helen, if this is too much, if you need to take today off, I understand."

Don't fucking *Helen* me at work.

"I'm fine, thank you, DCI Parker."

He flinches at the formality.

"This case should be very much join-up-the-dots, or I wouldn't have given it to you."

"Thanks for the vote of confidence," I snap back.

"That's not what I meant and you know it."

He sounds hurt, but I don't have time for his feelings.

"Is that all?" I ask curtly.

"Sure. But if you need anything, come to me."

He reaches out a hand towards me with a half-smile. His eyes offer more. God, it's so tempting. It'd be so easy. Just to give in like that. I want him to hold me. I want him to squeeze the pain away . . . No, I can't let him in again. He's the past. It's got to stay that way. I rebuild the barrier.

"Helen . . ."

I step back towards the door.

But we lock eyes.

"If you really want to help me," I say, fighting to keep my voice even, "bury me in work. Give me cases. Proper cases. Then I can't think about anything else."

* * *

Fifteen minutes later we're parking up at the allotments. The attending officer comes to meet us and introduces himself—Officer Stephens. He's quietly spoken and serious with slightly crossed eyes, so it's hard to tell exactly what he's looking at. We glove up, sign in the murder book then push past the police tape that ineffectually bars the entrance. A longlegged person could just step over the waist-height latch gate. Luckily, word hasn't spread yet, so the usual gaggle of reporters and rubberneckers hasn't had time to gather.

Stephens asks if we'd like to see the body first or to speak to the suspect, who's sitting, cuffed and quiet, in the back of his car. I tell him I want to see the vic.

The body lies on a path towards the rear of the allotments. A rotting shed hides it from view from the road, which explains the lack of passing interest. An elderly male, thin, balding, is splayed on his back next to a well-tended bed of what looks like cabbage. I don't get the point of allotments. Spending time at a ten-by-ten-metre patch of soil when you've got the whole open space of Richmond Park within easy walking distance. Maybe it's the desire to own land. To farm. Maybe it's genetically hard-wired into us. In the same way that hunting and killing is.

The vic's skin already has a greyish-blue colour. Stephens informs me that Forensics are on their way, but there's not really that much I need them to tell me. It's all pretty self-explanatory. A long section of dark-green hosepipe has been wrapped around the old man's neck and his tongue is swollen and protruding. The smell lets me know he's soiled himself before death.

I note down "death by strangulation".

Next to the allotment sits an old sleeping bag and a half-full plastic bag.

Stephens follows my gaze.

"Belongs to the suspect," he says. "He got quite agitated when I tried to look inside."

Dev bounces around at my heels like an overkeen puppy, asking for instructions.

"Look inside the bag," I say.

He does as I say, first rolling up his sleeves with a grimace. Heaven forbid he gets something on his nice new shirt. His energy dips as he pulls out a bundle of stained clothing, a mug and half a packet of Digestives.

Next I tell him to search the dead man's pockets for confirmation of identification. Dev extracts a battered leather wallet. Inside there's two twenty-pound notes, a bank card and a driving licence. Brian Benton. Seventy-one years old. Lives on Observatory Road. Tucked behind the driving licence is a faded photo of a woman in her forties, smiling. His wife probably, taken when she was a lot younger. The clothing is too old-fashioned for it to be his daughter.

I call Sandra to give her the address and wish her luck. I almost hope the wife predeceased him. That the photo is a keepsake from happier days. Breaking something like this to a spouse is never easy. Sandra is an amazing family liaison officer, she really has a gift for it, but it still takes its toll.

Hovering at the back of the allotments is the man, Harper, who discovered the body. He's in his forties, overweight, his round head stuck on top of his body like a snowman, with no allowance for a neck. His right hand is trembling; he's still shaken by his discovery.

He recounts what he saw. He points towards what looks like a bare patch at the back of the allotments with some sticks stood in it—apparently his. Another non-gardener, it seems. He'd just arrived to check on his seedlings when he noticed the body. He knew the deceased by sight and name, but not well. They'd exchanged pleasantries about plants in the past. Nothing more. He'd known something was wrong as Mr. Benton was lying on the ground. Well done, Sherlock. There was a man sitting next to the body, hands still on the hosepipe. Mr. Benton wasn't moving and appeared to be dead. Harper called 999.

"Did the man holding the hosepipe say anything?" I ask.

"He was talking to himself," Harper replies. "Over and over. And rocking slightly."

"And have you seen this man before?"

"No . . . Well, not here. I think I saw him on the high street once. Sitting outside the Costa. It might have been him. Shouting at passers-by. Getting quite angry."

I thank him, and Stephens steers me towards the car and the suspect. The suspect doesn't make eye contact and refuses to talk to us. He twitches slightly. I tell him that we're going to reach into his pocket to look for some ID. He tries to bite me as I do so, but Stephens and Dev grab an arm each and restrain him. You can get some nasty shit from bites.

There's a card in his pocket, so we have a name to run through the system. Stephens takes the suspect in and I leave Dev to wait for Forensics. I put the call in to social services and the community health workers.

The responses I get are sad but expected. A history of mental illness and erratic behaviour. He was on the waiting list for counselling. He'd left the shelter he was meant to be staying at. He should have been on someone's radar but wasn't. Same old, same old. The government underfunds and we clean up the mess.

Detective work is nothing like it is on TV. Chances are, the most obvious suspect is the person who did it. They might not always be sitting next to the body, but they're there. Nearby. It's just a question of working out who, then why. Of seeing the true personality underneath.

Natalie

The house has never seemed emptier. I'm jumpy. Nerves on edge. I swallow a couple of arnica to reduce the bruising from the fall and return to my laptop and try to finish the article, but the words don't come. I stare at the keys, trying to will them into submission, but still nothing. Graffiti suddenly seems so trivial. I don't care who owns it. Who defaces it. What the consequences are. Graffiti doesn't hurt people. It doesn't destroy lives. The yellow Post-it note is still there on the bookshelf, mocking me. In a flash of anger I rip it off, scrunch it up and deposit it in the bin under the desk.

I try completing mundane tasks. Anything small to focus on. I wash up the blender Ryan left on the side. He always makes a protein shake after a run. He also always says he'll wash up afterwards, but he never remembers and the powder sticks to the glass like glue if you don't rinse it off quick enough. You've got to wonder what it does to your insides. Ryan swears by them, but I won't touch them. There's that bitter taste that neither cocoa powder nor banana nor blueberries can ever properly disguise.

Disguise. Hide. Letters. Her . . .

My mind starts on a chain of free association and panic builds.

I leaf through the plant catalogue again, seeking solace in its pages. It doesn't come. The late-flowering chrysanthemums I was so interested in yesterday now seem cheap and flashy.

The colours begin to swim and the pixels threaten to return, but I can't let them.

I pick up my phone and try Rachel. It goes to voicemail.

I put the phone back down then curl up in a foetal ball on the sofa, arms wrapped around one of the velvet scatter cushions. My spine's curved, essential organs protected. But she's not targeting my organs. It's my mind she's coming for.

I want Ryan home. I no longer care about his pitch. His potential promotion.

I dial his mobile. Voicemail again.

The tingling is starting.

I call his office number.

"Ryan Campbell's office."

A young woman answers. It's not a voice I recognize. There's a lilt to it. A freshness. Someone who hasn't worked long enough for the office to have lost its sheen.

"Is Ryan there?" I ask, caught slightly off guard.

"Yes, who shall I say is calling?" The words are over-enunciated. I was right. She hasn't been saying them very long.

"Nat . . . Natalie . . . his wife."

". . . Oh . . . Sure." The composure's gone. Her training seems to have only covered the initial opener. Then she recovers. "I'll just fetch him for you, Mrs. Campbell." Perfectly professional again. I was being unfair.

There's a long pause and then Ryan answers.

"Nat?"

I can tell he's frazzled as soon as he speaks. His voice is tight. I can picture him: sleeves rolled up, top button undone and tie loosened in an attempt to increase airflow. To stop that feeling of being caged. I regret calling.

"I just wanted to hear your voice."

"Right. Of course. Are you OK? I'm sorry—I'm just in the middle of something . . ."

My eyes travel to the end of the sofa and then up to the side table. There's a photo there of us on our first holiday together in Florence fourteen years ago, the Ponte Vecchio in the background. Ryan used his best faltering Italian to cajole a passer-by into taking it. We're not looking at the camera though. We're staring into each other's eyes. We're each other's whole world.

". . . I'm fine," I say.

"Maybe get out of the house. You shouldn't be alone."

I don't say anything.

"Is there someone who can come round?"

No. The only other person I've told about my losing time is Rachel. And Rachel's not answering her phone.

"I'll be home as soon as I can, Nat. Go and sit in a café till then. Somewhere busy."

"But—"

"It'll distract you. Go to the new one on the corner. We've been talking about trying it."

Rachel's wrong. Ryan thinks I'm stronger than I am. He pushes me rather than holds me back.

* * *

I sit in the café at the bottom of the road till five, positioning myself at the small marble-topped table in the bay window. The owner keeps looking at me. He wants me to move on. I haven't eaten, my stomach too tight for food, so I'm occupying his prime piece of real estate just to drink herbal tea. But he can't say anything, can't be seen to be harassing a woman on her own. So he just looks, and every half-hour pointedly asks if I'd like to order anything else.

It's started to rain and I stare out the window, the raindrops smudging faces. Is she out there? One of the blurred people? The figure in front of the flower shop opposite? The woman who's tying her shoe by the bus stop? She'd be in her late fifties now. Would I even recognize her? Ten years can ravage a face.

Ryan picks me up on his way home. I see him before he sees me. He's walking up the street, face beaming under his black umbrella. It's been a while since I've seen him this happy. Today's gone well for him. His smile dims as he sees me through the window then rearranges itself into an expression of concern. His entrance is awkward. He struggles to fold his umbrella and a protruding spoke gets caught in the door. A trail of water follows him in and I can sense the owner's disapproval intensify.

"Are you OK?" he asks as he puts the umbrella down and reaches towards me. I burrow into his shoulder by way of answer, needing contact rather than words, then pull away.

"How did it go?" I ask, acting the part of supportive wife.

Ryan smiles. "The client loved it. It's too soon for a decision, but Paul was very positive."

"I'm so pleased," I say.

Ryan looks down and fiddles with his cuffs. It's his tell when he's nervous. I hadn't realized quite how important this promotion was for him. Maybe more's riding on it than he's let on.

Stratton

Back at the station, there's nothing to do but wait till the suspect's legal rep arrives. I doubt I'll get to question him at all. It'll probably just be a case of a psychiatric referral and a commitment hearing.

The building suddenly feels claustrophobic so I head out on to the smokers' balcony and shut the sliding door behind me. I quit smoking just over three years ago, along with Reynolds and Sandra, the other smokers on the team. Sandra's mum had been diagnosed with lung cancer. It was the wake-up call we needed and we made a pact and forced ourselves through it. Splitting Nicorette packets, holding and munching on carrot sticks, the works. As a result, the smokers' balcony now sits empty so it's a good place to go for some headspace.

Below, the traffic of the South Circular throbs and belches out fumes. I can as good as taste the nitrites in the air. Probably worse than bloody cigarette smoke. Ironically, it's got worse since the ULEZ zone. All the old cars are forced out of the city and on to the ring roads. There's a primary school a hundred odd metres up from us. It'd be a miracle if all the kids there don't develop asthma.

I try Angie. It rings and rings and I'm just about to hang up when someone eventually picks up. There's another delay as they fetch her from down the corridor.

"Hi, Helen, thanks for calling back."

Angie's voice is warm and rolling. She's my favourite of the carers there.

"How is she?"

"Not great . . . She bit a nurse. She's confused. She keeps asking for Karen."

Fuck.

"I'll be round after work," I say. "I'll come straight from the station."

"Thanks, Helen. It might help."

I should visit more. It's hard with my schedule. The hours don't allow for much in the way of anything else. But I also know I use the job as an excuse.

There's another briefing late afternoon. Everyone's mood is low. Like the weather. Grey. Damp. Maybe it's just caffeine withdrawal.

I fill everyone in on the Benton case, not that there's much to tell. Sandra's eyes are red-rimmed. The wife took it as badly as you'd expect. Sandra said she clung to her. She didn't let go until her daughter arrived, and then Sandra had to break the news a second time.

There's little in the way of other case updates to go over. Reynolds has a key suspect on the Williams case but is awaiting a report from Forensics. Parker waits till he's finished then calls Cooper to the front. Cooper hates attention so his face flushes as red as his hair. I'm going to miss him. We all are. Smart, capable, honest, a good detective through and through. He came from a posh background, could have done anything with his life, but he chose to be a copper. He hadn't lost anyone, been hurt, abused, none of that. He just wanted to make a difference.

That's what pisses me off most when there's so much crap in the papers about bad cops. Sure, there're some. The cop who turned up on our doorstep when Karen went missing was a lazy, patronizing arsehole. He didn't believe me. He looked at Mum like she was scum. If he'd tried harder, sought out and chased down leads, I'd be having a glass or two with Karen down the pub tonight, not wondering yet again where the hell she was and if she was still alive. Fuck. Don't cry. Don't fucking cry. But there're good cops too. Except the papers don't go out of their way to find them. They forget about those ones. And if they keep slagging off the force, then no one but dickheads will want to join.

"As you all know," Parker begins, "on Wednesday we have to say goodbye to DS Cooper. A dedicated and invaluable member of the team, he'll be sorely missed. Our loss is Newcastle's gain. They'd better appreciate you, or we'll be dragging you back."

Everyone laughs. Parker's popular. He's a good leader. Just a lousy human being.

"Whoop whoop," yells Sandra, and Reynolds punches Cooper in the arm. Cooper looks even more embarrassed now and his freckles seem to glow.

"He may be irreplaceable, but replace him we must," continues Parker. "Tomorrow, a new detective will be joining us. DS Hugh Bradley is coming from our colleagues in Kensal Rise, where he's been for just over a year."

"Why so short?" asks Reynolds, beating me to it. Most detectives stay in a team for at least two years. A one-year stint doesn't bode well.

"He's being fast-tracked," replies Parker.

A groan goes up. Fuck. Just what we need. Some head-up-their-arse fast-track kid. Someone with a degree in law or criminology or some such bollocks who thinks that makes them better able to catch murderers than someone who's worked the streets, worked the cases. Someone destined for leadership that they're shunting round the departments so they see how best to rule over us.

"Bradley will be partnering with DI Stratton"—fuck—"so he'll be with a safe pair of hands."

Dev and Sandra laugh.

Reynolds leans over to me. "Play nice. He might be OK."

Bollocks.

The fast-trackers are never OK.

Natalie

At night the dream returns.

I'm twenty-six. My hair's longer, my body tauter. I'm wearing a grey fitted dress and heels, hair down. I'm at the office, tasked with inserting the final changes into the Greensdale shopping mall contract. Gavin Scott, the senior partner in our property department, chose me, and I feel special. Noticed. The late hours, the all-nighters, vindicated. It's late, nearly midnight, the deal only just signed off after weeks of fraught negotiations. The rest of the floor is empty. The lighting has switched to motion-detector setting and every few minutes I have to flail my arms around to keep them from going out. There's a noise to my right and I look up to see Gavin walking towards me, a bottle and two glasses in his hand. He's fifty, but looks good for it; his hair is still thick, his navy suit well cut and expensive. He's tall, broad and his shoulders roll when he walks. He used to play rugby for the county. He tells everyone. It's what he's most proud of. Something about the way he looks at me as he approaches makes my back straighten, and there's a slight tightness in my shoulders. But I tell myself I'm being ridiculous. He's always been slightly tactile with everyone, an arm touch here, a slight invasion of body space there, but he's popular, well liked. He's just Gavin. No one takes it seriously. He's from a different generation. It's put down to age and to the entitlement that comes with being an equity partner.

He stops by my desk.

"Thought we should celebrate," he says, holding up the bottle. It's champagne. He doesn't break eye contact.

I smile. It's expected of me.

"Shouldn't we wait for the rest of the team?" I ask. "They're tucked up in bed—skivers, the lot of them," he jokes. His smile reveals rows of perfectly white, capped teeth. He had them done at Christmas. Close up, it gives him a lupine quality.

The lights go out, as we haven't moved, and I laugh at the awkwardness of the situation. He joins in, doing an exaggerated arm wave.

"Come on," he says, hand on my elbow. "Let's drink in my office. The lights at least stay on in there."

I don't want to go, but there is no reason to refuse. If I'm to succeed here, I need a good appraisal from him. A drink after a deal is customary. Part of the culture here. I don't want to seem churlish or prim.

He leads me into his office and shuts the door.

Instead of turning on the main overhead light he flicks on the side lighting and a lamp on the desk emits a warm amber glow.

"Easier on the eyes at this time of night, don't you think?" The glasses clink as he puts them down on his desk, then there's a pop from the cork as he opens the champagne. The label looks expensive. He fills the glasses generously and hands one to me. The dainty stem looks almost absurd in his huge hand.

"To Greensdale being signed off," he toasts. "To a dream team. P4, we salute you, although most of you are lazy buggers and already in bed . . ." I join in with an obligatory laugh. "And to Natalie, a very talented and very . . . beautiful solicitor." The tension in my shoulders increases and spreads to my jaw. He puts his glass down and takes mine off me. I don't protest. I don't know why.

I switch from participant to bystander. *Run, now.* I try to scream at myself. *Run.* But I don't. I can't. My eyes dart round the room.

He stands in front of me, his back towards the door. I'm trapped between him and the desk.

"I should probably be heading back soon," I say, forcing my voice to remain neutral. "Ryan will be starting to worry."

Gavin doesn't say anything. His eyes have taken on a hooded and hungry quality and he steps forward.

"You don't have to pretend any more. There's no one else around."

I swallow, my mouth suddenly dry.

"I really need to go."

"I've seen the way you look at me. The way you dress to make me notice you."

I try to step round him and he grabs my shoulders and forces me back towards the desk.

"You wanted to stay late. You knew it would just be the two of us."

"No—"

"We both know you want it."

He lifts me on to the desk and pushes up my dress.

I push at him with my hands, but he's too strong for me. He takes them both in one of his and he has me pinned.

I can't move. I cry out, but there's no one to hear me.

He rips my tights.

I twist and bite his arm.

He doesn't stop.

I bite harder.

He doesn't stop.

I taste blood.

He doesn't stop.

I start to come out of the dream. To surface.

I'm soaked in sweat and I'm shouting something. I don't even know what. Ryan's awake too and he opens his arms to comfort me but I flinch away. He tries to disguise the hurt in his eyes. But I don't want him to touch me. I don't want anyone to touch me.

I stagger out of bed and into the spare room.

Stratton

It's already dark as I finish writing up the Benton case, grinding my teeth as I fill in yet another form. My dentist warned me about it last check-up. Grinding leads to weakened enamel. Etc., etc. I told him I'll stop when half of policing stops being bureaucracy.

When it's finally done I pick up my coat.

"Drink?" suggests Cooper. They've just had their first kid and he looks exhausted, like someone's underlined his eyes in navy highlighter. His wife's family's in Newcastle. It's their main reason for moving up there. Free childcare and cheaper housing. I know he's offering for my sake rather than his. There's a sort of office pact: someone takes Stratton out for a drink on 18 March. They don't think I should be alone. Normally pity or sympathy of any kind really pisses me off, but this is different. They know me, and I know they mean well. And they're right. I shouldn't be alone. Luckily for him, tonight I won't be.

"Thanks, but no. Got to see Mum."

Cooper tries not to look relieved, and I head to the lift.

Forty minutes later I'm pulling into the car park of the Willows retirement home. The signage is of a weeping willow gently dipping its golden fronds into a stream. Like you're about to enter some idyllic place. A hotel slash spa for the silver surfers. It isn't. It's a low-level concrete number, the only running water in the vicinity the local drains. Still, it was the nicest one I could find. And afford. The staff, though they tend not to stick around long, are nice enough, and Mum, when she was with it enough to notice, used to join in with some of the group activities. Cards with Rita on a Tuesday. Quiz time with Charlie on a Friday. That's happening less and less now.

I sign in at the desk. The woman there smiles at me overbrightly, revealing lipstick-stained teeth, and greets me in a heavy Eastern European accent. Guess she's been told I'm a cop then. Thinks I might have the power to raid them and shut them down. Or, more likely, check everyone's visas are up to date. Poor fuck. I don't mind them being on their toes, though. You read horrific stories of negligence in homes.

Mum's in her room. "She didn't feel like mixing with the other residents." Code for "they kept her away". Thought she might bite someone else.

Angie's in her room with her, changing her nightie. The new one's a yellowish white with a high collar. I think they choose fabric colours that already look like they've been pissed on. Makes things easier. Angie explains Mum had an accident when she became "overwrought".

Fuck. The indignity of it. Old age. Dementia. Mum was the fiercest, proudest woman you could meet. She'd despise this version of herself. Life had already stolen her daughter. To then come for her mind is simply cruel. The Romans and Greeks had a better understanding of the Gods than anyone today. They knew people were their playthings. To be toyed with and laughed at. How they must be laughing now. No wonder Mum sometimes lashes out at people. I'd probably bite a few people if I was here too.

Mum hasn't registered me. I hold her hand, try to make eye contact, and speak softly to her.

"Mum, it's me, Helen. How are you doing?"

Mum's eyes travel over me. I give her time. I'm not sure if she recognizes me.

Then, eventually, there's the ghost of a spark and she leans in conspiratorially.

"Run away," she hisses. "You can't stay here. They steal children. They stole my Karen."

Fuck. Mum. Poor Mum. It's bad enough that it happened thirty years ago. But to have it happen over and over again in your head. To have that as your permanent present . . .

"Mum," I say, forcing myself to stay calm. "You're safe here. That was a long time ago. Try not to worry about that."

Her head snaps round.

"The coppers said not to worry. They said she'd come home. Are you a copper?" She spits on the floor. "You're a copper, aren't you?"

"I'm Helen. Your daughter." My right hand starts to tremble and Angie places a steadying hand on my shoulder. She knows how hard it is. And how important it is that I don't break in front of her.

"My younger daughter was a copper," Mum says, then stares out the window. "I don't know where she is."

"I'm right here, Mum."

Mum's eyes start to dart round the room, and I just sit there. I don't know what to say next. No one gives you training for this.

"Why don't you go and have a nice cup of tea?" Angie suggests. I nod and stand, but then suddenly Mum clutches my arm. Her grip is surprisingly strong. Her voice is high and pleading, her eyes wild.

"She didn't run away, my Karen. She was taken. I know what it looks like, but you're wrong. You have to believe me. You have to believe me."

Then, just as suddenly, she collapses in on herself and her eyes go out again. She doesn't say another word during my visit. I make tea and then we just sit together, the television on. Both watching images in our heads rather than on the screen.

TUESDAY, 19 MARCH

Natalie

Ryan doesn't wake me when he leaves; the sound of the front door closing does. I squint at the clock: 6.07. It's early even for him.

There's a note downstairs, pinned to the fridge. He wanted to let me rest, he says. He needs to make a start on a new pitch. He's really gunning for this promotion. He reminds me about the appointment he's booked with Dr. Browning. Six thirty. The address is scrawled underneath, hard to decipher. Ryan's always had the most appalling handwriting. I'll google it later to check.

The house is too empty. I can hear my own breathing. The clicking of the radiator. The hum of the fridge. I think about calling Ryan. Just to hear his voice, but he'll be on his bike.

I glance towards the hall and the front door. I can't be here. I can't sit here all morning, waiting for the post to come.

I feel weak. Powerless. I'd promised myself I'd never feel powerless again.

I turn on my phone and my email pings. Another article request from the magazine's editor. She sent it last night. This time she wants me to cover electronic billboard positioning and its potential to cause traffic accidents. I look at the deadline. It's due next week, nothing too pressing, so I accept.

My left eyelid starts to twitch. I think about going for a run in the woods to clear my head. Exercise is normally assigned to segment five—late afternoon—not first thing in the morning, but the segments seem to have fallen by the wayside. The glue they provided too thin to keep my life together.

I flex my right arm. It's still sore, but the bruising isn't too bad. I try a squat and my right leg survives, the bruising slight there too. The arnica must have helped. I imagine Ryan's face if I'd told him that. He has no stock with homeopathy. He'd have made some joke about the memory of bullshit. I smile. It's one of the few things we disagree on. Just because you don't know why something is happening doesn't mean it's not, does it?

The sky outside looks ominous, bruised too. It's not raining, but the clouds look saturated so it's only a matter of time. I check the weather on my phone. There's a ninety per cent chance of rain in the next hour so I swap thoughts of the woods for the gym.

I check my leather handbag for my gym card. It's not there. Surprised, I look through the drawer of the hall console table. We keep a few membership cards there. I find ones for Kew Gardens, National Trust, Wisley... but no gym card. I've just started searching our bedroom when my phone rings.

It's Ryan, just arrived, the noise of traffic in the background. He's reminding me again about Dr. Browning. Using his soft, encouraging voice. I know he means well and is worried about me, but there's a falsity to it that irritates me nonetheless.

"I thought we could maybe go out for dinner afterwards," he adds. "Somewhere nice. We haven't done that for a while."

"I'm sorry, I'd love to, but I'm meeting Rachel after," I say.

I'm sure I told him. I arranged it ages ago. He intentionally forgets anything to do with Rachel.

"Is that a good idea?" he says, his voice clipped.

I sigh. Not now. I can't deal with his animosity towards her on top of everything else that's going on. They used to get on. Not close, exactly, but fine. Then five years ago, soon after she got divorced, it all changed. I know she's become a lot more negative towards men, but that's understandable. It's not like she's poisoning me against Ryan. Telling me to leave him and join the singles club.

I decide to ignore his comment.

"We'll go out together soon," I say.

"Sure," he says. But I know I've disappointed him. Recently, I often get the feeling I'm disappointing him.

"What time do you think you'll be back?" he asks.

"I don't know," I say. "But knowing Rachel, it won't be that early."

As he hangs up I spot his gym card on our bedroom mantelpiece and I pocket that. Ryan won't mind if I borrow it. And they never check the cards anyway. The turnstile would let me through even if the photo were of an elderly bald man.

* * *

The gym is surprisingly busy—I hadn't realized so many people went before work—and I have to queue behind a group of immaculately groomed lycra-clad women, talking at an unnecessarily loud volume about the benefits of spin classes. I wait till the last has swished inside and then nod hello to the receptionist as I beep Ryan's card against the turnstile screen. She doesn't return my greeting but instead remains sat, eyes down, focused on her phone. Usually I'd turn right and head for the pool first, but I don't feel like swimming today. I want something harsher. I put my water bottle and towel in a corner and turn my attention to the free-weights stand. Not wanting to put too much strain on my still slightly sore right arm, I select two smallish dumbbells from the rack. The size I always use: 4kg. That feels about right. They look new. The whole rack does. I turn the dumbbells over in my hands, admiring the unblemished chrome, and catch my reflection in the middle section—nose flattened and exaggerated by the concave surface, the gym's logo, "Sparta", stamped across my eyes.

I have the sudden feeling that I might be being watched. That she could be here. Looking on. Choosing her moment. But I fight against the paranoia and force my mind to focus instead on the weight.

It is somehow comforting in its solidity.

Checking my posture in the mirror, I start with biceps curls before progressing on to upright rows and triceps kickbacks. With every repetition I feel stronger, more powerful.

Better able to keep the demons at bay.

Stratton

I GET TO work for eight fifteen. I couldn't really sleep last night so there was no point staying in bed anyway. Every time I drifted off, I'd dream of her, of Karen. Of someone strangling her with a hose. Her body splayed on the path down the allotment. Then, next dream, she's drowning. Sinking down, down, on to the ocean floor, with no one to help her. All alone. It's best not to sleep if you have dreams like that.

At least this way I should beat Fast-Track in. I want him to feel like he's entering my home turf. That I'm in charge. They're always arrogant, these fast-track kids. Need putting in their place.

I hang my coat over the back of my chair then head to the kitchenette. There's a maintenance guy in there—late twenties, I'd say—plugging in a Nespresso machine. Nice. Maybe Parker's finally listened to everyone moaning about the instant coffee and having to fork out three quid at the Costa across the road and got management to cough up for one. The guy smiles at me. He's attractive in an obvious way. Prominent cheekbones, short-cropped brown hair, hazel eyes. I find myself wishing I'd worn a better top. A tighter one. More make-up. I know I still look OK. My face hasn't aged too badly. I exercise. I have to, for the job. But still, a little extra never hurts as the years add up.

He seems too clean almost for a maintenance guy—good skin, ironed shirt, polished shoes. But maybe he has a mum like mine who taught him right. *Dress well if you want to get on in life. No one's going to think you have a smart mind if you don't look smart on the outside.* Mum could have set up one of those motivational cushions companies. Maybe not. Her sayings were always a lot more tough love than reassuring crap.

He keeps eye contact. OK. He's a forward one. Everyone thinks young guys are only interested in young women, but a surprising number pitch older. They like a woman with a bit of experience.

I smile back. He's younger than I normally go for, but I could make an exception. Maybe he could help me sleep tonight. It's like fate has thrown me a little pick-me-up. I've sworn off cops for a while, it's too messy, but it's not like I'd bump into the coffee-machine guy every day.

"Hi," I say, looking him directly in the eye. "Are you planning on sticking around a while?"

I keep the wording vague. Then throw in a smile. People who work on pick-up lines are wasting their time. The words themselves are unimportant. It's the eyes that do the real talking. The eyes and the lips.

"I hope so." His voice is RP. Posh. His smile deepens and he sticks out a hand. "DS Bradley, I'm new." He waves a hand towards the coffee machine. "My little gift to the team. Don't know about you, but I hate bad coffee."

Fuck. Fuck. Fuckity. Fuck. He's not a coffee-machine guy. He's stick-up-his-backside Fast-Track. I was starting to hit on Fast-Track. I shake his hand. It's warm. The grip firm.

The coffee machine lights up and purrs.

"Looks like she works then."

That confirms it. He's a dickhead. Anyone who assigns a gender to an inanimate object is clearly a dickhead. And who the hell does he think he is, to buy the team a fucking coffee machine? Is he trying to rub his money in everyone's face? Is he so confident in a future littered with promotions and pay rises that he can drop a hundred quid just to curry favour? Want people to like you? Buy a tray of fucking doughnuts.

And don't hit on the boss.

He's looking at me strangely, and I realize I haven't said anything. Haven't introduced myself.

"DI Stratton," I say tightly.

He smiles.

"I think we're partnering together, right? I've heard a lot about you. All good, of course."

He's trying to seem friendly. Likeable. Too likeable. I'm not sure that I trust him.

There's a noise from the main floor. It's Sandra and Reynolds clocking in. I introduce Bradley and notice how broadly Sandra smiles at him. Reynolds, too. Reynolds even takes off his glasses for a moment, pretending to clean them, but really trying to dazzle Fast-Track with his bright green eyes. New boy suits all tastes apparently.

Fast-Track offers to make everyone coffee and Reynolds and Sandra accept gratefully.

"Stratton?"

"No, thanks," I say. "I prefer instant."

Sandra snorts, and Fast-Track shoots me an amused "suit yourself" glance before heading back into the kitchenette.

"Thought you were going to play nice?" Sandra whispers.

I glare at her and she laughs and rolls her eyes.

"I like him." She smiles.

"Thought you'd just got engaged," I snap.

"A girl can look, can't she?" She laughs.

I head to the ladies and catch sight of my reflection in the mirror. Fuck. My trouser suit looks old—sagging at the shoulders. My skin looks paler than normal and I've got worse eye bags than bloody Cooper. There's no way Fast-Track was hitting on me unless he has some weird fucking mother issues. He was just being friendly to an older colleague. Trying to make a good impression on his new partner.

I rummage in my bag and pull out some foundation and mascara. It's never good to look old and tired at work. Men can get away with it. Grey hair and a sagging face in a man supposedly show experience. It actually gets you respect. In women, look tired or haggard and you're washed up. Past it. I spend the rest of the day showing Fast-Track round the department. He picks things up quickly enough, not that anything's rocket science. All the software's the same as at MIT 2, so it's just a question of where everything's kept and meeting the rest of the team. It's annoying how quickly everyone seems to take to him. Like all it takes to be a good detective is some cheekbones and a smile. Even Cooper seems to warm to his replacement.

"Join us tomorrow night? It's my leaving drinks at the Stag's Head. Seven onwards."

"Thanks, I'll be there."

"Good man." Cooper slaps him on the back.

Sandra corners me later when Fast-Track's with Parker. "How's it going with your new hot partner? DS Bradley."

"I'm not sure. I thought all you youngsters liked to use your first names. What does that say about him?"

"That he's a bit old-school. I thought you preferred that?" she mocks.

"I don't trust him," I say.

Sandra laughs. "You don't trust anyone."

"That's not fair."

"It took you three months to believe I wasn't some stupid blonde airhead but a damn good FLO."

She's right. It took me a while to see past Sandra's big blue eyes and blonde curls. To recognize the sharp mind that lay beneath.

"OK. OK. I'm slow to trust. Kill me."

"Just give him a chance."

I decide she's right. If I'm going to be partnered with this guy for the next year, I need to try and make it work. As a weird kind of peace offering I head to the kitchenette and insert a capsule into the Nespresso machine. I watch the thick black liquid ooze out into a mug. I have to admit, it does smell good. Then I replace the mug and insert a second capsule.

Bradley is back on the floor when I return with the mugs so I deposit one on his desk.

"Thanks," he says. I hope he sees the coffee for the olive branch that it is.

"Thought you preferred instant?" he adds with one eyebrow raised. Followed by a smile.

"Nah," I say. "Can't stand the shit."

Natalie

THE GYM SESSION leaves me tired in a good way—the peace of physical rather than mental exertion—and I feel positive and engaged as I start working on the article. I'm just sending a query to my editor when the letterbox shakes and there's the thud of mail hitting the doormat in the hall.

Then there's a discordant ringing sound. It takes me a moment to place it before I realize it's my left foot tapping against the metal desk leg.

Wrapping my cardigan tighter round my waist as if for protection, I force myself into the hall and pick up the bundle of letters. Today they're held together by a thin brown elastic band, which accounts for the single, louder than usual thud.

Hands shaking, I leaf through them. Clothing catalogue. A voter registration reminder. A council garden collection renewal letter. And a Tesco Clubcard statement.

Nothing more.

I wait for a feeling of relief to come. For the air to feel thinner, the pressure released, but it doesn't, for all I can think is, if not today, what about tomorrow? Or the day after that? She knows where I live now. It's not going to stop.

I try to stay focused on the article for the rest of the day, but my concentration is erratic. My mind wanders. And spirals.

Finally, it's six o'clock and time to leave for Dr. Browning's.

He's based at the top of an old Victorian building at the end of Ship Lane which he shares with a couple of other therapists and an acupuncturist. Ryan used to come here for his back. Opposite the building lies a square of communal grass edged by benches that ends in a small playground. I didn't want to be late so I've allowed far too much time to walk here and now have ten minutes to kill before the appointment starts. It's a nice evening, not too cold, so I sit myself on a bench with my back to the playground, watching the sun complete its daily arc. There are no children out. They'll all be having dinner or starting their bedtime regime, so that at least is a blessing. I need to keep my mood up. To see this session as an opportunity. To be willing to accept that it could be a turning point.

* * *

Dr Browning is a lot smaller in person than he seemed from the photograph on his website. I know you can't judge height from a face, but his features seemed somehow to belong to a taller man than the one now ushering me into his room and offering a chair with a slightly beatific smile.

Silence disproportionally amplifies the sound of him shuffling the notes from his last appointment, before he files them in his desk and fixes his eyes on me.

I feel the tension rise and set in my shoulders and try to relax. He's here to help me, I tell myself. Not to judge.

His voice is soft. Intended to reassure. But the perversity in me immediately starts to distrust it. No one is naturally this calm, so the calmness must be an act. A lie. How can someone help me if they're lying about who they are?

He pulls a fresh notepad out of a drawer.

"Let's begin with a brief history, shall we?" he says, pen raised and forehead creased, the perfect picture of concern.

"Are you on any medication?"

I hesitate before telling him about the pills. The ones I need to sleep, to function. I feel the shame rising up in me as I admit this, to a stranger.

He notes this diligently. He has beady eyes. Like a robin. Chasing morsels of information rather than garden worms. "There's nothing to feel ashamed about," he says, looking up. "A heart patient wouldn't feel embarrassed about taking a statin, would they? The brain is just another organ. We medicate when organs need a little help. It doesn't matter which one. The divide between physical and mental is entirely artificial."

I nod. I've heard it all before, but hearing and believing are two very different things. Society tells you there's a difference. Society makes you feel the difference.

"And your husband said you've suffered an episode of dissociative amnesia?" he asks. "In layman's parlance, a blackout."

"I know what it means," I say tersely.

"Tell me about it," he says. His eyes bore into me. I look at the floor. Then I tell him about losing time and waking up in the garden.

His eyes shoot up. Ryan hadn't told him about the letter.

"And have you experienced similar episodes before?"

"Around ten years ago."

"After similar letters?"

I nod. "And . . ." Breathe. "More generally as well."

"All incidents being after the court case?" My mind starts to swim. And float.

"Natalie?"

He calls me back into the room.

"Sorry."

He clicks his pen.

"So you've suffered dissociative moments on and off for ten years."

"No," I correct him. "They stopped. I hadn't had one for over eight years. I thought . . . I thought they'd stopped." I choke back tears.

Wordlessly, he reaches forward and offers me a box of tissues. The design is of wild geese flying in formation. I take one and wipe my eyes.

"I see. And have you been seeing a therapist during this time?"

"At first I did," I say. He leans his head to one side.

"Why did you stop?"

"I didn't need one any more," I say.

We moved house. I devised my system. My segments. I arranged my life so that I could cope. I didn't need anyone else.

"Yet you're here now," he says gently. "You can't run from trauma. It always catches up with you." He clicks his pen again. It's starting to get on my nerves.

Silence stretches. I think he expects me to fill it. I don't.

"Natalie, I understand that this is a very distressing time for you. Dissociative amnesia can be a symptom of PTSD." He steeples his fingers in front of his mouth. The skin surrounding his nails whitens. "It's rare . . ."

Does he doubt me? Anger makes me spit back, "I know that. But that doesn't make it any better."

He nods sagely.

"Can you remember anything that happens at all during these episodes?"

I shake my head.

"And how long are you usually out for?"

"I don't know," I reply honestly. "Sometimes it's just a couple of minutes. Sometimes an hour or more."

"You said that you regained awareness in the garden. Do you normally travel while in your dissociative state?"

"Sometimes. I did initially."

"Was there any pattern to the places you'd wake up in?"

I shift in the chair. I don't like talking about this.

Dr Browning can sense my discomfort.

"I can't help you if you don't let me in," he says softly.

I take a deep breath.

"It would normally be somewhere in the house. An enclosed space. A wardrobe or a bathroom."

"I see. Possibly somewhere you felt safe. A womb, if you like." I flinch. He writes something down. "And if you travelled further?"

I cast my mind back. To waking up by the station I used to commute to work from. To waking up outside a children's clothes shop on the high street. I had a baby blanket in my hand, the receipt in my wallet. It was the softest lemon yellow. I remember the feel of it against my cheek. The new-wool smell. Ryan made me return it. Said it would only distress me further.

"Somewhere connected to . . . to the attack. Or connected to the loss I felt."

"I see."

Then I think about the roses. Coming to at the bottom of the garden and seeing the secateurs in my hand. That wasn't connected to what happened. I'd been meaning to prune them for days, but hadn't got round to it, hadn't allowed myself the time.

I ask him about it warily. "How could that fit?"

"A fulfilment of a subconscious desire," he asserts confidently. If only humans were that simple. I think he sees the look on my face. "Is the garden a refuge for you, Natalie?"

"Yes," I reply. Maybe that's the simpler truth. It wasn't about desire. It was about safety.

He straightens the notepad and clicks his pen again. I clench my teeth and look round the room. There are two framed diplomas on the wall. And an abstract print of the river. Blues and greys. Intentionally calming.

"I will review your medication over the course of our sessions together. I don't want to recommend any immediate changes while you're under stress, as it's important that your anxiety doesn't worsen. How is everything else at home? Your marriage?"

"Fine," I say. Then change my answer to "good". And try to ignore the twinge of sadness. Before . . . before *him*, our marriage, our relationship, didn't use to be good. It used to be great. Almost overwhelmingly so. Ryan and I never argued. We couldn't keep our hands off each other. Other people used to envy us. I know Rachel did. She never said anything, but I knew. I'd catch her looking at us sometimes, her smile only arriving when she realized I was returning her gaze. And I have to admit that part of me liked her jealousy. Liked the way it made me feel. That the glamorous, radiant Rachel was jealous of *me*. That the moon had for once eclipsed the sun.

"And your sex life?"

He drops his voice as if a hushed tone somehow confers delicacy.

I don't know how to reply.

I can't remember the last time we had sex. That's terrible. But it's the truth. It's been nine months at least. And we'd had difficulties before that. At first it was me. Turning away. Not in the mood. I never knew when his touch would trigger me. Ryan would try to disguise the hurt in his eyes as his wife recoiled from him, but I always saw it. It was always there.

I think the final blow came when we ran out of specialists. When my infertility had been confirmed over and over again. When we were young, first together, sex for procreation was the last thing on our minds. A fear rather than a goal. We took every step to avoid it. Once, before I was on the pill, a condom split and I remember queuing in the local chemist's. Asking for the morning-after pill. Not meeting the pharmacist's eye.

But when all your friends are reproducing, sex with no end other than itself feels somehow hollow, lifeless. An imitation of the real thing. An AstroTurf lawn that's shiny and perfect from a distance but inevitably disappointing close up. Ryan kept trying for a while. Skirting the line between supportive and insistent. Then he stopped trying too. Stopped asking. I'll wake occasionally and he'll be taking care of himself, the mattress shaking slightly, the dim light from his phone as he watches porn. I'll close my eyes and pretend to be asleep. We never speak about it.

But I don't say any of this to Dr. Browning. How can I? Instead I mumble, "It's complicated," and he scribbles something down.

"Your parents. Are they supportive?"

I swallow. "They died. When I was at university."

"I see." He nods and writes something else.

"And children. Any children?" he asks.

"No," I reply. "We don't have any children." My voice begins to waver.

"Any plans to?"

Therapists are supposed to be perceptive. They're supposed to be able to read between the lines. But they're not. They don't. They just poke at wounds and make them bleed again. He's not going to help me. They never help me.

"I can't have children," I say, staring at the corner of the room. There's a cobweb there. Small, but noticeable. "I had an abortion and . . . well, it went wrong and I can't have children." The voice seems separate to me. Someone else is talking now. I'm with the spider in the corner. It's spinning me into its web.

"When was this?"

"About ten years ago."

"After the incident?"

Incident? It wasn't an incident. It was an attack. A violation.

But I don't say that. Yes, the head nods. My head nods. I return to my body.

"I think we need to talk about the case, Natalie."

Stratton

I can't work Fast-Track out. He's nice. Everyone seems to warm to him, but there's an uptightness too, sitting there under the manufactured charm. It's there with most fast-trackers. They know they're just passing through. They're never a member of the team. They just see you as a leg-up to something better.

I wait till Parker calls him into his office for a first-day debrief and then head out to the smokers' balcony. It's noisier than normal. No other people, but they've started digging up a section of road fifty metres or so west of here and there's a dull drilling sound that really worms its way into your head. Searching through my contacts on my phone, I pull up the number for Reggie Thompson. He transferred from here to the Kensal Rise MIT a couple of years back. He might be able to give me the unfiltered low-down on my new partner. Thompson picks up instantly. Cops always do. We shoot the breeze for ten minutes—I fill him in on all the team's gossip—Sandra's engagement, Cooper moving on—and ask after his three kids; the oldest, Shania, is thirteen now—fuck, how did that happen?—then I cut to the chase.

"Bradley. What's he like?"

"'Course. He's moved to MIT 8."

"Yup. Partnering with yours truly. So?"

". . . He's a good cop."

I heard the pause. We both heard the pause.

"But?"

"No buts."

"Thompson, I know you. There's a but."

"OK . . . Don't say that I said this, but he's very by the book."

"I'm by the book."

I'm offended now. He makes me sound like some dodgy plant-the-evidence, shit-for-morals copper.

"He's more by the book, believe me. He believes in the rights of defendants. Solicitors. Paperwork. That sort of thing."

I inhale angrily.

"I don't go after innocent people."

"I'm not saying that. You're one of the best. Everyone knows it. It's just . . . you and I know you have to sometimes play the system to get the job done. To keep the scum off the streets. I'm just saying be careful around him. He'll report anything he thinks isn't one hundred per cent kosher. Watch your back. That's all."

Natalie

"This is a safe space," Dr. Browning says, sensing my discomfort. "The incident is obviously a trigger for you. Understandably so. So it's important that we examine it carefully. That I even ask some uncomfortable questions. Do you understand?"

I nod. I think of Ryan. I'm doing this for Ryan.

"Your attacker was found not guilty, is that correct?"

And in an instant I'm back there. Sat in the stand, fighting back the tears pricking at the corners of my eyes . . . I won't let him see me cry. I meet the prosecutor's gaze and remember her words. *Keep your answers simple. Stick to exactly what happened. Don't let them trip you up.*

I don't let myself look at Gavin Scott.

The defence counsel stands and looks at me with a simulacrum of concern. And then presses play.

A large TV screen sits in front of the court facing the judge and jury. It's the CCTV footage from that night. There's no sound. They watch Gavin walking towards me and me smiling. The footage is too grainy to show that the smile doesn't reach my eyes. They see me laughing as the lights come back on. They watch me walk apparently happily into his office, his hand on my elbow, champagne bottle dangling by his waist.

"You would have us believe that you were an unwilling participant," the defence counsel asks, as if genuinely bemused. "But you do not appear very unwilling here."

I try to stick to the facts, to say exactly what happened, but I can feel the jury's eyes on me. They don't believe me. I know they don't believe me.

The prosecutor tries to mend the damage. There's the later footage of me re-crossing the floor, carrying my shoes, my head bent low. But you can't see my face. Can't see the tears. And there's no CCTV in his office. No sound recording.

"Natalie . . ."

Dr Browning's voice. I'm back in the present. He wants an answer. An acknowledgement.

The word lodges in my throat, but then I manage to spit it out. "Yes, he was found not guilty."

"Right." Dr. Browning leans forward, pinches the bridge of his nose and then lets go again.

"And it's his wife who wrote the letters?"

I nod.

Fiona Scott. Her face is burnt on to my retina. Sitting there in the gallery behind her husband, next to their teenage son. Her son stares into his lap, but it's like she can sense my attention. She takes her eyes off her husband and fixes them on me instead. She hated me. Hates me still. I've never felt such pure, distilled hatred.

At the end of the trial she accosted me outside the courthouse, her brown eyes boring into mine as she grabbed the sleeve of my coat. Ryan hurried over and pulled me away, but she spat a single word at my back.

"Liar!"

"Because she thinks you falsely accused her husband?" Dr. Browning cuts into my memories.

"Yes . . ." I confirm. ". . . And because he died."

"I'm sorry?"

"He died. He had a heart attack. The day after the verdict."

Stratton

Everyone else has gone home. I should too—all my official work's done—but there's nothing waiting for me at home. No one. Not even a bloody cat. And anyway, I've got my weekly ritual to complete.

I open up the music files on my laptop and *La Traviata* starts playing. The 1963 Decca recording. It's my favourite version. No one can match Joan Sutherland as Violetta. The sound echoes round the empty office.

I hadn't heard any opera growing up—it wasn't exactly what everyone listened to on the estate—and I thought I'd hate it. I thought it'd all be pretty and poncy, but there's death and grit and pain there too. It gets under your skin if you let it.

It was Grayson, known to everyone as Pavarotti, the team's go-to forensic pathologist, who first introduced me to opera. He'd got his nickname partly from looking like the big man himself, but also from his encyclopaedic knowledge of the stuff. It was well over twenty years ago and I was new to the force—all fresh and shiny; hair scraped back, boots polished so hard you could see my fucking face in them. It was my first visit to the morgue. DI Jones, my then supervisor, steered me in front of a tall man with a large belly and a black goatee. "Stratton, meet Pavarotti," Jones chortled, and I made the mistake of looking confused.

"You know . . . Pavarotti? Jesus. She hasn't even bloody heard of Pavarotti."

Jones laughed at my ignorance. Grayson didn't. He sent a CD of *La Bohème* to the station, addressed to me, with a note saying it was the first step in what would be a lifelong education.

Grayson plays it in the morgue. Says it helps him focus. I think it's also because he thinks it impresses the cops who turn up. I only ever listen to opera alone. I don't like to admit it, but some small part of me, the part that never left the estate, still thinks that someone will laugh at me if they see.

I feel my eyelids grow heavy so make myself another coffee—Fast-Track's gift is proving annoyingly useful—and then open up the nationwide "recent cases" search function. Bodies are found depressingly regularly. Mainly women. Many aren't identified. At least not at first.

And one of them might be Karen.

Natalie

I'M SUDDENLY NAUSEOUS. Remembering it all. The court. Him. Fiona Scott. All of it. I have to leave. I can't breathe in here.

The edges of my vision start to pixellate.

Then there's a sharp pressure on my hand. A squeezing. A loud voice.

"Natalie . . . ? Natalie."

My vision stabilizes.

"I'm sorry," I say.

Dr Browning waits a moment then releases pressure on my hand.

"It was starting, wasn't it?" he asks, curious, peering at me like I'm a dead frog in a biology class. Like he wants to dissect me. Find out how I work.

I nod.

"Interesting. There are techniques we can try. Pressure. Pain. Things that jolt the mind. Reminders of the external world. Do your episodes tend to happen when you're alone?"

I nod again.

"Try and find ways to introduce external stimuli."

Easier said than done. When they happen I lose control of my body. Of my mind.

"And keep a record of any that happen. Timings, triggers, where you travel to."

He thinks they're going to keep happening. They're not going to stop. Tears start to fill my eyes.

"Don't despair," he says gently. "There've been some exciting developments in treating PTSD these past years. A centre in the Netherlands is producing some impressive results with psychedelics. There are avenues to explore. In the meantime, try to avoid stressful situations. Triggers."

That's what I've been doing, I want to shout.

"I need to go now," I say, pushing myself out of the chair. My legs threaten to buckle as I stand. I want my home. I want Ryan.

Dr Browning's saying something about a follow-up appointment, and I nod vaguely, but I'm trying to block him out. Focus on what I can control. The door handle. My turning it. The stairs. The sound of my footsteps clattering down them. A latch. I fumble with it. Then I'm out, on the pavement, and I'm gulping air.

Tears are now streaming down my face and I roughly wipe them away with a coat sleeve. Talking doesn't help. Talking just brings it all back.

A middle-aged woman stops to ask if I'm OK.

"Yes," I lie. "I'm fine."

She doesn't believe me but she walks on, throwing a worried glance over her shoulder at me when she reaches the other side of the crossing and pauses outside Tesco.

My phone vibrates with a text. Rachel. She's finished work earlier than she thought and she's about to get the tube over. She's just checking I'm not cancelling before she makes the trip. I have a habit of cancelling.

I picture the evening. The bar's crowded, strangers pressing up against me. Rachel is drinking too much, her voice loud and carrying. Men edge nearer, wanting to be close to her. She's enjoying the attention, encouraging them with the occasional glance. She's asking me questions, grilling me about why I won't go for the professional support lawyer job. No. I can't do it. I need to be home tonight. To feel safe. I want Ryan.

I text Rachel back. "Sorry. Got a migraine. I'll call you tmrw."

I can explain everything then. I read an article once that said small lies aren't always bad. Sometimes they're just a more efficient means of communication.

The night suddenly feels a lot colder than it did half an hour ago and I wrap my coat more tightly round me as I walk home. Drizzle hangs suspended in the air. Anxiety heightens my senses and every shadow, every footstep, registers as a threat.

My heart rate only starts to slow as I turn into Sheen Common Road and its stretch of painted terraced houses. Ours is halfway down on the left: the palest green with a dark grey door. The colour was one of the reasons we chose it. Ryan said it was an omen. Our first date had ended with ice cream and we'd both chosen pistachio. This was supposed to be somewhere we could start again. Be how we used to be. Before.

The downstairs lights are on. Good. I was worried Ryan might have gone out for a drink, thinking I wouldn't be home till late.

I insert the key and turn.

There's a noise from the kitchen and I head there, not even bothering to remove my coat or shoes.

As I open the door, I see them. The ceiling spots are off and they're sat there, at the table, bathed in a pool of golden light from the overhead pendants. They're so close their legs are almost touching. They're laughing, Ryan showing too many teeth. Next to him is a girl I've never seen before. She's in her early twenties. Pretty. Really annoyingly, effortlessly, pretty. Her limbs long and languid. Her eyes large. Her lips full. Make-up a frosting rather than a necessity. She's wearing a pencil skirt with a white shirt but the top buttons are undone and she's leaning forward. Leaning towards him.

They're so absorbed in each other's company they don't even know I'm there.

I take a step back in shock and, in doing so, lean on the door, which squeaks. Ryan spins round.

"Nat," he says, startled. There's panic in his eyes. "Are you OK?"

I don't answer.

Ryan's now on his feet. "This is Alice," he says, introducing us. She stands too and, after a second's pause, reaches across a hand. I shake it. There's no alternative. She looks uncomfortable. But not so much guilty as confused.

"Alice has just started at the firm," Ryan explains. "She's helping me with the last touches of the package we're putting together for the client."

"Right," I say, forcing a smile. "I'm Natalie, Ryan's wife." I immediately regret the emphasis.

I cast a forensic eye over the scene.

There are files spread over the table in front of them, substantiating the work premise, but there are also two wine glasses. They're drinking red. Lipstick stains the rim of Alice's. The bottle is open on the table. A Saint-Émilion. It's one of our good ones. The ones we save for special occasions.

"Nat, are you OK?" Ryan repeats. "I thought you were seeing Rachel?" He takes a step closer, reaches out a hand, and I flinch away from him. A look of disappointment flashes in his eyes. Disappointment mingled with anger. He always takes rejection harder when he's been drinking. He sucks in his breath.

Alice is looking at me with something resembling pity. I imagine myself through her eyes. My hair flattened by the damp, my mascara smeared. She must wonder why Ryan's with me. I can't start slinging accusations. I'll be known as the crazy wife. The liability.

God. Get it together. I'm probably over-reacting. I've had a horrible evening and I wanted Ryan to myself. But there's nothing wrong with him inviting a colleague back to work here. He's had Dave and Ash round before. It's not his fault Alice is so attractive and so bloody young.

"I need to go to bed," I say. "I've got a migraine."

"I can go," says Alice. "What do you want me to do?" She makes eye contact and doesn't break it. I end up looking away.

What an odd way to phrase it. I stare at her. I can't quite work her out.

"No. Finish your work." I manage a smile and turn to Ryan. "We'll talk in the morning."

I feel his eyes follow me as I leave the room.

I think I won't sleep, but I do.

Until I'm woken at midnight by the sound of the front door slamming.

Stratton

I KEEP SCROLLING down the list.

A woman, Claire Atwood, 37, was killed in Liverpool by her ex. Not Karen.

A woman was found dead near Newcastle. Unidentified. Looks like a drug overdose. I click for more details. Late sixties. Brown eyes. Not Karen.

Bones were found buried under a garage in Fulham. They were discovered by the new owners, who then called the police. Best estimate was that they belonged to a female in her mid-twenties. I do the maths. Ten years till she was mid-twenties. Another ten years for a body to fully decay . . . My heart speeds up. It could be Karen. Kept by someone then killed. I know the odds are low, but it could be. I click for further information. The remains have been taken to Fulham Mortuary. It's not far.

Then I click on the latest data tab. A hair sample was found attached to the skull. Dark-brown. Afro-Caribbean.

Not Karen.

I'm lost in a wave of emotion and I can't tell if it's disappointment or relief. I'm so caught up in it that I don't hear Fast-Track come over until he's standing right beside me. He looks as surprised to see me as I am him.

"Sorry—didn't know there was still work to do," he says. "I would have stayed."

He fixes his eyes on the screen. Bollocks. What I'm doing isn't exactly wrong. But I know I'm searching police records for personal use. Karen's disappearance isn't on my list of active cases. The last thing I need is Fast-Track ratting me out on this and someone high up shutting me down.

I try to close the search window, but I'm not fast enough. He's seen.

Fast-Track shoots me a confused look.

"Are we working this murder?" he asks. "I haven't been briefed."

". . . Not exactly."

His lips narrow and his eyes shine brighter. Fuck.

"Then I don't understand." His voice is clipped.

I don't have a choice. I have to tell him. Appeal to his better side, if he has one.

"My . . . my sister went missing when I was young," I say quietly. "The police logged her as a runaway. She wasn't. Someone took her. If she was alive, if she was free, she'd have come home . . ." I swallow and blink rapidly. ". . . She never came home."

He nods slowly and I think I see a flicker of understanding.

"And you thought that could be her?" he says.

I nod. And wait . . .

He swallows and it's like his face glitches as a wave of emotion washes over it.

"Let me know if there's anything I can do to help," he says quietly.

I look up at him, surprised. This was the last reaction I expected.

He's lost someone too. I can tell. Someone he was close to. It leaves scars that other scarred people can see.

And I feel guilty for dismissing him so quickly. The preppy boy persona is partly an act. He's not just sprinting towards the top. He wants to make a difference too. He's more like me than I thought.

I look up at him curiously, but he's not looking back. He's staring out the window. When he speaks again it's as much to the street as to me.

"Family matters," he says. "Family is the most important thing."

WEDNESDAY, 20 MARCH

Natalie

Ryan wakes me with a tea then hovers by the side of the bed, not saying anything. His hair is wet. He's showered unusually early and smells of the new shower gel I bought him. Sea salt and mint. He's also wearing the tie I gave him last Christmas. The one I know he doesn't like but won't return for fear of offending me. He's trying to please me by wearing it now. Why? His eyes flit from my face to the floor. There's something he wants to say but doesn't. He's making me feel uncomfortable.

Finally he asks me. "How did it go with Dr. Browning?"

". . . Difficult," I say. "He asked about the case. About the verdict. About why we couldn't have kids."

Ryan wraps me in his arms.

"Are you going to see him again?"

"I don't know," I say. My voice comes out as barely a whisper.

His hug tightens and emotion chokes his voice when he speaks. "Oh, Nat. I should have been there for you. I should have sent Alice home."

I've been so caught up in recalling Dr. Browning that it takes a second for my brain to shelve one bad memory and then dredge up the next.

Ryan sitting in a pool of golden light with the impossibly pretty girl.

"It's OK," I say. "You had to work."

"I'd have stopped if you'd just asked."

His face is a picture of guilt and my heart goes out to him. He doesn't deserve my insecurities. My paranoia. I was just upset after talking about the past. Seeing things that weren't there. Projecting. Not all men are monsters. He's been there for me through everything. He understood without being told why I can't be around young children. Why, as a result, I had to walk away from certain friendships. Why we had to move house. He changed his life—everything—for me.

Yet still the questions come.

"How long's she been working with you?" I keep my voice casual.

"Alice? Just a couple of weeks."

"And she's in your department?"

"My new assistant, actually."

". . . I saw you opened the Saint-Émilion?"

"We just had a small glass each. It seemed like the polite thing to offer. It was the first bottle I found."

"Right."

I tell myself that he drinks with all of his colleagues. He always says that the best marketing ideas lie at the bottom of a bottle of wine.

He's staring out the window. Apparently fascinated by something happening on the street.

She must have been the girl on the phone. I was right that she'd just started. I picture her again. Long-limbed, and that face. She's in his office every day. He'll look at her every day. I'm being unfair. He probably didn't choose her. Recruitment's an HR thing. She might be very good at her job. I don't want to become one of those bitter women who hate pretty girls.

Nevertheless the question slips out unbidden.

"I don't need to worry about her, do I?"

"Alice? No. God, no. Don't be absurd."

He kisses me and leaves.

On his path to the door his right hand adjusts his cuffs and my stomach contracts.

I try to reassure myself that nothing's wrong. Ryan probably just felt awkward that he hadn't told me about her. He'd normally mention something like a new assistant. But maybe he'd been worried about how I'd react. After all, what sane man would tell their wife that an impossibly beautiful twenty-year-old had just started at work?

I begin my morning routine, and the distraction helps. I start researching relevant case law around the positioning of and liability surrounding billboards. This is my favourite stage. The gathering. The processing. However, by ten my mind starts to wander. There's a chill in the air that's starting to settle into my bones. I go to the window seat in the living room to fetch the orange-and-blue check blanket that I always leave there for moments like this. I like to drape it over my legs for warmth. I don't let Ryan see—it makes me look the wrong side of sixty—so he thinks it's purely decorative. But today it's not there. He must have moved it. Maybe he uses it in secret too. The idea makes me smile. The strange little things you hide from your partner.

I check the weather on my phone. It says it's 14 degrees outside—I thought it'd be lower. Still, there's a slight draught in the air. Strange. I stand and pad around downstairs, looking for the source. Eventually I find it. The window in the loo is open. I never leave it open. You could see it from the road. It wouldn't take a ninja to access it. Silently I curse Ryan. He's left it ajar before and he promised he'd never make the same mistake again. There may not have been a letter for a couple of days, but it doesn't change the fact that she's out there. Mrs. Scott. She knows where we live and he's leaving downstairs windows open like an invitation to enter. I close the window a little too forcefully and the glass rattles in the frame. I want to let it go, to try to, but the annoyance lingers, amplified by the memory of him and that girl.

"You left the window open again," I text him.

There's no reply. I check again five minutes later. Two ticks tell me he's got the message and read it, just not responded. Maybe for the best. He'll think I was being petty. Some things are better left unanswered.

The rest of the morning passes uneventfully. There's no mail today—aside from a couple of flyers—and for lunch I concoct myself a rather delicious nasi goreng from a leftover roast chicken leg.

I have the radio on as I'm washing up, so it takes a lull in the song for me to realize there are footsteps in the hall. I freeze rigid. Maybe the letter was just a warning. Maybe there was only going to be one more letter. This is the next stage. She's crawled through the window. She's here, in our house. Instinctively, I take a knife from the rack and hold it, pointing towards the door, hand shaking.

"I'm calling the police," I say loudly, taking my phone out of my pocket.

I keep the knife pointing forwards as I dial 999 with my thumb. The kitchen door opens.

"I have a knife," I call.

Then drop it to the floor. Ryan's standing there. Or rather a shell of Ryan. His face looks grey, his shoulders stooped. He's been crying.

"Hello. Operator. Which service do you require?"

"No. Nothing. Sorry, I made a mistake."

I hang up the phone and rush over to Ryan.

He's pulled out a chair and folded his body down into it. He's not talking.

Something terrible's happened. It's written all over him. My brain goes to dark places. What has he been keeping from me? Doctor's appointments? He's ill. Cancer. I know two men of a similar age who've died of cancer. One prostate. One brain.

"Ryan . . ."

He needs to tell me. If he tells me, I can help. We'll find the best doctor. Waiting lists are terrible, but we can go private, sell the house if we have to.

"Nat." Ryan finally opens his mouth. Then chokes. "I'm so sorry, Nat."

"Are you . . . are you ill?"

He shakes his head slowly.

Relief doesn't come. His body language tells me that relief isn't the right emotion.

The fridge hums.

"Why aren't you at work?"

"I . . . they . . . they sent me home."

". . . Why?"

Ryan stares down at the floor and his body convulses again.

"Ryan . . . what's going on?"

"There's going to be an investigation."

"What investigation?" My words are tight. I don't understand what's happening.

"Alice . . ."

The radiator clicks. *Click. Click. Click.*

"Alice?"

"She said I . . . raped her. For fuck's sake, Nat. She said I raped her."

Stratton

Robert Fenton's died. I don't know the name, but looking around the briefing room I see that it registers with the old-timers. Parker lays out the background. Fenton was shot outside a nightclub back in 2007—three years before I joined MIT8. Reynolds shakes his head sadly, he remembers the guy—an innocent bystander caught up in a gang-related turf war, left with serious injuries and unable to communicate or leave his bed. His death turns it into a murder investigation. At least I'll have something to do now. It'll be a straightforward case—the facts aren't really in dispute. It'll be a good one to gauge how Fast-Track works.

"DI Reynolds will take the lead on this one," Parker says, then shuts his file. I feel the anger build up in me. Fuck Parker. Reynolds might have the time, but I told Parker I needed to work.

I give Parker enough time to go back to his office then knock on the door. I enter without waiting for permission.

"What the hell was that?" I hiss, stalking towards him.

"What do you mean?" Parker leans back in his chair, looping his fingers through his belt. Dickhead.

"You said you'd give me cases."

"No, you asked for cases." Pompous twat. How the hell can he do this to me? He said he'd help and now he's denying me the one thing I need.

"Mark—" Fuck. I meant to say *Parker* but the *Mark* slipped out. Old habits. ". . . I told you I needed this."

Parker manages to look a little ashamed. He lowers his voice to a more coaxing tone. "You're not in the right frame of mind. You look exhausted. The allotments murder was one thing. It couldn't have been more straightforward. Even that was probably a mistake though. Take some time to settle Bradley in. Show him how we do things round here."

"I've shown him. He knows. I'm a detective, not a babysitter."

"It's an order."

He's puffed up his chest now, meaning he's not going to back down. He's always been a little bit afraid of me, not that he'd ever admit it, and he won't want to give way now, as it'd make him feel small.

"Then the next case?" I keep my tone level. Not friendly exactly, but with less of a bite.

"The next case is yours."

Natalie

RYAN BANGS HIS fist down on the table. The room starts to dissolve. Tile by tile. Floorboard by floorboard. My home disintegrates.

I bite my lip to try to wake up but I taste something wet and metallic. I'm not dreaming.

He grabs my shoulders and forces me to look into his eyes. "You don't believe her, do you? You don't think I could do something like that? Not after what happened to you. Not after everything we've been through."

I can't look at him. I don't want to look at him.

"Women don't lie about things like that," I say quietly.

"She does. I don't know why, but she's lying."

I give in and glance up.

His eyes are desperate. They bore into mine. Pleading.

"Why aren't the police here?" I ask.

"She told HR she wanted twenty-four hours to see if she wanted to involve them. Which makes no sense. If I'm the monster she claims I am, she'd go to the police straight away, right? She wants to fuck with me. Draw it out."

"Going to the police isn't easy," I snap.

"God. You think I did it, don't you?" Ryan stands up and steps away. He's staring at me. "I've always believed you. Always backed you. Every time. Without question. I love you, so I believe you. And yet some woman says something and you take her word over mine."

He doesn't understand. I want to believe him. All I want is to believe him.

"Swear nothing happened," I say. "Swear on your life . . . no, on my life . . . swear on my life that nothing happened."

He falters. The fucker falters.

"She . . . OK. Just before you got home last night, she kissed me."

I wasn't imagining things. I sensed there was something going on.

"And you kissed her back?" I fight to keep the emotion out of my voice.

". . . Yes . . . I was flattered, Nat. She's young, attractive. I know it was wrong . . ."

I picture the two of them again, bathed in that golden light. His smile. His bloody toothy smile. The axis of my world tilts. Gravity shifts. My husband kissed another woman. A girl, practically. He's wearing the tie I gave him to make up for the fact he kissed a girl. Such twisted, childish logic. It's almost funny. Except it's not. Not remotely.

"And . . . ?"

"Well . . . after you went to bed she kissed me again."

His eyes flit. He adjusts his cuffs. He's holding back. There's more.

"And . . . ?" I repeat.

"And I slept with her, OK?" His voice is raised now, as if I'm the one who's angered *him*. "Is that what you want to hear? I slept with her on the sofa while you were upstairs in bed. I should never have done it. It shouldn't have happened. I'm the worst fucking husband, I know it, and I can't tell you how much I regret it, but it meant nothing. It was one moment of weakness. She made me feel attractive. It's been so long since I've felt attractive. You never want me to touch you . . ."

So it's my fault. I wondered how long it would be before it was my fault.

I don't say anything. I try to take myself away. I stare at the orange paint. Maybe green would have been better. Or a duck-egg blue. Ryan had wanted a duck-egg blue.

"Aren't you going to say something?" Ryan says, the fight completely gone from his voice.

I turn and look at him.

"What's there to say?"

"I didn't force her, Nat. I promise I didn't. I told her nothing more could happen between us, and that must have annoyed her, the rejection. But at the time she wanted it. It was all her. She wanted it as much as I did, Nat. She seduced me."

I'm transported back to the witness box. Gavin Scott's words mirrored back at me through my husband's mouth.

My vision starts to blur, but I fight against it. I will not lose time now.

I don't know what to think. It's Ryan. He wouldn't attack someone. But then, five minutes ago, I'd have laughed at the idea that he could have slept with someone else. That he could have ever done anything to hurt me. I can't believe that I ever thought we could read each other's minds. That we had a special connection. Any connection we ever had, anything special, he's broken it.

I leave the room, leave Ryan slumped at the table.

If he's telling the truth, I get that she might be angry. Feel used, even. But to lie about rape? I picture her next to him. She seemed uncomfortable, but that was only after she'd noticed me. Did she feel she had to come back with him? That she had to have a drink with him? That her job depended on it? Did he then take advantage?

I rewind the image. Before she saw me, she was leaning towards him. She was smiling.

But just a few hours later the front door slammed.

I don't know. Fuck. I just don't know.

I pick up my bag and walk out of the house.

I wish he'd had fucking cancer. I want to strangle him with that fucking tie.

Stratton

There's nothing for me to do on the Fenton case. Reynolds and Dev have it covered. All I can do is sit and stew and think about how it should have been mine.

I try scrolling through the news to distract myself. Cheery reading. The economy's fucked . . . more cuts to services . . . a mother of three dies because the ambulance didn't get there in time. Depressingly familiar stuff. Further down the page something catches my eye. The Manchester Strangler has been sent down. Life without parole. I remember the case when it first hit the news. Everyone on the force will. The general public too. The body of a teenage girl was unearthed on a building site. Developers had been sitting on the land for six years, waiting for prices to rise. When they finally decided to exploit it and bring the diggers in, they found more than they'd bargained for. The case stood out as it wasn't your run-of-the-mill domestic-violence murder. The vic, when she was finally identified, was single. She'd been killed on her way home from work. And here's the media-bait bit—she'd been strangled with her own bra. There was no discernible motive, just a sicko on the loose. Understandably it had caused panic at the time, even though the actual murder had happened years earlier. Mothers tried to stop their daughters going out, installed location checkers on their phones.

I stare at the photo of the man they've convicted. It's a profile shot; his head is down. He's late sixties, grey hair, thicker on the sides than on top. He's in his caretaker's uniform. There's nothing remarkable about him. Nothing at all. Nothing to put you on alert. A man, used to being invisible, blending into the background. Using that time-honed skill. It was a neat murder. That struck me too. No broken bones, no deep defensive wounds. A single deep laceration round the neck where the underwire had cut into the vic's larynx. He'd known what he was doing.

I put my phone down. Me sticking around isn't helping anyone and it's doing bad things for my blood pressure so I tell Parker I'm ducking out to see Mum.

I think he might react. Get annoyed—who the hell visits their mum's care home in the middle of the bloody work day?—and to be honest, part of my motivation was to provoke him. But instead he smiles patronizingly and says he thinks it's a good idea for me to take a couple of hours out. For my "wellbeing". It makes me hate him even more.

As I start my car I think I should have told Fast-Track I was taking off, but I don't think of him as my partner yet. That'll take some getting used to. I'll apologize at Cooper's drinks tonight.

Mum is asleep when I get there. Asleep at two in the bloody afternoon. I know she's old, but it makes me wonder if they put something in their lunch. To give the carers a little bit of time off. No. I know I'm being unfair.

I'm deciding whether to bother staying when Angie puts her head round the door.

"Good to see you here, Helen. Two visits within a week. That's quite something." The level of surprise in her voice makes me feel guilty. Are my visits really so rare? I try to count how many times I've been since Christmas. Then stop as it just makes me feel worse.

"Not much point though, is there?" I say, nodding towards Mum's sleeping form.

"Oh, you'd be surprised," Angie says. "She'll still know you're here. She'll register your presence. Talk to her. Even while she sleeps. It'll do wonders."

Angie leaves and I stare at Mum. Her chest rises and falls beneath her thick polycotton nightgown. OK, I think, if coma victims can hear you then maybe sleeping old women can too.

"Mum," I say, quietly, feeling like a bit of a pratt, "it's me, Helen." She doesn't stir.

"I hope you've had a better morning . . ." What the fuck do you say to someone who doesn't answer back? I wish I had a book to read to her or something. ". . . It's a bit tricky at work. My boss won't give me the cases I need." She doesn't know the history. I never told her about Mark. She wouldn't have approved. To her, marriage was sacrosanct. I tell her about Fast-Track, about Cooper retiring, and somehow it feels good. Her being asleep allows me to say things I normally wouldn't be able to. Things that are usually too real and raw to say out loud.

"I'm so sorry about what's happened to you, Mum." My voice starts to crack. "It's not fair, what you've been through. I'm going to find out what happened to Karen though, I swear it."

Mum moves slightly and I think she's about to wake when, instead, she just shifts position and her breathing turns nasal. There's a crucifix on the wall above her bed. Mum's—from her old flat. She was brought up staunchly Catholic and tried to raise us in the same mould. It didn't stick. I was never very malleable. I never could understand why she kept going to church, even after Karen was taken. Surely if anything was proof that God doesn't give a fuck, that was. But she'd go. Religiously. Sit at the front. Watch the vicar and then get down on creaking arthritic knees to pray.

The room is warm, the air close. Triple-glazed windows keep out the day outside. I keep staring at the cross. It's like it's daring me.

Right, you fucker, here goes. I haven't prayed since I was fourteen. I close my eyes. I'm not getting on my knees, though. That's one step too far. OK, what next? With my eyes closed I suddenly feel very alone. And less confident in my rejection of God. Brainwashing runs deep. I think what I want to say and try not to swear . . .

Dear God. It's me, Helen. But I guess you know that anyway or there's no f—no chance of you helping me. I've spent my life finding murdered women and bringing their killers to justice. Please, please, let me find Karen. I know she probably isn't still alive, but let me at least find her body and lay her to rest. I'll even throw in a Catholic burial. How about that? Another soul saved? I know you're probably not that used to bargaining, but I've got an offer for you. A case for a case. If I solve one more murder, help one more murdered girl, you help me? You show me Karen. That's it. That's my offer.

A girl for a girl.

Natalie

It's starting to drizzle and I wish I had my raincoat.
   Our black Qashqai is parked right outside. It's possible my raincoat's in there. I don't think I took it out after our trip to the garden centre the other day.

I reach inside my bag, but I can't find my car keys. I think about going back inside to look for them, but I can't face seeing Ryan again yet.

There's only one way to know for sure what happened, and that's to confront her. Alice. She won't be able to lie to my face. She'll give herself away. It'd be something she says, a light in her eyes: whatever it is, I'll know.

I set off towards Mortlake station. The drizzle dies down so I don't get too wet. There's a five-minute wait during which I pretend to read the *Metro*, and then I'm on the train, crawling towards Waterloo. I hold my bag tighter than I need to, my fingernails wrapping 360 degrees around the handle and then digging into my palm. The slight pain helps keep me focused, stops my vision from pixellating. I can't pass out now. Lose time. It's too important. I need to talk to Alice before she goes to the police.

I change at Vauxhall, descending into the Victoria line before changing at Oxford Circus on to the Central line. The air is thick and heavy; I can feel particles of pollution being drawn down into my lungs. The carriage is busy and I claim the one empty seat, next to the doors. Opposite me sits a mother with a young girl, four or five I think. They're doing a sticker book. The theme seems to be Space. Every time the girl peels and places a planet sticker on the page, she looks up at her mother for approval. The mother smiles back encouragement. I turn away, as it hurts too much. They have everything. They think it's normal, but it's everything.

My mind's tumbling so much I nearly miss the stop: Holborn. I stagger out and walk the fifty metres down the Viaduct to stand outside Ryan's office in Waterlane Square.

What to do now? She's probably not even there still. She'll have made her allegations then gone home. I feel like an idiot. I think about going in, but I don't want to see Ryan's colleagues. I don't want their questions, or their pity. They'd probably ask me to leave anyway—afraid I'd "compromise" their internal investigation.

Frank's on security duty, standing near reception, but I don't think he's seen me. I stand in the shadows to the right of the courtyard entrance and wait. Hoping she'll come.

I'm about to give up when she finally emerges. Dressed in shades, a white long-sleeve tee and cropped pink trousers—the length that makes anyone with normal legs look dumpy. For some reason, that annoys me. Irrationally angers me that she's parading her perfect long legs. No. I can't think like that. That's blame-the-victim mentality. That's what each of those jurors thought about me.

Alice stalks out the building just after four and heads towards the Viaduct.

I step out of the shadows.

"Alice," I hiss.

She keeps walking.

"Alice," I say, louder this time.

She spins round and sees me. Then stops. Her body's tight. Wary.

"Tell me the truth," I say. My voice is louder than I want it to be. "I need to know. Did he force you? Did he really do it?"

I mean to be calm. All I want to do is talk to her. Ask her some questions. But she just stands there, shades on, saying nothing.

I step towards her and, next thing I know, I'm forcing off her shades. I need to see her eyes.

"Tell me!"

She stares back. Scared and confused. Blinking as her pupils adjust to the light.

"I don't understand."

"What's there to understand?" I yell. "Did he rape you? Did my husband rape you?"

Then a pair of strong arms are wrapping round me and pulling me backwards.

"Easy there, Mrs. Campbell." I turn my neck around to see Frank. He looks apologetic, but still waits till Alice is out the courtyard before releasing me.

"Sorry," I say, realizing how deranged I must look. "I didn't want to hurt her."

"I know," he says. "It's an emotional time."

I assure him that I won't be back, that this was a one-time thing, and he lets me go.

Straightening my clothes, I head back on to the Viaduct and scan right and left. There it is. A flash of pink trouser leg heading down the steps to the tube. I follow.

I clatter down the steps. Where is she? Ahead, pink legs descend the escalator. I scramble after. I can't let her get on a train without me. I'd never find her then.

Running down the escalator, past an obstacle course of elbows and briefcases, I reach the platform. Which way? I mentally toss a coin. Heads eastbound; tails west. Heads. Damn. She's not on the eastbound platform. The whoosh of carriage doors opening comes from the westbound platform. I run. And just make it, throwing myself through the closing gap to glares of disapproval from the other passengers.

Where is she?

I spot her at the other end of the carriage. Pink legs crossed. Sunglasses still on. I don't think she's seen me. I consider walking up, confronting her here when she has nowhere to run to, but quickly reject the idea. The carriage is busy; it's too public. Someone might intervene. Someone might call the transport police.

I wait.

She stands at Wood Lane and I follow her off, keeping my distance. She doesn't look back. I trail her up steps and then down a second set on to the Hammersmith and City line. All the time, I'm analysing her body language. Does she walk like someone who's been attacked? Does she walk like a liar? How would a liar walk?

The tube passengers change. As we head away from the City there are fewer business people, more teens.

We approach Latimer Road and she stands again. I wait till a group of teens also stands and block her eyeline and then I get up too. Alice is first off. Then the teens. They light up on the platform and a cloud of weed shrouds them.

I follow them out on to St. Ann's Road and get my bearings. I've never been here before. Grenfell Tower stands to the right, a charred monument to institutional failure, yet I'm pretty sure the luxury houses of Holland Park are only a few blocks ahead. The juxtaposition of poverty and wealth jars. They would have seen people fall from their Georgian sash windows.

The pink trousers light the way ahead. She'll be home soon. No doubt in some flat Daddy bought her.

I increase my pace, working up the courage to confront her. The longer I leave it, the stranger it's going to seem when I reveal myself. But she picks up pace too as she passes a crowded street corner, her trousers standing out like a beacon against the muted greys and browns of concrete and cheap brick. A dog barks and a man wolf-whistles, and I'm trapped in the role of pursuer.

Finally Alice turns left down a path to a run-down block of flats. She stops in front of a door: 114B—blue in a sea of blue doors and matching railings—the council must buy paint in bulk. This isn't anything like where I'd thought she'd live. I'm hidden from sight by a tree, so she doesn't see me as she glances over her shoulder before opening the door. Now's my chance. I have her trapped. All I need to do is walk up and ring the bell. She'll have to talk to me. But then I catch my reflection in the window of a neighbouring flat. I'm stood, flattened behind a treetrunk, having stalked a girl home. Shame burns in my cheeks. What the hell am I doing? I'm like Fiona Scott. I'm no better than Fiona Scott.

Lost, I call Rachel. She picks up on the third ring.

"Wondered when you were going to call," she says. "How was the therapist? How's the migraine?" It takes a second to click. I hadn't called her back after ditching her last night.

I don't have time to tell her about Dr. Browning now. Instead I tell her about Ryan. About Alice.

"What do I do?" I conclude.

"Fuck," she says. "You're outside her flat, aren't you?"

"What?" How does she know that?

"I've got you on location tracker, remember?" She laughs. "I'm not stalking you."

Of course. I forgot. We gave each other access a while ago. After there was that stuff in the papers about the strangler killer. You can never be too careful—a woman walking home by herself. At least I've got Ryan looking out for me. After the divorce, Rachel's got no one.

"Yes."

"Leave, Nat. You're just going to get yourself in a world of trouble. She'll call the police on you. And she'd be right to."

"But—"

"If you want, you can come and stay with me for a few days. Clear your head."

As tempting as it is, I can't. I can't run away from what's happening.

"No. Thanks, but no."

"Then go home. Talk to Ryan."

I hesitate and then ask the question I'm not sure I want an answer to.

"Do you . . . do you think he could have done it?"

"Nat, you know I'm not the right person to ask."

"But do you?"

". . . I don't know, Nat. I don't know."

Stratton

THE STAG'S HEAD is crowded by seven thirty. Cooper was always popular and cops have turned out from across the London MITs to give him a decent send-off. Sandra has changed into tight jeans and a low-cut red top and is collecting lots of admiring glances. I haven't made much effort, but I've let my hair fall loose and added lipstick. Anything more seemed like overkill for a place where your feet stick to the floor and which primarily plays nineties rock ballads. Reynolds is buying and lining up shots. While I'm chatting to Dev, I spot Bradley, standing alone at the bar. It surprises me that I've started to think of him as Bradley. Not just Fast-Track any more. He looks exactly the same as in the office. Most of the guys have loosened a few buttons, rolled up their sleeves, but Boy Scout here looks as perfect as ever. Tan chinos. Bright white shirt, buttoned to the collar. Like a bloody M&S advert.

Right. He didn't rat me out like I thought he might. Least I can do is make an effort. I take a shot and walk over. Bradley looks up as I place the shot glass down in front of him with a clink.

"Courtesy of Reynolds," I say. "Don't know what the fuck it is, but he's cheap, so it won't taste nice and it'll burn your throat."

"Thanks," he says, but doesn't pick up the glass.

"I wouldn't let it get any warmer," I say.

"I don't drink, actually," he replies, pushing the shot glass back towards me. "It's all yours."

"Scout leader not approve?"

His smile doesn't reach his eyes.

God. Maybe I was right first time. Can't trust a guy in this job who doesn't drink. How the fuck else are you supposed to wipe away the things that we see?

"Suit yourself," I say, then knock the shot back. Fuck. I shake my neck in a reflex reaction. I was right: it tastes awful and it burns.

But then it numbs.

Bradley just stands there.

I have one more try. "Come over, join the team," I say, indicating Sandra, Dev and Reynolds, all clustered round a table in the corner.

"Thanks. I will in a moment," he says. And it pisses me off. I'm his superior. He's the one who should be making an effort, he's the one who should be ingratiating himself with the team. I'm about to walk off in a huff when a pretty girl with big hair and very red lipstick walks up and stands on the other side of him. I recognize her. Kelly, I think. She's a friend of Sandra's—an FLO from another team.

"Hi, Helen," she says, then sidles in closer to Bradley like a dog marking her turf. "Where were we?" she continues, turning to him.

Bradley looks embarrassed. OK. I misjudged him. Less unfriendly, more on the pull. And to think I felt sorry for him all alone.

I return to the others, and another line of shots appears. Parker was buying this time, I think. Then another turns up. Sandra is laughing at something Dev says. The room gets warmer. Fuzzier. The pain, the hurt, duller. Karen's face no longer lurks at the edge of my vision. Parker makes a long and rambling toast to Cooper and we all cheer.

Another shot.

Bradley has the right idea. I want someone to hold me. Someone to fuck away all the pain.

I glance round the bar. I can't see Bradley any more. Probably slunk off with the girl with big hair and a too-red mouth.

I can feel Mark looking at me. Edging closer. I know that look. No . . . I'm not going back there.

Then DI Green from MIT4 approaches. Smiling. He's hammered too. I can tell by the way he's walking—like his limbs are slightly fluid. We had a one-night thing a couple of years back. He's all right.

All right for one night anyway. And, as far as I know, he's not married.

He places another shot glass in front of me.

"You look like someone in need of a tequila," he says with a smile. Then he runs a line of salt along his hand, places a lime segment between his teeth and winks at me.

Green wants a repeat. I can see it in his eyes. It's an easy option. Mark shifts uncomfortably. He's annoyed, but there's nothing he can do.

Minutes later we're in a cab on the way back to mine.

Natalie

I DON'T GO home. I can't face him yet. Instead, I walk. Up Holland Park Avenue towards Notting Hill Gate, and then down towards High Street Kensington. After that, I don't focus on where I'm going, I just register the impact of my feet against the pavement.

My phone keeps ringing. It's Ryan. I don't answer. After the fourth call, I turn it off.

Dusk turns to dark, and streetlamps throw down oases of amber light. Hours bleed into one another. I walk past couples sitting in restaurant windows, groups of men pouring into pubs, families out late.

My legs eventually tire before my mind does and I start the journey home.

It's just after nine when I get off the train back at Mortlake. The walk up the road takes me longer than normal. I'm dreading my arrival.

Ryan is sat on a chair in the kitchen, lacing up his trainers.

"Where did you go?" he asks quietly, not meeting my eye. "It's been hours. I called and called."

"I went to talk to her," I reply.

He lets out a sound halfway between a cough and a laugh.

"Did you? And what did she say? What did a complete stranger say to make you believe her over your partner of fourteen years?"

"She didn't say anything. I followed her. Then I went for a walk."

"And?"

"What?"

"Do you believe me now?"

He stares me straight in the eye, and I stare back. They're eyes you can drown in. I look for deceit, for cruelty, but I don't find it. I just see sadness.

And I feel guilty. A mix of guilt and relief. He cheated on me. I still have to process that. But he's no rapist. I should have believed him. He's always believed me. Stood as my protector against the world.

But then I think of Fiona Scott. The world is littered with wives and girlfriends who looked into their partners' eyes and found innocence.

Women who "knew".

Women who were wrong.

"I'm going for a run," he says. "In the woods."

"At this time?" I ask.

"I need to clear my head. I might be a while."

When he leaves, I change into track pants and a sweater and go to curl up on the sofa, knees pulled up to my chest. A wildlife programme's on. Animals strolling across the Serengeti. I try to watch it. To turn my brain off, but I can't. A vulture swoops down and picks at a sun-bleached carcass. Images swirl in my head. It's like they've found me now I've stopped. Gavin Scott on the stand saying I'd seduced him. The security footage of me next to him, laughing. Then Alice. And Ryan. His toothy grin. His look of shock when he saw me in the kitchen. The door slamming late at night.

Then it hits me. The sofa. Where we normally sit together every night. Where I'm sitting now. This is where he had sex with her. Right here. Bile rises up my throat.

The grey of the sofa fabric pixellates first, tunnelling my vision. I try to pinch my hand, to dig my nails in, but I can't. I've lost control of my muscles.

The floorboards blur.

My stomach drops.

Then blackness.

* * *

It's cold. I'm cold. And wet. I'm sat on something hard. Wooden. It's dark, but there's a harsh white light to my right. And a low, rumbling noise in the distance. My brain starts slowly ticking. Piecing the world back together like a jigsaw puzzle.

"Are you all right?"

A figure stops next to me and leans in. A male voice. I flinch and the footsteps speed up and away.

Tick tick tick.

The wood becomes the base of a bench at the edge of the pavement, the harsh light a street lamp, the rumbling the sound of traffic on the main road a few blocks behind me. The road I'm on is quiet. It leads up to the park and there's no reason for anyone but residents to use it after dark. Further up it joins Fife Road, where there's an entrance to the woods another hundred metres or so along. It's where I usually walk. I used to walk there every day. Less so now. Now there are too many dogs.

I check my watch: 11.03 p.m. I've lost around an hour and I'm half a mile from home. I haven't travelled this far while losing time since the first time it ever happened. And in the rain? And why here? I like the woods, I walk here to relax, but at night? Did I follow Ryan? Do I now feel the subconscious need to monitor his every move? Or is he still my place of safety, my refuge, in spite of everything? I'm going crazy. I'm going slowly crazy.

Repressing a sob, I stand to walk home. My trainers are muddy—my hands wet too. Bits of leaves stick to the bottom of my track pants. God knows what route I took to walk here. I must have wandered off the pavement into gutters or possibly on to front lawns. Please don't let any neighbours have seen. There isn't enough for old people to do round here other than gossip. A juicy titbit like this would fuel them for a week. *Did you see Natalie Campbell staggering around last night? She must have been drunk. Her poor husband.* I imagine the pings of the neighbourhood WhatsApp group echoing round the streets.

Keeping my head down, I walk quickly home, trying to stay in the shadows, picking up pace as I cross front drives, cringing when security lights throw beams towards the pavement.

I reach the front door without having to talk to anyone. Ryan still isn't back. I hope he took his head torch. It's far too dark to be running in the woods without one.

Then I catch myself. How can I hold two completely different thoughts in my head at the same time? I can fear he might have attacked a girl and yet worry about him bumping into trees.

It doesn't make sense. The whole situation is ludicrous.

I don't want to wait up for him and the inevitable further arguments. I don't want to lie next to him, not until I've worked out what he is, what I'm dealing with. So I go to bed in the spare room. This time, sleep doesn't come and I'm still awake when he returns. I don't say anything though. I just lie on the pillow, facing away from the door, keeping completely still when he tries to turn the handle, when I hear his grunt of hurt surprise to find it locked. It's only the white noise of the blender downstairs followed by the shower running that finally sends me to sleep.

THURSDAY, 21 MARCH

Stratton

WHAT'S THAT NOISE?
I half wake and stare around myself.

It goes again. Drilling into my brain.

Fuck.

My phone.

I swivel my head towards the clock. Just that slight movement makes me want to gag. The digits glow in the dark: 6 a.m.

It's work. Got to be. No one else calls at 6 a.m.

There's a groan next to me. It's Green, face crumpled into the pillow. Bollocks. I'd forgotten he was even here. Bringing him back was a mistake.

My phone's not on the bedside table. It's still tucked in my trouser pocket on the floor at the end of the bed. I head towards it. The rolling, lurching feeling continues. How much did I drink?

I pick it up.

"Stratton."

"You've got a case." It's Parker's voice. He sounds rough too. I wonder how late he stayed. "Suspected homicide. Sheen Woods. Uniform are already at the scene and the HAT car is on its way. Forensics too. Bradley will pick you up in ten."

"I can drive myself," I say angrily.

"Didn't think you'd pass a breathalyser," he quips. "Just be grateful you've got the case. It's against my better judgement."

He hangs up. Damn. I don't want to sit passenger to Fast-Track. As I walk over to my chest of drawers, the room buckles again slightly. Maybe Parker has a point.

I pull on navy trousers and a grey vest, then layer a tan polo neck on top—sensible, appropriate clothing—knock back a couple of aspirin with a glass of water and put a pair of shades in my pocket. I crave coffee and a bacon sandwich, but they'll have to wait.

Bradley knocks on the door exactly ten minutes later. No surprise there. He strikes me as someone who's always exactly on time. He looks fresh. Trousers neatly pressed, an ironed shirt and navy jacket, hair brushed back, coffee in his hand. He must have been tucked up in bed nice and early. Probably after a bit of plain vanilla sex with Kelly. Wonder if she's still in his apartment. He probably made her an omelette in the morning and brought her tea in bed. He looks the sort. But then again, he has the benefit of youth. I could have stayed up all night at his age and finally passed out in a dumpster and it wouldn't mark me. Not like now.

He takes one look at me. It doesn't take an expert in body language to tell he doesn't approve.

"You OK to do this?"

"Yes. Get in the car."

"I've brought you a coffee." He hands it over.

"Thanks."

I take a sip. It's milkier than I like, but it's still welcome.

I wear my sunglasses in the car. I tell him the sun's lower in the morning so the glare hurts my eyes. We both know it's to deaden the hangover. The whole car stinks of pine. He's got one of those bloody air-fresheners hanging from the rear-view mirror. Shaped like a fucking Christmas tree. I have to open the window or I'll retch.

We park on Christchurch Road in front of the main entrance to the woods. Uniform have already wrapped the gates with police tape. Whoever found the body has been less discreet than at the allotments and a gaggle of dog-walking busybodies have gathered in front and are clamouring for details. Rubbernecking fuckers. A couple even have their phones out in case they're lucky enough to see someone else murdered in front of them. True-crime podcast junkies, no doubt. Need to get off on something bad happening to give some meaning to their empty lives. Maybe they should just stay in bed a bit longer in the morning. Or get a job. They might find that boosts their sero-fucking-tonin levels a bit more than a local murder. The homicide assessment detective spots us and ushers us through, writing our names in the log as we pass the tape. It's Collins. Good. He's dependable. It's his job to preserve the crime scene and he's taking it seriously.

We follow Collins down the path. My head's starting to hurt less now. The aspirin's kicking in and the adrenaline's starting to build. It always does at a crime scene. Senses heighten. Blood rushes to the brain.

I automatically start to note the surroundings. It's not too cold. Dry now, but it rained last night and the ground's still damp. The air too. A slight drop in temperature and it will rain again. The path's churned-up mud—a jumble of stretched-out human and paw prints running in both directions. Chances of getting any usable prints are negligible.

"Give me the low-down," I say to Collins as we head deeper into the wood.

"Vic's female. Twenties. Discovered by a dog-walker. Dog started whining and barking. Exposed the vic's face. The walker phoned it in. Coroner's been informed."

I like Collins. He's curt, to the point. No extraneous crap.

I drill down on the details.

"What time?"

"Five twenty."

Who the fuck walks their dog at five twenty in the morning?!

"Did the walker see the perp? Or anyone else near the scene?"

"No. They only saw another dog-walker when they exited the wood. They're giving a statement to Uniform now, but short story is they didn't see anything of use."

"Any ID?" Bradley asks.

"Not as yet. We're waiting for Forensics before we uncover more of the body."

I nod approvingly.

We take a left-hand fork and the path is blocked by a second line of police tape. An extra precaution. Ahead sits a white tent erected approximately four metres to the right of the path, just where the holly bushes thicken and the shrubland starts. Good. A tent's a necessity on a day like this. Stops prying eyes if the tape line is breached and protects the scene from the elements. If anyone finds Karen in the ground, I hope to God they give her a tent. Fuck. Don't go there. Stay here. Focus.

Collins stops by a bag and hands me and Bradley shoe covers, overalls, face masks and latex gloves. Only then are we allowed to enter the crime scene proper.

"Uniform have started a sweep of the area," Collins says, "and Forensics should be here any minute. I don't need to tell you not to touch anything." He looks at Bradley as he says this. Bradley looks annoyed, and I don't blame him. Don't touch anything is rule 101 of detective work. Fast-Track may be young, but he doesn't strike me as a total moron.

We approach the tent at a diagonal from the main path, to minimize the chances that we'll cross and disturb the perp's tracks.

Collins holds open a tent flap and we duck inside.

The tent covers a patch of ground two metres by three metres. The vic's body lies straight, legs and arms parallel, almost like she's sleeping, or on display in an open casket. She's covered by a blanket of branches, twigs and leaves, but her face is exposed and she stares up sightlessly.

I stare back. Fuck. It still gets me every time like a sucker punch. You think you'd get used to it, but you never do. The cops you have to watch are the ones that aren't bothered any more. Not the ones that joke; I don't mean them. Jokes are just a coping mechanism. They still care, it still bothers them, so they act like childish dicks and joke about it so they don't throw up or cry. I glance over at Bradley. He looks pale, like he might throw up. Good.

"The dog had a largish branch in its mouth," Collins says. "Chances are that's what had been placed over the vic's face."

I edge round the walls of the tent, making sure I don't damage whatever prints there are. Just in case.

The vic was pretty. Remarkably so. Even covered in a dusting of soil and dirt from the branches you can tell that. It shouldn't matter. A life's a life. Age—that should matter—how many years have been stolen from them—but not looks. Yet somehow it always does. If the vic's female and pretty there's always a different feel at the scene. I guess it's the way we're programmed. To care for young and pretty things—like babies. It's hard to find a truly ugly baby. It's also why a campaign to save lion cubs can raise millions, whereas no one's flocking to save the bloody proboscis monkey with its flaccid-cock nose.

She also hasn't been dead long. Her skin's greyish but there's no sign of decay. Her hair, long and blonde, hasn't faded.

The cause of death seems obvious. The right side of her head is caved in, just above her ear. The hair is matted there, and splinters of bone protrude. But I've been doing this long enough to know better than to jump to conclusions. We'll know more when Forensics have examined the scene. Whether the blow was pre- or post-mortem. A surprising number of sickos get off on harming a corpse.

I stare at her again. All I can think is she's been left so close to the path. No attempt's been made to bury the body. The leafy covering is token at best. No one could have thought it would hide her properly. I poke the ground with my toe and the soil gives. It's hardly baked dry. A spade or any digging tool could easily cut through it. And the undergrowth between the trees gets quite dense only a few feet further in. If they'd dug there—four feet deep or so—the body could have stayed undisturbed for months. At least until a missing person's report or something had triggered a full search of the area.

There's a sound to my right and I remember I'm not alone. I look over to see Bradley staring at the ground as intensely as I am.

"What do you make of it?" I ask him.

"I can't work it out," he says. "No grave has been dug, which points towards a spontaneous act or the perp being disturbed . . ."

"But . . ." I prompt.

"If someone had witnessed the murder, they'd have reported it. And even though she's not buried, the killer has had time to arrange the body and cover it."

I nod. My thoughts exactly.

"Which suggests the covering is more a mark of respect than an attempt to conceal."

I nod again. He's not bad.

Bradley waits a minute before continuing. Then meets my eyes and says slowly, "It's like they wanted her to be found."

I nod. Yes, that's exactly what it's like.

"Stratton!" A bellowing voice from behind makes me turn round.

The tent flaps open again and Grayson walks in, his stomach straining against his white coverall.

"You'd better not be messing up my crime scene."

His eye creases tell me he's smiling under the mask.

Collins fills him in, and then Grayson asks for some space.

"I need to remove the rest of the stuff covering the body so we can see exactly what we're dealing with here. Looks like a blow to the head, but we can't jump to conclusions now, can we?"

I nod my go-ahead, but Bradley lingers.

"Shouldn't we be documenting all of this?"

"Who's this then?" Grayson asks, his voice mocking. "We haven't met. I'm Grayson, but everyone here calls me Pavarotti."

"Detective Sergeant Bradley."

"New?" he asks me, rather than Bradley.

"He's being fast-tracked."

"Bully for you," he says ironically. "Well, Detective Sergeant Bradley, you don't need to worry. Collins here will document, and I'll take extensive photographs of every stage, as I've done for the last thirty years. Are you happy with that?"

Bradley's eyes narrow, but he follows me out.

I don't have time to deal with his crushed ego now. We've got work to do.

There's no single set of prints leading off the path towards the grave. The perp's will be there, but probably also the dogwalker's and no doubt Uniform's. The path itself is an unreadable muddle. The woods are popular. Hundreds must visit every day. No way of telling from which direction the perp approached or left. There's no direct car access. If the perp drove here, then the closest entrance to the road is the main one. If they came by foot they could have entered via Richmond Park, which then opens it up to half a dozen areas. Alternatively, they could have come through the alley that runs here from Richmond behind the cemetery. Fuck. It's the woods, so there's no CCTV. We'll check nearest CCTV points when we're back at the station, but there don't tend to be many away from the high streets and arterial roads.

I finish scribbling in my notebook then turn to Bradley. "Right. Call the station. We need CCTV footage of the area, focusing on all the entry points. Close as we can get. We're looking for someone on foot. Potentially carrying a bag concealing a weapon of some kind. Possibly two people—one of which would be a female, early twenties, Caucasian, slim build, long hair. Also look for any vehicles heading up to the woods. Sheen Lane, Sheen Common Drive, Hertford Avenue. Any of those. Pull all the ULEZ cameras too. And reinterview the dog-walker. I want to double-check the vic was completely covered before her dog started pulling off sticks."

My phone rings. It's Pavarotti.

"Stratton."

"We have the body uncovered."

* * *

She's taller than I thought. Long, thin legs in tight-fitting jeans. No sign the jeans had been ripped or removed. One small mercy. Trainers on her feet and an oversized sweat-shirt. She wasn't dressed up to go out. She doesn't look like a hooker on her way to a client. She also doesn't look like she was out for a run. Maybe she was walking and it was an opportunistic, random act. A deranged killer waiting in the shadows. Or maybe she was brought here. Either already dead or killed where she lies. So many maybes . . .

"It is likely that the blow to the head was the cause of death," Pavarotti says. "There are no other obvious external injuries. I'll be able to confirm when I get her on the table."

"What about time of death?" I ask.

"I'd say sometime from around ten o'clock last night to one this morning. It's difficult to be more exact as she's been outside in the cold, so her temperature will have dropped faster than normal and rigor mortis set in more quickly."

"Was she killed here?" Bradley asks.

"Again, I'll have to get her on the table to be sure."

We open the tent to leave when there's a crackle on the radio and a shout from outside. Uniform's found something.

A PC steps out of the shrub on to the path ahead, brandishing something, triumphantly. It's a bag. A brown leather shoulder bag. I hope to fuck he's wearing gloves.

Collins reaches him before we do and enters the discovery into the log before handing it over to us to examine.

"Where did you find it?" I ask the PC.

"In the undergrowth," he replies, indicating behind him. God he's young. Sounds like his voice has only just broken. "Just ten metres or so in. Under that holly tree there." A smile of pride spreads across his freckled face. "I saw it cos the buckle caught the light. It was glintin', like. I didn't touch the handle. I kept my gloves on."

I resist the urge to give him a little hug.

Bradley stands by, phone on camera mode, as I unzip the bag. Keys . . . a book—*The Fundamentals of Property Law*—strange choice: she doesn't look like a lawyer. There's something hard in the corner . . . a wallet. Trying not to get my hopes up too much, I retrieve it and open it, pausing to let Bradley document each stage. There's about seventy quid cash inside. That rules out a mugging gone wrong. There's a couple of cards in the credit card section. I remove them, one by one, careful to only touch the outside edges. A Tesco Clubcard. A debit card. We have a name. An ID. Great. That will save us hours of leg work, scouring through missing persons reports, putting out inquiries. I turn over the final card. It's a driver's licence. The face of the dead girl stares back out of the left-hand side. A name and address. It's almost too easy. Bradley's eyes narrow, and I can see he's thinking that too. I used to make that mistake when I first joined. Seeing an easy win as suspicious. But the longer you're on the job, the more you realize there are very few highly intelligent killers out there. You're generally dealing with pissed-off, angry people lashing out, or the mentally ill. There aren't many Hannibal Lecters. You don't need to be Sherlock Holmes."

"Right." I turn to Bradley. "Call Sandra. Tell her to find the next of kin of . . ." I double-check the card. "Alice. Alice Lytton."

Natalie

I DIDN'T SET an alarm and the world is fully awake before I am. Birds chirp in the trees outside and planes take off and land from Heathrow with relentless frequency. My life may have been turned upside down, but everything else continues as normal. I don't know whether I should feel thrown or reassured.

At least I woke up here, at home. Part of me feared I'd lose time again during the night and come to God knows where. Small mercies.

Today we find out if Alice is going to the police. If she's going to tell Ryan's work, then the police and then the world that my husband is a rapist. I glance out of the window, half expecting to see flashing blue lights and officers in uniform assembling on the front drive. No. Nothing. Not yet.

I can hear Ryan downstairs, and my anxiety builds. I can't avoid my husband, but is the man downstairs really my husband? What I thought my husband was? Or was "my husband" always merely a construct of my imagination? A fiction cloaking a flawed and dangerous man?

I would have known. Surely, I would have had some inkling. There'd have been some part of my subconscious ringing out a warning. You can't spend that much time with someone and not know.

"Nat?" Ryan calls upstairs. He must have heard me moving about.

"I'm coming down," I call back. I pull on my thick green dressing gown and tie the belt tightly round my waist.

Ryan's standing at the bottom of the stairs, fully dressed in work clothes, holding a protein shake in one hand and a cup of tea, handle turned out in my direction, in the other. I take the cup from him.

"Have you been for another run this morning?" I ask, surprised, looking at the shake.

"No, just last night. But I'm trying to up my protein. Get in shape."

He looks at me for approval, but all I can think is *you slept with another woman. Who says you forced her.* How are we talking about protein?

"Oh," I say flatly. I don't know how to do this. How to talk to him.

He runs a hand through his hair.

"What route did you go last night?" I ask. I want to check if he saw me. If someone knew where I'd been and what I'd been doing. But then he'd have mentioned it already, wouldn't he?

"Along Fife, and then through the woods into the park and back. It was cold and wet," he says with a short laugh. "But I think it helped." He's acting like nothing's wrong. Like nothing's changed. Like he's about to kiss me goodbye and then head into work to deliver a presentation. I'm not sure if he's performing for me or for himself. Probably for the both of us. He runs his hand through his hair a second time. "How are you doing?" he asks. "Your coat was soaking when I got in. I didn't know you were going out."

I debate whether or not I should tell him. He's always been my confidant. But now everything's different. One evening. One act. He's ruined everything.

My mouth decides before my mind does.

"I . . . lost time again. I . . . I was here, then I woke up on the bench on Sheen Lane."

Just telling him somehow eases the pressure, and I find myself irritated that I rely on him so much. It makes me feel vulnerable that no one else understands me quite as well.

Ryan stares at me. Pity and guilt filling his eyes.

"God, Nat, I'm sorry. It's all my fault. What I've put you through, the stress . . ."

He moves towards me, but I back away. I'm not ready for him to touch me yet. Even if I let myself believe he isn't a rapist, he still cheated on me. He cheated with her in our home while I was upstairs in our bed. I'm not sure I can ever forgive that.

"Have you heard anything from work yet?" I ask, looking at his suit again. It's hardly "stay at home and wait" attire.

Ryan looks away and his whole body sags.

"No. No one will be in yet though." He sounds small. And scared. I know he needs me to put my arms round him, but I can't bring myself to.

He gives himself a little shake as if to snap out of it, then offers to make me breakfast.

"Thanks, but I'll make my own."

Rejected, shoulders hunched towards his ears, Ryan heads into the utility room and I hear the tap run.

I pour myself a bowl of Alpen. Images start to flash through my head once more. Alice. Ryan smiling. The door slamming. I switch on the radio to drown them out. They're playing "Super Trouper". God, I hate ABBA. Ryan does too. That had been our one stipulation to the DJ at our wedding: no ABBA. The DJ didn't listen though. He'd thought he knew better. Third song in, he'd played "Dancing Queen". A half-smile forms on my lips and then fades. Is this what life is going to be like? Glimpses of almost happiness that then drown?

I'm about to turn the radio off when the news comes on. The newsreader leads with an item about stalling trade talks. I only half listen. Politics has always bored me. Half-truths, calculated displays of sincerity and horse trading. But then the newsreader says something that makes me freeze, my spoon stuck in midair on its trajectory towards my mouth.

"The body of a young woman has been found in the woods in East Sheen in south-west London. The police are treating the death as suspicious. The woman has not yet been identified. Police are asking anyone who might have seen something to come forward."

Sheen Woods? A dead body in Sheen Woods? I can't quite believe it. The worst thing that'd happened there before was when the natural playground was closed because of oak processionary moth. From moths to murder? It's somehow absurd. Like it shouldn't happen round here. The leafy gardens and high property prices are designed to insulate you from it. Push it back towards grittier territory. The neighbourhood WhatsApp group will be pinging with furious delight.

I put down the spoon and push away the cereal bowl, no longer hungry, and wonder whether Ryan's heard anything. Then I remember he was in the woods. God. He could have seen the killer. Jogged right past them.

"Ryan?"

He doesn't answer. He probably can't hear over the sound of the running water. I poke my head round the utility room door.

"Ryan?"

He looks up from what he's doing with a start. His trainers are in the sink and he's scrubbing them with a nail brush.

"Sorry, you startled me. Did you say something?"

I stare at the stream of reddish-brown water that swirls down the plughole.

"Did you hear? A body's been found in Sheen Woods. A young woman."

Ryan looks shocked, his eyebrows raised in disbelief. "Sheen Woods? Are you sure?"

I nod.

"God, Nat. You walk there. I always worried about you alone there."

"Did you see anything?" I say.

"Sorry?"

"Last night. Did you see anyone?"

"Um . . . I don't know. I think there were a few other runners. It was dark. It was raining. I had a lot on my mind."

I can't stop staring at his trainers. He never washes his trainers.

He must feel my gaze as he pauses, brush in hand. "Trod on something. Dog shit, I think. There are too many dogs in the woods now."

I nod. There are too many dogs.

I fetch him the anti-bac spray from under the kitchen sink.

* * *

At my insistence, Ryan tries his work at 8.30 a.m. They won't talk to him. They won't even tell him if Alice is in yet. I suggest he messages Bob instead. Bob's always the first exec in. They've known each other for years. Bob might bend the rules for a friend.

There's a five-minute wait before Bob replies.

"No show yet."

"What time is she normally in?" I ask.

"Assistants don't have to be in before nine, unless there's a client conference."

Eight forty-five comes round. Then nine.

I can feel the tension building and building. Everything lies in the hands of a young woman, ten years my junior. A victim or a liar.

And then I think, what if she doesn't go in? What happens if she never goes back? It won't necessarily mean Ryan's telling the truth. She might just have got scared. The enormity of the ordeal—the idea of the police, court, cross-examination, all of it—it might have overwhelmed her. Then I'll never know. There'll always be a tiny seed of doubt buried in the back of my mind. I realize if I'm ever going to find peace, I need to hear her account of what happened last night. And I need to see her face when she says it.

I shouldn't have listened to Rachel. I should have knocked on Alice's door last night. It was the perfect moment to confront her. *Tell me the truth about my husband.* She would have had to talk to me. I could have waited outside until she did. What does Rachel know? She's never been in this position.

If I leave now, I can be there before ten.

"Nat?"

Ryan calls after me as I grab my coat from the stand, pick up my keys from the console table and hurry out the door.

"Nat, I need you today."

"I'll be back before twelve," I say. I don't say *in case the police come.* But the look in his eyes shows he heard the unspoken words anyway.

* * *

I leave the car at the Castlenau end of Barnes and then walk across Hammersmith Bridge. The wind whips waves on to the Thames's grey surface as the temporary boarding bounces underfoot. Will they ever repair the bridge? It's been causing havoc for years now. Then I catch myself and marvel again at the brain's ability to compartmentalize. That I can feel anger towards the council at the same time that I'm heading to discover if my husband raped a woman. Such is the human psyche. Do our distant relatives the apes have to go through this? Does a female mountain gorilla care if the silverback she thought was hers took his pleasure in another gorilla with or without her consent? Is this a particularly human torment?

On the other side of the bridge at Hammersmith, I hurry to the tube entrance off King Street and take the Hammersmith and City line to Latimer Road. Then I retrace my steps from yesterday.

Before I know it, I'm walking down St. Ann's Road towards Alice's flat.

I stop by a tree, a few feet from the front path, stare at the door—and compose myself. Am I doing the right thing?

The door opens and a female police officer leaves. She has a friendly face and blonde curly hair. She calls back to someone that she'll get them a bite to eat and be back soon. I flatten myself into the treetrunk. I don't think she's seen me. Then it hits me, full force. Alice has done it. She's called the police. I know I should go. That I shouldn't even attempt to speak to Alice. I'd be interfering with an investigation. Pressurizing the witness. Or whatever the correct phrase is, rather than one pilfered from a terrible TV drama.

The police officer steps on to the pavement. I edge round the trunk away from her. She heads up the road in the direction of the tube.

I contemplate turning back and fleeing home. Warning Ryan. But then I think: *I'm here*. Alice's allegations are now official. It already feels like I've lost everything, so one step further seems insignificant.

Taking a deep breath, I march up the path and knock on the door.

A woman in her early thirties answers. She's wrapped in a dressing gown, her eyes swollen from crying.

It's not Alice, but there's a trace of family resemblance around the nose and mouth. A sister, maybe.

She stares out at me angrily.

"Are you a fucking reporter? Get lost. You're vultures, you know that."

Oh my God. The press know. The police and the press. Reporters are already starting to circle.

"I'm not a reporter," I say quietly. "I need to speak to Alice. It's important. Is she in?"

She raises her face and meets my eyes. The suspicion still present, but less barbed.

"I haven't seen you before . . . Are you friends?"

"I . . . We know each other," I say cautiously.

Her right hand is shaking and she's leaning against the doorframe. Her lips have a bluish tinge.

"Are you OK?" I ask. "Do you need me to call a doctor?"

She shakes her head and forces herself to control her breathing. In. Out. In. Out.

Then she stares me directly in the eye.

"Alice is dead," she whispers.

Stratton

We've only just finished briefing the team at the station when Pavarotti calls. He's about to begin the autopsy. We need to be there. Bradley goes to get the car. I tell him to pull over at Ron's en route, where they do a decent bacon bap for three fifty. It's one of the last few proper caffs round here. Where you can get a fry-up all day without them calling it fucking brunch and charging you a tenner for the privilege. The hangover's starting to kick in again as the adrenaline wears off and I'm going to feel like shit in about ten minutes if I don't eat. I offer to get one for Bradley, but he says he isn't hungry. Probably thinks he'll be able to eat after the autopsy. Rookie. He can't have attended many in his last posting. Hasn't learned yet what those things do to your appetite.

Ron greets me with a smile. We go way back. He takes out an extra rasher, on top of the normal three, and fills me in on business as the bacon starts to spit on the griddle.

"It's mainly Poles now. Poles and guys up from Kent and Essex. Locals are too good for us," he says with a smile, like he's joking. But we both know he's not. It's changed round here. I spot a photo of Kev, his oldest, stuck to the coffee machine. A good kid. Used to see him helping his dad out on the occasional Saturdays I'd pop in for a greasy pick-me-up. Big smile. Huge bottle-top NHS glasses, the kind that distort your face.

"How's Kev?" I ask as Ron layers the bacon on to the bap and smothers it in ketchup.

"Off to uni in September," he says with a proud smile. Even his chest puffs up a little. The first kid in a family going to uni is a big deal.

"Good for him."

"Studying to be an optician," he adds. Figures.

I congratulate him and put a fiver in the tip jar. "For Kev," I say.

The bacon is working its magic as we pull into the mortuary car park.

"It's fine if you need to leave at any point," I say to Bradley. I get the impression he doesn't particularly like advice, but I'm his supervisor. It's my job to look out for him.

"I'll be fine," he says with a tight smile. My instincts were correct. He leaves his jacket in the car.

"You're not taking it?" I say.

"It's not that cold today."

I think about saying something, but it's not such a bad thing if Fast-Track gets taken down a peg or two.

As we walk up the steps to the morgue, we bump into Sandra leaving with a woman in her thirties. Her whole body is slumped. Must be the next of kin—here to formally identify the body before we cut her open. Poor woman. She's just had her world sledge-hammered. The rest of her life shunted on to a different track.

Sandra introduces us, her voice soft but not patronizing. She's got a gift for it. Not many have.

"Ms Lytton, this is DI Stratton. She's leading the investigation into Alice's death. You're in good hands. She's one of the best."

I nod hello and say I'm sorry for her loss. I feel it's best to say the words. People never knew how to react around me after Karen went missing. They didn't want to feel like they were intruding, so they didn't say anything, in the hope that was better. It wasn't. If something awful happens, you want it acknowledged.

Ms Lytton doesn't reply, but then I didn't expect her to. That wasn't the point.

"I'll be coming to ask you some questions about Alice in a bit," I say. "Is that all right?"

She still doesn't speak. She's in the denial stage. Anger will kick in soon.

My phone vibrates. Pavarotti's getting impatient.

"Why don't you take Ms. Lytton home and make her a nice cup of tea?" I say. "We'll be over in a couple of hours."

Sandra nods and steers Ms. Lytton towards the car park as me and Bradley continue into the building.

Dressed once again in scrubs, masks and shoe covers, we enter the autopsy room. The cold hits us as soon as we close the door. It's got to be cold to slow decomposition. I glance over and see Bradley shivering and allow myself a little smile.

The Marriage of Figaro starts playing at low volume.

"Thought I'd make it a bit classier for you, Fast-Track," Pavarotti says with a rumbling laugh. "We're not all uneducated heathens, you know."

"Never said you were," replies Bradley tightly. I can't tell if he's embarrassed or angry. Probably both.

The music and bickering are making my headache worse. "Enough," I say, marching towards the table where the vic's body lies covered by a white sheet, only her head and neck exposed. "Music off, please."

Pavarotti does as I ask.

I take out a notebook and pen. Bradley presses record on his phone. Kids today, worried they'll get hand sprain if they actually write stuff down.

Pavarotti takes his place at the vic's head and tilts it to show the right temple wound more clearly. Placing fresh damp cotton between tweezers, he swabs the wound.

"The cause of death is the blow to the head," he says. "The bruising and tissue damage are consistent with the vic being alive at time of impact. The wound was heavily coated in soil. There are no obvious fibres or other extraneous material, but obviously I'll send away samples for analysis to see if the microscope picks up what the lowly eye cannot. It'll give us more of an idea whether she was killed in the woods, or somewhere else and then dumped. The dirt runs deep into the wound, which suggests that if she was murdered elsewhere, it was not long before. There was no time for substantial clotting or scabbing.

"The size and shape of the indent suggests a heavy, curved surface, probably metallic or stone. Wood is more likely to leave trace splinters. It is frontal rather than posterior, suggesting that the attacker was facing the victim at the point of striking."

I visualize the scene.

"Would that make the attacker left-handed then?" I ask.

He nods. "They could have used their right hand, but it would be a less natural sweeping motion. I think left-handed is probable."

I scribble in the notebook. God, my handwriting's awful. Maybe I should use a recording app after all.

"What about the height of the attacker?"

"It depends if the vic was seated or standing at the moment of impact. And on the length of the weapon and therefore its arc of travel."

"So, basically, we can't tell. Can't rule anyone out."

"Exactly."

Pavarotti peels the sheet down to the vic's waist.

And what I see next makes me flinch.

The vic's upper right arm is branded with a trio of faded circular burns—spaced at regular intervals, a couple of centimetres apart—and both her arms show faint needle tracks. There're some things you learn to recognize quickly if you're on the force.

Alice, what happened to you?

"I thought you said that there was just one wound?"

"The burns occurred earlier—see how they have scabbed over. They're most likely a minimum of two or three weeks old."

"Cigarettes?"

"Most likely."

"Could they be self-inflicted?" I ask. The track marks suggest a troubled girl.

"Unlikely. Self-harm usually takes the form of scratching or cutting. Cigarette burns hurt. Really hurt. If someone tried it once, they're unlikely to do it again. I'd wager that this was done to her. And see here . . ."

Pavarotti indicates marks at the top of the same arm and just above the elbow. Leaning in, I make out very faint yellowish bruising.

". . . Likely remnants of bruising from when she was held as she was burnt. The discoid nature suggests they were caused by finger pressure."

I wrap my right hand round my left upper arm and squeeze. I see how the fingers pinch down on the wool of my polo neck sleeves.

"Exactly," Pavarotti observes.

Something strikes me. She was held in two places. Two hands used up.

"She must have been restrained by someone and burnt by someone else," I say.

"Good. I've taught you well."

I roll my eyes at him.

"And the needle marks?"

"Again, they're faded, so older. Exactly how old, it's difficult to say. We'll do the blood work. See what turns up in her system."

So an addict. Or recovering addict. Her face looks so innocent. I catch myself. I've been away from the estate too long. Thinking addiction is somehow deserved. Something that bad, dirty people bring upon themselves.

Pavarotti shifts his attention to the vic's hands.

"We'll swab the nails for DNA in case she fought and scratched her attacker," he says. "But what do you notice about them?"

I look at them. They're painted a pale pink but otherwise quite normal. I've never been into nails. Don't really see the point. I want them long enough to pick at the end of Sellotape if it gets stuck to the side of the roll but short enough so they don't get in the way.

Bradley speaks up. I'd almost forgotten he was there.

"They're painted, suggesting she cares about her appearance."

"Well done, Fast-Track," Pavarotti says. "Anything else?"

And then it strikes me. They're cut like I cut nails. Short, no particular care or thought about shape. Someone who paints their nails wouldn't cut them like that.

"Could they have been cut by the perp at the scene?" I say. "To get rid of any DNA evidence in case she scratched them?"

"My thoughts exactly."

I scribble again, forming the words more carefully this time, like I'm back in primary-school handwriting class.

Pavarotti now pulls the rest of the sheet down.

"No vaginal or anal tearing, but there is some evidence that the vic was engaged in sexual activity in the forty-eight hours prior to her death. I'll send off swabs and we can see if we get a DNA match. I'll call you when we know anything."

"There are no other burn marks or bruising?" I ask, scanning the vic's body.

"None," Pavarotti confirms.

I turn to Bradley. "What does that tell us?"

He pauses in thought. "She wasn't tied up or held forcefully enough to cause bruising. Which suggests two possibilities. One—it was a random attack on a stranger that happened on site in the wood. He didn't have to restrain her—he hit her before she knew what was happening."

I nod. His comments are thoughtful and considered.

"Or . . ."

"Or she knew her attacker. She went willingly. Or willingly enough to walk unrestrained. Then he killed her."

I nod again. He's reaching the same conclusions as I have.

"Just one thing," I say. "Avoid assumptions. What assumption have you made?"

He looks at me.

"You said 'he'. There's no reason the perp can't be female."

* * *

The air tastes fresher than normal when we're back outside the morgue, even though we're right by an A-road. The dead give off a different kind of pollution. It clings to you and seeps under your skin.

A little shiver runs through me, but this time it's not the hangover. Everything's normally clearer after an autopsy. You have manner of death. Time of death. Later, chemical analysis, fibre analysis. The blanks start to be filled in.

But this time I'm feeling more confused. What started looking like a random attack looks less like it. Did the same person who killed her inflict cigarette burns on her two or three weeks earlier? What perp is careful enough to cut a vic's fingernails to remove DNA traces but then only tokenly covers the body in branches and leaves her bag metres away where it can easily be found?

The vic's bag. That's something else that's been troubling me. It had nearly everything you'd expect in it. Keys. Wallet. A book. But something was missing. Her phone. It's highly unlikely she didn't have one. So why go out without it? Did she leave it at home by accident, or did the perp take it? And, if so, why would a perp take her phone but nothing else?

Natalie

I'M ON AUTOPILOT on the way home. I hardly remember making my way back to Latimer Road, let alone changing tubes or walking back over the bridge. All I can think is that Alice is dead. Alice. Is. Dead. Probably got hit by a car. Someone who'd had one too many drinks at a party yet decided they were fine to drive home. One of those rare horror stories that normally make me pause for a moment—imagining myself both in role of victim and perpetrator—selfish concern masquerading as empathy—before carrying on, largely unaffected.

And the most secret part of me, the part I want to pretend to myself that I can't hear, doesn't think about the girl at all, doesn't think about the life full of promise and adventure cut short. Instead, it whispers. *She died before she could press charges. Now you'll never know. You'll never know the truth about her and Ryan. You'll never find peace.*

As I open the front door I hear the indistinct murmur of the TV coming from the living room. Damn, Ryan's still home. Of course he's still home. Where else would he be? I wonder if he knows yet? If news of Alice's death will have filtered through to work and then back to him? What will it mean for him? They can't keep investigating without her testimony. He can't be left on hold at home indefinitely, can he? To fire him without evidence would be unfair dismissal. No company wants to be wrapped up in legal proceedings. So the only other option is surely automatic reinstatement. But under a cloud of suspicion that will never lift.

I stay put, feet glued to the hall floor. If Ryan doesn't know, I don't want to be the one to tell him, to see his reaction. If he looks devastated, I'll know he really cared about her. If he seems relieved, then I'll think him a monster.

I think about leaving again. He might not have heard the key turn. I could step back outside. Go to the coffee shop. Return later. When he knows. When someone else has told him.

"Nat?"

Too late.

I walk towards the living room. He's sat on the sofa. The news is on. His eyes are red and his face is pale.

I have the sudden urge to comfort him as one would a lost child. To wrap my arms round him and make everything all right.

"Nat, look."

He gestures at the screen.

It takes me a second to register what I'm seeing. A reporter stands in front of a low barrier criss-crossed with police tape. Trees cluster in the rear of the shot. I can make out a cricket pavilion.

It's Sheen Woods. The murdered girl has made it national. Subtitles chase each other across the bottom of the screen. "Murdered woman found in Sheen Woods has been identified as Alice Lytton. Please come forward if you have any evidence relating to the case."

"It's her, Nat," Ryan whispers. "The dead girl is Alice."

Stratton

ALICE'S SISTER'S FLAT is small but neat. Nothing's expensive, but the care and fierce pride of its owner means that nothing looks cheap. It reminds me of Mum's old place. There are well-watered plants on the windowsill, the lino floor is spotless, and there are framed photos on a dust-free dresser. Most are of Alice.

Sandra's worked her magic, and Ms. Lytton is now talking, a freshly made cup of tea steaming on a coaster next to her. A plate of biscuits too, but that's untouched. The light's still out in her eyes, but she's communicating, at least. Some don't. The first few hours of any murder investigation are the most important. The faster you can get the information, the more likely you are to get the bastard who did it.

I start softly. Rush them, they get flustered and omit key details. Either that, or they feel they're being interrogated and they get defensive and clam up. Slowly, softly. It's the best way.

"She was a very beautiful girl," I say.

The "was" makes her stiffen. Fuck. But then she sniffs and nods and I breathe again.

"Alice was always the looker of the family," she says quietly. "Boys followed her everywhere. 'Like wasps at a picnic,' our mum used to say. Ever since she turned fourteen."

Bradley opens his mouth to ask a question, but I glare at him, signalling to let her talk. We'll end up with a better picture of Alice if

Ms. Lytton leads this first bit herself. She might say something we don't think to ask.

"Bright, too. Not that she ever really applied herself. Too easily distracted. She could have done anything if she put her mind to it. Mum was heartbroken when she dropped out of school. Alice wanted to be an actress, you see. She had the looks for it, of course, but it's a cruel profession. Messes with young girls' heads."

I nod and make a sympathetic noise, forcing myself to wait and listen.

"She was going back to college, did you know that? To study law, of all things . . ." Her voice fades out.

That explains the textbook we found in her bag. I smile encouragingly, but groan inside. She's given us nothing to work with. The dead girl was beautiful and clever. All families say that. As soon as the vic is cold, their journey to sainthood begins. OK, this time the pretty part is true—it often isn't—but it doesn't get us anywhere. It's time to start the questions.

Bradley senses this and asks if she'd mind if he recorded their conversation. "Just to make sure we have all the facts straight."

She looks at him blankly then nods her consent.

"Ms Lytton, when did you last see Alice?"

She doesn't have to think. She must have been playing it out over and over in her head.

"Nine thirty last night. I know as she left when we were halfway through *Celebrity Big Brother*. We always watch it together."

"That's quite late to be going out. Did she say where she was going?"

"She just said she needed a walk to clear her head. That she might be a while, but not to worry about her."

"So she wasn't meeting anyone?"

"Not that I knew of. She wasn't dressed up or anything."

I recall her outfit. Jeans. Oversized sweatshirt. Perfectly plausible late-night-walk clothing.

"Did she often do that? Walk in the evening?" I probe.

"Sometimes. Not normally that late. Sometimes she'd get anxious. A walk would help calm her down."

I make a note.

"Did she seem particularly anxious last night?"

Ms Lytton nods. "Something was up. She didn't want to tell me what. Said she'd tell me when it was over."

"When it was over?"

"Those were her words."

I make another note in my book.

"And you didn't see or hear from her later that evening?"

Ms Lytton shakes her head, her lower lip starting to quiver.

"No."

"What time did you go to bed?"

"Ten. I always go to bed at ten. I'm a nurse. My shifts start early. That's unless I'm working nights. I shouldn't have, though, should I? Gone to bed? I should have known something was wrong. Gone and found her. Brought her home."

She collapses into sobs and we wait as she takes the time she needs for the wave to pass.

Bradley speaks softly. "There's nothing you could have done."

It's compassionate. He understands grief. And it works. The sobs slowly subside and I can resume my questioning.

"As far as you know, was Alice seeing anyone? A boyfriend, perhaps?"

"No. She didn't bring anyone back here, at least, and I'd have known if she was spending nights away. Alice set her sights high. She was going to save up. Finish college, go to university. A 'mature student', she'd call herself. We'd laugh about that." Her eyes mist over and I think we've lost her, then she starts speaking again.

"She'd just got a job. An assistant at a marketing firm. Fancy place."

"Can you remember the name?" Bradley asks.

Ms Lytton pauses. And looks confused.

"Sorry . . . I can't remember. Oh . . . I'm letting her down, aren't I? I should know that . . ."

"It doesn't matter, Ms. Lytton," I say calmly. I don't want her to panic. I can't lose her now. "We can easily find that out. So, as you said, she'd started work at a marketing firm . . ."

"Yes. Two weeks ago. The pay was good. She wore smart clothes. Really looked the part. But that wasn't enough for her. She wanted a proper job. Professional, like. And then a proper husband. In that order. She had a plan, did Alice."

"Did she talk about anyone she'd met at the firm?"

"No." Her answer is quick and final and her eyes flick up and left. She's not telling me everything. I want to ask her more, but I know that'll shut her down. She has something of the prey animal about her. Poke more now and she'll disappear down her rabbit hole.

"What about someone outside of work? Someone she'd turned down, rejected?"

"Plenty of those. But no one who'd hold a grudge. Alice was charming, you see. You'd forgive her anything."

I bite back a sigh and smile again. We're back to St. Alice territory. It doesn't help us catch her killer. And it doesn't square with what we know. What about the needle tracks down her arm? What about the burns? I have to tread carefully.

"Ms Lytton. I'm going to ask a few difficult questions. It would really help us catch Alice's killer if you can answer them as honestly as possible. Do you understand?"

She nods, her eyes wary.

"Was Alice troubled in any way?"

I've struck a nerve. There's a new tension to her body, her mouth the thin straight line in the middle of a no-entry sign. "Ms Lytton, I only ask because we saw the needle marks on her arms."

"Alice was a good girl."

"It would really help us understand what happened to her."

"She's not using any more. She stopped. It half killed her. Made her do some really stupid stuff. But she stopped. Hasn't used for two months now. Weaned herself off that filth. She moved in here, with me. I helped her."

Her arms are folded across her chest. She's on the defensive. I need to get her back on side, but the next questions I'm going to ask are only going to push her further away.

"Did she ever . . ." I swallow. There's no easy way to ask this, but I have to. "Did she ever have sex for money?"

Ms Lytton grips the cup handle, and her knuckles whiten. She looks like she wants to smack me one.

"I'm sorry, but it's relevant. We need to understand why she was in the woods. Why she might have been alone out there. Or why she might have got in someone's car. Someone who then took her there."

Ms Lytton swallows then juts out her chin.

"She did some stupid things when she was on the drugs. To get her next hit. But she's clean now. She doesn't do that any more."

She stares at me as if daring me to challenge her. I don't. I can hear the truth in it.

"How did the drugs start?" I ask.

Ms Lytton sighs heavily.

"She was going through a bad patch. We all were. Mum died. Dad's a piece of work. Walked out on us when we were little. I was working long shifts. I didn't know how much it had affected Alice. Her dream of acting was falling apart and, as far as she was concerned, she'd lost her family. She needed to escape life. Check out for a bit."

"And the burns?"

The first flash of fire sparks in her eyes. This is new information to her.

"Burns? What burns? Are you saying that someone burnt her?"

Her anger and surprise aren't faked. Her fist is clenched and she looks ready to stand. Stand and thump whoever hurt her baby sister.

"I don't want to add to your distress, but yes, someone inflicted a number of cigarette burns on her. Best estimate two or more weeks ago."

"That bastard. That murdering, bloody bastard."

Her voice is raised and shrill.

"Who are you referring to, Ms. Lytton?" Bradley this time.

"Angel, of course. Her dealer. Ex-dealer. He's evil. Pure evil. He got her hooked on the stuff. She owed him money. Quite a lot of money."

"How much, Ms. Lytton?" I press. It's always best to know the details.

"Ten thousand," she replies quietly. I repress a whistle.

"I knew he was threatening her. But I didn't know he'd hurt her. Alice didn't tell me."

Her fingers perform a beadless rosary as she stares at the photo on the dresser.

"Alice, why didn't you tell me . . ."

She turns back to me and grabs my hand tightly.

"Find him. Promise me you'll find him and make him pay."

"We'll find him," I say, standing. Bradley takes my cue and stands too. Before we leave we need to look round the rest of the apartment. Search through Alice's things.

"But first, please could we see her room?" I say.

Ms Lytton tenses again. She doesn't want us in there.

Thinks we'll somehow desecrate the place.

"We'll be very careful," I say reassuringly. "We won't touch anything without gloves on. And we'll leave it exactly as it is."

Ms Lytton sniffs and then nods her consent.

We glove up and then Bradley opens the door. The room is small; a single bed pushed against the wall, a chest of drawers at the end and then just enough room to walk around. Everything's neat and ordered; it has to be—there's no room for mess. It's not surprising that Alice didn't bring anyone back here. It is more like a kid's bedroom than somewhere you'd take a man back to. There's a patch of mould on the wall—the small window at the top providing insufficient ventilation. You can smell the faint odour of damp in the air. A shout from the flat next door makes Bradley jump. It's so loud it's like the bloody neighbours are in the room too. God, the walls are thin. Fast-Track won't be used to that. Probably grew up in some large detached house in leafy suburbia where you only meet neighbours while pruning your fucking roses or in the village deli.

I open the drawers. Sometimes you might find a diary. Or a phone. Or the drugs the vic had supposedly given up. No. Nothing here. The drawers told their own story though. Only a few clothes. All nice, but the labels weren't expensive. They'd been carefully chosen. Neatly ironed. All projecting the image of a richer girl. Stacked next to the bed was a pile of books. Classics. Nabokov. Dickens. Brontë. Hardy. Ms. Lytton was right. Alice was trying to better herself. Aiming for the education she'd missed out on. I remember doing the same, encouraged by Mum. No one was going to tell me I was uncultured, uneducated. If you can read, you can educate yourself. End of story. "If you've read what they've read, they've got nothing over you," she'd say. "You're every bit their equal. Doesn't matter if you read it in a fancy school, or in your bedroom. A book's a book."

I think I would have liked you, Alice. What happened to you?

There's nowhere else to look, so I nod to Bradley that it's time to go.

"Just one more thing, Ms. Lytton," I say as we walk back into the living room.

"Yes?"

"Did Alice have a mobile phone?"

"'Course. An iPhone something or other. Rose-gold case."

"And have you seen it anywhere?"

"No. No, I don't think so." She creases her forehead as if desperately trying to remember. "She always had it with her."

"Right. And do you know her number?"

"Yes. Of course. It's stored in my phone."

I wait for her to retrieve it, but she remains rooted to the spot.

Grief does that. The surprise of it. It messes with your brain's wiring so logical connections no longer work. A doesn't lead to B any more. Two plus two makes whatever the fuck you want it to. I couldn't think for weeks after Karen was taken. A fog descended. My brain shut down.

I don't want to push it, but we really need the number. It'll give us an insight into who contacted her last and who she called or messaged. How and why she ended up halfway across London in the woods in the middle of the night. I ask again as gently as I can, and Ms. Lytton gives herself a little shake into action and pulls her phone out of her pocket. She opens her contacts and we have a number. It's not much, but it's a start.

I sense we've nearly used up the questions she's prepared to answer today, but there's a couple more I need to ask.

"And are there any friends of Alice we could speak to?"

It's amazing how many people share things with friends that they keep from their family. Blood bonds, but it also judges. Friends hold you to lower standards. They can also be ditched if you regret oversharing. It's harder to escape from family.

Ms Lytton pauses.

"Alice doesn't have that many friends left," she admits. "She lost most of her old friends when things got . . . difficult, and I've encouraged her to break off with the newer ones. The bad influences. Alice thought I was being cruel, keeping her for myself. But it wasn't like that. You can't expect to get clean if you're with people who aren't, can you? I'll have a think if there's anyone. I think she might still see Katie. Katie's a good girl. Nice. Done well for herself."

"Thank you, Ms. Lytton. If you could find a number for Katie, that would be really helpful. And, one last thing—would we be able to take a recent photo of Alice? We'll copy and return the original, of course."

She nods and walks towards the mantelpiece, grabbing the back of the settee to steady herself as she sways. With shaking hands she carefully selects one. It's of Alice in a simple white T-shirt and jeans. Her hair is down and she's staring straight at the camera and smiling. She looks like a girl in a preppy American film. Ms. Lytton presses the photo into my hands and I hold it carefully, knowing how much it means to her. My photo of Karen is the most precious thing I own.

It's time to go. Sandra catches my glance and follows us to the doorstep so we can have a private word.

"See if you can jog her memory about the marketing firm. Have a look round. There may well be some paperwork from them here. Either way, call me."

"Will do."

Bradley follows me to the car.

As the doors shut I turn to him.

"So, what do you think?"

"We look into this Angel."

"Angry drug lord she's heavily in debt to. Good, hadn't thought of that. And?"

He ignores the sarcasm.

"There's something she's not saying. She looked cagey when we mentioned Alice's work and whether she'd met anyone there."

I nod approvingly. Good, he'd seen it too. I was worried he'd be so by the rules there'd be no room for intuition. You sometimes need a little intuition if you're going to break a case. Detective work isn't a science. It's an art form.

"Agreed. We'll check out this Angel then push her for more. Call the station. See if someone can track down an address for us."

"Will do."

"And then check in with Sandra. See if she's got the name of the marketing company yet, or a number for the friend."

I leave my shades off as we drive. The headache is fading. The adrenaline of the case keeping it at bay.

We've got a lead. A good fucking lead. Follow it, we might find her killer. And a voice in my head whispers *you might find Karen*. But something about it doesn't quite feel right. Why would Alice travel from Latimer Road all the way to Sheen in the middle of the night to meet someone in a wood? And if she didn't go voluntarily, if she was taken—why take her there to kill her or dump her body? There must be closer places. Easier places.

I'm missing pieces of the puzzle.

Natalie

Ryan doesn't look relieved, at least. Nor grieving.
He's not a monster.
He's not in love with her.
I wait for a feeling of relief, but it doesn't come. Because he looks scared. Really, really scared. And I start to feel it too. Absorbing the emotion as if by osmosis.
"She's dead, Nat. She's dead."
I reach my hand out and he grips it so hard it hurts.
"What are you going to do?" I ask.
"What do you mean?" His eyes are wider than normal, a line of white topping the iris.
"They're asking for information," I say. "On the news. You knew her."
Ryan looks at me like I'm crazy and then throws back his head and bark-laughs.
"Nat, think. Yes, I knew her. I *knew* her. What do you think the police will do with that?"
He puts on the voice he always uses when he acts out scenes, the vein in his forehead becoming more pronounced with every sentence.
Oh, hello, Officer. Yes, I knew the victim.
How?
She worked for me.

I see. And when did you last see her?
Two nights ago. When she says I raped her on my sofa.
Did she press charges?
No, she was waiting till the next morning.
So she was killed before she had the chance? Isn't that FUCKING convenient?

He's so worked up now that little bits of spittle are leaving his mouth as a fine mist.

I wait till he's calmed slightly, then ask hesitantly, "Did you see anything in the woods?"

"What do you mean?" He's on guard, hackles raised.

"In the woods? Last night? When you went for your run? Did you see anything at all? Anyone? Something that could help point them towards who did it?"

He runs his hands through his hair. It stands up in tufts until he smooths it down again. "No, nothing. I've been over and over it while waiting for you. I didn't see anyone. Didn't hear anything."

He breaks down and starts sobbing.

"I know how it looks," he says. "I can't call the police, Nat, I just can't. She said I raped her. She's been killed ten minutes from our house, while I was out there. I call the police, I might as well put myself in handcuffs."

"Work will inform them about Alice's allegations. You know that, Ryan," I say gently.

"I know," he says. It's little more than a whisper.

I sit to steady myself. Next to Ryan, my leg pressed against his. The enormity of it slams into me. Winding me. He's right. He's going to be the prime suspect. Who else would they focus in on? Who else would have such a strong motive? He can't tell them he was out last night, right where she was killed.

I glance over. His eyes are fixed on the floor.

Ryan. A killer? No, ridiculous. He couldn't have done it. Taken a life. Murdered someone. He even looks away when there's too much blood on screen. Whether it's a horror film or *Last Kingdom*, he always offers to get up and make me a cup of tea when things get too violent. He pretends he's looking after me, but we both know the sight of it makes him sick. When we had mice in our kitchen a couple of years back he wouldn't even buy a trap that killed them. He insisted we got a humane one—one where the mouse was trapped in a baited clear cylinder that we could then release into the garden. I swear we kept catching and releasing the same mouse. Over and over. Until it died of old age. If you can't kill a mouse, how could you kill a person?

But then that part of my brain I don't want to listen to starts its whispering again.

You never thought he could cheat on you.

He probably would never have even told you about it if he hadn't been suspended.

Alice says he raped her. Women don't lie about that.

And then an image flashes into my head and my stomach flips. Ryan standing at the utility sink this morning. Scrubbing his running shoes. Scrubbing and scrubbing. Over and over. The red-brown water spiralling down the plughole.

Stratton

BRADLEY CHASES DOWN an address for Angel. He's focused, gets the job done, and I start feeling pleased he's my partner. It's a strange sensation.

When our station drew a blank on Angel he was straight on the phone to the MIT in the Latimer Road area. He'd had a case crossover with them in his Kensal Rise posting. A member of Angel's gang had taken out a rival on their home turf—a land grab that went wrong. It was supposed to be a "bagging"—a horrific "well-aimed" stab wound leaving the vic in need of a colostomy bag for the rest of their life. It's so depressing they come up with this stuff. Minds that should be busy with schoolwork find other things to focus on. Other creative outlets. This time the perp stuck the knife in too far and it turned into a murder.

He didn't rat out Angel though, despite the team squeezing him as hard as they could. A stupid, misplaced sense of loyalty, or maybe just a survival instinct. If he'd talked, chances are someone would have come after his family. The perp is now in jail. His family safe. And Angel still at large. Always the way.

Bradley's phone pings. The detective he spoke to has sent across Angel's photo and his rap sheet.

We both stare at the face. Angel. Born Stanley Richard Turner. It's nothing remarkable. But then evil never is. Hair longish, and dirty blond. Eyes grey-blue. Nose flat with a kink in it. Gold right front tooth. The ends of a tattoo spread out from under T-shirt sleeves.

I peer in. My close-up vision, already shot, has nosedived in the last two years. I'm going to have to give in and get reading glasses soon. Then I'll look properly fucking old.

"Are they feathers?" I ask.

"Wings," Bradley states simply. "Angel wings."

* * *

As we enter the estate we're met by wolf whistles and jeers. We're not in uniform, but they know who we are. It's like a sixth sense. A kid, no more than ten, stares at us over a balcony and then lobs a ball of spit down at us. An older boy, standing next to him, his brother most likely, cackles, looking proud. Bradley spins round, angry, but I just feel sad. They're kids. They should both be in school. What hope do the poor little fuckers have in life?

"Should we call for back up?" Bradley asks. Boy Scout seems out of his depth for once.

"No. Their bark is worse than their bite. Make a big deal out of it and no one will talk to us."

Angel's flat is on the third floor, accessed by a stairway that winds up the outside of the building like a concrete snake. Bradley stands back and I knock on the door.

A young woman, early twenties, in a crop top and tiny denim shorts, opens the door. She's attractive in an upfront way, her breasts so large they're almost spilling out. She's high, her pupils dilated and a faraway look in her eyes.

"Is Angel in?" I ask, trying to sound friendly. "We just want a chat. Nothing serious."

I try to peer deeper into the flat, but I can't see past the settee.

She smiles slowly, absorbing the words rather than hearing them.

A guy barges past her from behind and comes to the door. He's wiry, aggressive, a muscle in his neck jumping. He looks like he's gagging for a fight. A release.

"What d'you want?"

"We need to speak to Angel. Is he there?"

"Nah. He's out."

There's a clatter of feet on the stairs. A couple of young boys clutching a ball. They freeze at the end of the walkway that runs past the third-floor flats and stare at us suspiciously. I wave them on with a smile. The suspicion doesn't leave their eyes. I turn back to the wiry guy.

"Do you know when he'll be back? Or where he might be?"

"Nah." He spits at the floor. I feel Bradley tense behind me and start to move forward, but I block him. Last thing we need is for things to kick off.

"Mind if we come in and wait?"

There's another noise on the stairs behind me. Feet smacking concrete. This time someone's coming up rather than down. Wiry guy's about to tell me to piss off, but then I see a different expression flash across his face. A tiny headshake. It's not me he's looking at.

Bradley's noticed it too. We both spin round.

A man stands stock still. One foot on the stairs, one on the walkway leading to the flat. He has dirty-blond hair tied up in a topknot. His flat nose has a kink in it.

Angel.

In a flash his foot has left the walkway and he's scrambling down the staircase.

And we're after him.

He reaches the bottom. We're gaining on him. Bradley is just behind and I'm on his heels. I may hate them, but the enforced gym sessions have been paying off. He ducks to the right and then vaults over the bike racks. Bradley's legs are moving like pistons. He's hardly broken into a sweat. Fuck, he's fitter than me. He vaults after him, while I sprint round the outside. Vaulting is for the young.

A dog tied up outside strains at its leash, its teeth bared and growling.

Angel swerves and sprints down an alley to the right, Bradley on his tail. I force myself after them. A cyclist coming in the other direction flies past Angel but then nearly crashes into me. He slams on the brakes as I throw myself at the wall and curse at him. Bradley looks back.

"You OK?" he yells, slowing his pace.

"Fine—go!" I shout.

We can't lose him. If he reaches the main road, there are so many ways he could go. Bradley was right. We should have brought back-up.

I force myself faster, using reserves I didn't know I had. My heart's pounding and my legs are killing me, but I don't let myself stop. Rounding the corner, I see Bradley up ahead. He's only metres behind Angel now. *Come on!* Bradley increases speed. Angel glances back and his eyes widen. Then, with a final burst of speed, Bradley careers into Angel's back and brings him to the floor.

Natalie

I WANT TO get out of here. Our house, never on the large side, feels small, claustrophobic even. The walls beginning a creeping advance towards the centre of the room, stealing air.

I think about calling Rachel, asking if I can take her up on her offer and crash at hers for a few days, but then I know it would destroy Ryan, send him over the edge. It would read like I didn't believe him. That I thought him a rapist and a murderer.

I don't know what I think.

I close my eyes and the image of him standing in our bedroom wearing that tie assaults me. Him telling me I had nothing to worry about with Alice. If she hadn't accused him, I probably would have never even known he'd cheated on me.

I wish I had a mum to call. A dad to fall back on. Someone to comfort me and let me revert to the role of child.

But I don't. And I can't just sit here and do nothing. I finally understand Ryan's need sometimes to just act. That acting in itself, in some way, alleviates the problem.

I need to approach this like I would a legal article. Collect facts, consider precedents. Don't be clouded by subjective feelings. Distrust intuition. Ignore emotion and the little voice in my head that says *girls don't lie about things like that*.

Here goes. I breathe deeply and focus. The panic, the fluttering in my chest, subsides.

Ryan says he didn't rape Alice. Ryan says he didn't murder Alice. Ryan, as far as I know, has always told me the truth in the past. OK, he didn't initially tell me about sleeping with Alice, but he admitted to it when pushed and is adamant that it was consensual. Ryan's fear of blood, his abhorrence of violence, suggest he didn't kill her. The only thing I know for sure that Ryan did wrong is to cheat on me. He doesn't deserve to be arrested for that. Possibly Alice was troubled. A pathological liar, or delusional. Maybe she'd been hurt before and Ryan represented men. He was to be the sacrificial lamb. He was to pay for all men's sins.

In any event, it seems the case has not been made for Ryan's arrest. So that's what we need to prevent.

I put on the kettle and make two cups of coffee then put one down in front of Ryan.

"You need to call work," I say.

"And say what?"

"They'll expect you to have seen the news. They'll expect you to have heard about Alice. You need to call and express your shock and dismay and find out what the next steps are for your return."

"Won't that look suspicious?"

"It'll look a fuck of a lot more suspicious if you cower at home and do nothing," I snap.

Ryan looks at me warily. I hardly ever swear, and my anger surprises me as much as him.

I take a deep breath. "This isn't going away, Ryan."

He swallows. His Adam's apple ripples out and back in again.

Then he picks up the phone.

I'm watching, listening. I'm trying to be the supportive wife. But I'm judging, analysing his every move.

The receptionist is clearly uncomfortable when she hears his name. He asks to be put through to his boss but is told he's unavailable. The Adam's apple repeats its trajectory.

Then he asks for HR. There's a pause and hold music, then the receptionist is back. She's terribly sorry but there's no one available to speak to him at the moment. Someone will call him back very soon.

Ryan hangs up the phone then thumps his fist full force against the wall, releasing a primal scream as he does. Snail trails of blood stain the freshly painted plaster. His hand will bruise. I resist the urge to offer him arnica.

I put my hand on his back. It's the closest I can manage to a hug. He flinches away.

"I'm going for a run," he says.

"Are you sure that's a good idea?" I say.

"Don't worry," he snipes back. "I'm not going to go and kill anyone."

He goes upstairs to change and I stand by the window seat, immobile. I can't even gauge my emotions. Things are happening around me that I don't understand, like life's a play and I've just walked on to the wrong stage, where the lines I've learned don't correspond in any way to the action.

When Ryan's out of earshot, I take out my phone and call Dr. Browning's office.

I didn't particularly like him. But I didn't like Dr. Thomas either. Maybe I'm not built to warm to any therapist. I don't want to tell him about Ryan. About Alice. That's too personal. Too raw. I'm not ready to share. What I want is more practical than that. He stopped me blacking out when he squeezed my hand. It didn't work when I tried it, but maybe he'll have other techniques that actually work. I can't break. I can't start regularly blacking out again. Not now.

His secretary answers. My voice cracks as I ask for a follow-up appointment. If she notices, she doesn't say anything. The secretary says his next available slot is after the weekend. Tuesday at three. I take it.

Stratton

ANGEL SITS IN Interview Room 2, flanked by his lawyer, Priya Khinda. She specializes in representing scum. Can afford the fancy car, smart clothes and probably a top-of-the-range memory-foam mattress to help her sleep at night. I thought we could get in a few questions, a few jibes before she arrived, but Bradley insisted on waiting. Defendants' rights need to be respected. Otherwise we're no better than them. He had a zealous gleam in his eye as he said it. He might as well have had a bloody prefect badge pinned to his lapel. As if asking a few perfectly reasonable questions suddenly tips me into the bracket of drug lord and woman-burner.

I press record, remind Angel of his rights and re-introduce everyone in the room for the benefit of the tape. It's not Bradley's presence that makes me follow the rulebook when I'm recording. I always make sure I do everything right. No one's throwing out my tapes at trial. Instinctively I glance at the two-way glass. I bet Parker's there, listening. It's turned into a high-profile case. The youth and looks of the vic have mobilized the public. She could be their friend/sister/daughter, and they want justice.

I place a picture of Alice on the table in front of Angel. It's the one I took from her sister's mantelpiece.

"Do you know her?"

Khinda places a hand on her client's arm.

Angel remains silent.

"For the record, Mr. Turner has not responded."

I put another picture down on top. This time from the woods. Lifeless, dusted in dirt.

"What about now?"

Khinda interrupts. "There is no need for the theatrics, thank you."

"I have a list of people who will testify that you knew Alice Lytton. So shall we do this the easy way or the hard way?"

"I knew her."

Khinda scowls. Her client isn't following her instructions. That's the thing about drug lords. They can pay top dollar for lawyers, but their machismo, their need to dominate the proceedings and play top dog then stops them from following their advice.

"Good. How did you know her? Bear in mind we already know the answer. We're really only asking out of courtesy."

Khinda objects again, but Angel looks at me and smiles. His gold tooth glints.

"She used to buy drugs from some people in the area."

"And did she pay these people or was she a little behind?"

"I wouldn't know."

"That surprises me. I thought you knew everything about what happened in your area."

I stare at him. He doesn't take the bait.

Bradley picks up the questioning. "We heard she was a lot behind. Ten grand behind, in fact. It's a lot of money, isn't it? Ten thousand pounds. Has a nice ring to it. Can't let someone fall into debt like that, can you? It isn't good business. Might encourage others to do the same."

Angel spreads out his hands wide, palms up.

"I wouldn't know."

He looks like he's almost enjoying this. Fuck. We need something. We need to rattle him. I try another tack.

"Do you get a kick out of burning girls?"

Khinda interrupts, but I shut her down.

"There were recent cigarette burns on the deceased's right arm. Three. And bruises where she was held down so you could do it."

I see a flash of disgust in Khinda's eyes. Good. Accept what you're dealing with. Who pays you your money.

"Is that what turns you on?" I press. "Burning girls then killing them? We can get witnesses to testify that you burnt her. Imagine how that will play with a jury. She owed you money. You burnt her. Look at you! How big a leap will it be in their minds to work out you killed her?"

"You're not pinning this on me." He's rattled. Finally, he's rattled.

"You're our number-one suspect. You have motive. You have means."

Khinda tries to stop the interview but Angel waves her away. We've got through to him and he's scared. He wants to talk.

"She paid me back."

"Sorry?"

"Alice may have owed me some money for . . . commercial reasons but she paid me back. The whole ten grand."

"When?"

He rolls his shoulders back then sits up a little straighter. His feeling of control is returning.

"Ninth of March."

"Very precise."

"What can I say? I'm a businessman. I have a head for dates and figures. Yours isn't too bad."

He puts his head to the side and shoots me a leer. The bravado is returning. I have to re-establish my authority.

"So she just turned up with a big bag of cash and handed it over. Out of the blue? That's very convenient. Did she say where she got the money from?"

"No. And I didn't ask. Ten grand is ten grand."

"Can you prove this?" Bradley asks.

Angel laughs hollowly at him. "What do you want? A receipt? To look at my fucking accounts? This isn't exactly a receipts business."

"What about last night?" I ask. "Where were you between the hours of 10 p.m. and one in the morning?"

"I was at my sister's."

"Where's that?"

"Harrow Road. It was her kid's birthday. I slept on the couch."

"Do you have a number and address for her?"

Bradley passes Angel a pen and pad of paper and he scribbles the information down.

I end the interview but say we'll hold Angel for another few hours, until we've checked out the alibi.

"What do you think?" Bradley asks as we stand in the corridor outside.

I hesitate. As much as I want it to be him, I don't think it is.

"I think he's a sick bastard, but he's telling the truth."

"Me too. What now?"

"Get some sleep. I want everyone in early tomorrow."

Natalie

Ryan's left for his run, slamming the door behind him, but he'll be back soon. And it's like his presence still lingers, watching me. Admonishing me for my lack of support.

I call Rachel. She says she can't meet, she's caught up in something at work, but then my voice trembles and she relents.

"It's nothing that I can't finish later. I'll meet you at the Hare and Hounds. It'll take me forty-five minutes, but go there now and wait for me."

I do as she says. Sometimes, when everything goes wrong, it's good to be led. It's easier to put one foot in front of the other if someone tells you where to tread.

A glance in the hall mirror floors me. My eyes have a wary, haunted quality I recognize from a decade ago and my face looks drawn. Mascara smudges augment eye bags.

I wash my face, reapply foundation and pinch some colour into my cheeks. The eyes remain haunted. There's nothing I can do about those.

I put on my thickest winter coat. It's not that cold outside, but it's like my circulation has shut down. Blood no longer warms skin. The walk to the pub is all downhill and I keep my eyes on the pavement, studying cracks as I did when I was a young child and thought a monster might rise up through one. Before I knew that the monsters are already here.

I'm ensconced in a dark green leather chair in the corner when Rachel arrives. I've been pretending to read so that I don't need to meet people's eyes. A woman reading on her own in the pub is either independent or eccentric. A woman sitting alone, looking around, is an object of pity or prey.

"Another one?" she asks, pointing at my glass and hanging her coat over the back of the chair opposite. She smells the quinine. "G&T?"

"Just tonic, please," I reply.

"Suit yourself."

She heads towards the bar, her fitted black work dress revealing her enviable figure.

Rachel is served quickly, as always, and returns bearing a tonic water and a fishbowl-sized gin and tonic for herself.

"Right." Rachel stares at me.

I don't know what to say. There's nothing to say. I've already told Rachel the facts as far as I'm aware of them. What's to add?

But Rachel keeps the conversation going. She distracts me. Keeps the conversation away from Ryan. Away from Alice. Instead she reminisces about old times. Easier times. Before Ryan and Adam, her ex. Before Gavin Scott.

She ends up refuelling and becomes louder and slightly slurred in her recollections. Traces of her Midlands accent sneak back in as, face flushed, she reminds me about the time she slept with one of our uni professors in the library. "Fucked", as she puts it. She likes to shock. It was in the second year and he was lecturing on tort. He was probably only in his early thirties, but that seemed ancient to us then.

". . . and as he was about to come he asked me to call him 'your Honour. Yes, your Honour. Yes, your Honour.'"

She's laughing, head thrown back, but I'm not. Instead of picturing the professor I start picturing Ryan. Ryan and Alice. I half gag.

Rachel sees my reaction and her hand flies to her mouth.

"Oh God, sorry, Nat. It was a stupid, thoughtless choice of story. I was just trying to cheer you up."

As the barman rings the bell for last orders she leans in and says, "To be honest, Natalie, you're probably better off without him. Even if he didn't force her, he's a cheating bastard. My life's so much better without Adam. I'm free, my own person again."

I don't know what to say. I don't want to be without Ryan. My old Ryan. I just want to leave this parallel world I've shifted into.

"It's not all Ryan's fault," I say. "We don't have sex any more—"

"No," Rachel says firmly. "Stop there. Do not do the whole victim-blaming-herself thing. You're better than that. It is Ryan's fault. Ryan . . ."

"What?"

Rachel puts down her drink and forces a smile.

". . . It's just you might be better off without him."

FRIDAY, 22 MARCH

Stratton

I HAVE TO fight my way through a crowd of reporters just to get into the station. Fucking vultures. Serving up death as entertainment.

"Any news on the Alice case?" shouts one, a short fat guy who thrusts a microphone into my face. I push it away and climb the steps.

"Any suspects yet?" calls out another. I close the door in his face.

Minutes later, I stand in front of the morning meeting. Everyone working the Lytton case is present. Reynolds and Bradley in the front row, Sandra and Dev behind. Parker keeping his distance at the back, making it clear he's here to observe and judge, rather than join in. All eyes are on me and the air is charged and static. It's not just the media attention. There's something about this case that has got under all of our skins. The ceiling spot is still flickering. Strobing on and off. Are they going to wait till someone has a bloody epileptic fit before they change it? It's doing my head in so I ask Dev to turn the lights off. There's enough daylight through the panel of side windows anyway.

The room feels hot and my jacket's tight under my arms, but I keep it on. I want its added authority. Parker's presence is making me uneasy.

"Right," I say. "Let's summarize where we're at so far. The vic owed a drug dealer, Angel, ten grand, but according to him she paid him back, in cash, eleven days before she was killed."

"Doesn't mean he didn't do it," Reynolds says.

"Of course. But he does have an alibi—his sister."

Reynolds groans.

"OK, obviously not watertight, but we still can't ignore it. Dev—did you manage to get hold of her?"

Dev consults his notes. "I spoke to her first thing. She said Angel was there all evening. Came at seven—brought a present for her kid—a PlayStation 5—and then they all got wasted so he slept on the sofa."

"OK," I say. "See if you can get any neighbours to confirm. And I want us to look into this money. Seems like rather a big coincidence that Alice suddenly comes into ten grand cash, and then is murdered. Where did the money come from? Is there any more of it? We didn't see any in her room, but maybe we need a second look. Sandra, can you ask the sister?"

"What if the sister provided the cash?" Dev suggests.

"No. She'd have given her the money in a heartbeat if she had it, but money was tight and when we spoke to her she still thought Alice was in debt. Dev—pull her bank accounts to verify. Have we got Alice's yet? I want to know about any surprising credits or large cash withdrawals. If there aren't any, we need to figure out who the mysterious donor is and why. Sandra—any luck with the friend"—I glance down at my notepad and squint as I try to decipher my own writing—"Kate? Could Alice have reached out to her?"

"Katie. Katie Roberts. Ms. Lytton found the number," Sandra replies. "I called, but it went straight to voicemail. The recorded message said she's away till the 25th—Monday—and won't be checking her messages. I left one anyway, explaining it was urgent. She might be checking occasionally and just be screening work calls, so I'll try again this morning."

"Good. Thanks. Reynolds—where are we in general with phone records? This needs to be top priority."

Reynolds adjusts his glasses. It's a tic he has to focus his mind. "We've just been given access by the provider and are starting to go through them. The last call she received was at nine twenty-five that night. It was from a burner. The same number contacted her regularly in the preceding week. I tried the number, but there was no dial tone. Seems the SIM's been taken out."

"A burner? Right. See if you can find out where it was sold and if they remember the purchaser at all."

Reynolds groans and I know it's a long shot. Lots of places don't keep records and memories suddenly all become blurred around burners.

"The sister swore Alice was now clean," I continue, "but her being in contact with someone on a burner suggests she might not have been. The timing of the call fits with what the sister said about Alice suddenly going out at nine thirty. It appears that she might well have been meeting someone. Possibly a new dealer. Possibly the murderer. Or it could have been a random attack."

I glance at the back of the room. Parker's hands are in his pockets; he's looking unimpressed. I've basically summarized that the killer could be fucking anyone.

"OK. Step one. Let's find out if Alice is using again? Have we got the blood tox results back yet?"

"I'll chase Grayson after the briefing," Bradley says. "Sandra—any luck with the name of the marketing firm Alice was working for?"

"The sister couldn't remember, but I found an engagement letter in the console table. Hunter and Harris."

"Great. Bradley—call their HR. Give them a heads up that we're on our way. We need to speak to everyone there who had contact with Alice. If they're in a meeting the other side of the country, they need to pull them out. No debate."

Bradley nods.

"Have we heard anything from Uniform about the weapon?"

"No." Reynolds speaks up. "They've done a detailed sweep of the area, on foot and with dog-handlers and have come up with nothing. The perp either buried it or took it with them. The dogs did go crazy on the path next to where the body was found, which suggests she might have been killed there and they were reacting to blood spatter."

I feel that same unsettled sensation again. Something about this death just doesn't sit right. The cutting of the fingernails, the careful disposal of the murder weapon. How does that fit with the token covering of the body and the casual disposal of the handbag? I don't understand it, and I hate it when I don't understand.

There's a hum as people start talking. Damn it, I've zoned out, lost focus. Parker's face is stony.

"And CCTV?" I ask, a bit too loudly, to overcompensate. "Have we picked up Alice at all?"

It's Dev who fields this one. "We've got her entering Latimer Road station at 9.45 p.m. We're going through all the underground footage to see where she went next."

"Good. Let me know when you have something."

I wrap up the meeting, instructing everyone to keep me abreast of any new developments.

Parker waits for everyone else to leave the meeting then waylays me.

"Was this a mistake?" he asks.

"What do you mean?" I say, feigning ignorance. I know exactly what the prick means.

"Can you handle this? The case is getting a lot of heat. I need to know if you're up to the job."

I control my breathing. Withhold the words I want to say.

"I can do this," I say. "Better than anyone else."

He only looks half convinced. I hope to God I'm right. A girl has been murdered. She deserves justice. *As does Karen*, a little voice whispers in my ear. I wish now that I'd never conflated the two cases. It makes it harder. I don't need the additional pressure.

Bradley follows me out to the car.

I drive this time. I get Bradley to dial Pavarotti and put him on speaker. I want to hear what he has to say too.

Pavarotti answers and the car fills with the tinny echo of Puccini bounced off steel tables.

"What can I do for my favourite detective? Name the opera and I'll tell you everything you want to know," Pavarotti booms.

"Where are we on testing?" I ask. It's *La Traviata*, but I'm not in the mood for games.

"OK. Straight down to business it is."

"Have we got the blood tox results back yet?"

"You're in luck. They've just landed in my inbox. Let me have a look . . ."

There's the sound of breathing interspersed with the occasional key tap.

"Right. Well, she's clean. No drugs in her system. Legal or illegal. That would mean she hasn't been using for at least a week. No alcohol either."

Good. The fact that she stayed clean has a bitter-sweetness to it. She was finally getting her life back on track. Which meant she had more stolen from her.

"No traces of chloroform, so she wasn't chemically incapacitated," Pavarotti continues.

"What about the wound and clothes? Anything to suggest whether she was killed in a car or in the wood or somewhere else altogether?"

"The wound only has a few fibres in it. The main contaminant is soil."

"So she was killed in the wood?"

Pavarotti laughs his rumbling laugh. "You know I can't be as definite as that. I live in a world of probabilities and statistical relevance. You do the alchemy and turn it into fact."

I roll my eyes at him, even though he's not there to see it.

"But, you'd expect to find more fibres if she'd been killed and dumped in the boot of a car?"

"Indeed. In that eventuality there'd likely be more fibres from the car-boot lining present in the wound."

It's like pulling teeth.

Bradley leans in for a question and I gesture for him to go ahead.

"What about her clothing? Were there any unexpected fibres attached to her clothing?"

Pavarotti hums and the keyboard noise taps again.

"Yes. Actually there were. On the victim's sweatshirt we found high traces of an unusual fibre. I examined them under the microscope myself. The fibres are woollen and flecked with orange and blue."

Natalie

WE HAVE BREAKFAST sat opposite each other at the kitchen table. Separated by a green chair, ninety centimetres of grey-washed oak and a million miles. The light spills in through the window, throwing long shadows off the pot plants that line the sill. My two favourites sit in the middle: the taller Sansevieria and the squat, trailing Devil's Ivy.

I watch Ryan spoon milk-sodden Weetabix into his mouth in between sips of a blueberry protein shake. And scrutinize him. There's a slight slurp after each mouthful. The fact I thought he could have assaulted Alice, that I was thinking he could even have had something to do with her death, seems absurd in the morning sunlight.

I don't know why Alice would lie, but maybe she had a reason. Maybe she'd suffered a trauma. Damaged by someone else and so was inflicting payback against all men.

I think it was just sex. Consensual, adulterous sex.

The question is can I forgive him?

Spoon. Slurp. Spoon. Slurp.

Is Rachel right? Would I be better off without this man? We've been together for fourteen years. You don't abandon fourteen years' worth of history for one mistake. Rachel said I shouldn't blame myself, but she's my friend, so she would say that, wouldn't she? We weren't sleeping together. Ryan has needs. His conjugal rights. If

Alice offered, isn't it only human that he accepted? Ryan's right. Rachel's wary of men after her split with Adam. What's the opposite of rose-tinted glasses?

Ryan wants to atone. He won't hurt me again, he's promised me that, and I think I believe him. We can find a couple's therapist, he says. I could keep seeing Dr. Browning on my own—"only if you want to, of course"—and we could find a new one for the two of us. Get us back on track. If we're heading for divorce anyway, what's there to lose? We just need to get through the next weeks, together. Keep Ryan out of police custody. I bet they'd love to pin this on someone like him. Middle-class white male.

We can get through this.

I need to believe we can get through this.

Ryan's firm is still ignoring him so after breakfast he sets out for yet another run.

"You'll be ready for your half-marathon soon," I say, trying to keep the tone light.

He smiles mechanically, but we're both going through the motions.

He leaves and I head to my office room. To my sanctuary. But try as I might, I can't do it. I can't pretend everything's OK. Can't will it better. My article sits on the computer screen. I've only managed a four-line paragraph in the last hour and I'm not even dressed yet. My mind won't still. My daily segments, abandoned. My life, unmoored.

The sound of the doorbell breaks my reverie. I go to open it, grateful for the distraction. Matt stands there, smiling his chemically induced grin. I glance at my watch: 10.25 a.m. He's slightly later than normal.

"Thanks," I say as I take the letters and small parcel from him. It's from a second-hand bookshop. Ryan will spend huge amounts of money on cycling gadgets but will scour the internet to save two pounds on a book.

I close the door and start picking through the letters. A car insurance renewal letter. I open it. The cheek of them. My insurance will automatically renew in three weeks' time for £150 more than the current price, despite my having an extra year's no claims bonus. I'll sort that out later. Next up is a water bill. A flyer about a roof specialist operating in my area and an estate agent offering to value my house on a "no obligation" basis. Then I reach the fifth letter in the pile and my stomach contracts.

It's white, A5, the name and address typed neatly on a sticky label.

I'm stuck between laughing and crying. Don't I have enough to deal with? My husband slept with someone else. My husband is or is not a rapist. My husband is or is not a murderer.

No, please not now. I'm not strong enough for this to be happening now.

I think about putting the letter down and waiting for Ryan, but I know that will almost be worse. To have it sitting there, spreading its poison. And Ryan—what exactly would Ryan do? He's no longer the shield he once was.

With shaking fingers, I rip open the top of the envelope and pull out the letter inside. It's on the same thick cream paper, the same mix of lower- and upper-case letters neatly cut out and glued to its surface.

Blood pounding in my ears, I force myself to focus and read the words.

WHAT GOES AROUND COMES AROUND

I bite my cheek, but the sensation—the pain—is not enough. I hardly feel it.

I fight to stay present. To stay here.

But the hall carpet starts to pixellate.

The console table warps then disappears.

A rushing sound.

Then blackness.

* * *

I come to in the dark. My eyes adjust. No, it's not completely dark. There are horizontal stripes of lights. I'm inside. Something soft brushes my upper arm. My cheek presses against something hard.

Slowly my brain re-engages. I'm in the bedroom wardrobe. The stripes of light come through the slatted doors. My dresses hang above me, the fabric of the longest one reaching my arm. My face was buried in a pair of my shoes. To my right sit Ryan's clothes, Ryan's shoes.

Why here? I think back to what Dr. Browning said. Somewhere significant? Hardly. Somewhere I feel safe, cocooned? Possibly. It is a small, enclosed space. It fits with past behaviour.

I have no idea how much time I've lost. It's still light outside, so that's something. Stumbling out of the wardrobe into the bedroom, I check my watch: 11.07 a.m. Half an hour, give or take a few minutes. I lost half an hour.

I start shaking all over, then catch sight of myself in the full-length mirror. Pale. Dishevelled. Wide-eyed. No. No. I won't be like this. I won't let other people do this to me.

If I'm going to survive I need my routine back. My segments. Otherwise I'll crumble. I'll cease to exist. I step into the shower, turn up the pressure and then mercilessly turn down the temperature so I gasp. I force myself to stand there. To freeze. To feel.

Ryan returns as I'm drying my hair. I don't hear the key over the hairdryer but I do hear his voice. Raised to a cry. A bellow.

"Nat? Nat? . . . NATALIE?"

He's seen the letter. I must have dropped it in the hall.

I know I should call back to him. Let him know I'm safe, but instead I turn up the hairdryer to max. Let the whirring drown him out.

Finally he bursts into the room, his face red and sweaty, emotions running across it.

"Oh. Thank God, Nat." Relief. "I've been calling." Concern. "And calling." Anger.

Stratton

We walk through the brass revolving doors and into the reception of Hunter and Harris. What a joke of a place. It's clearly been designed to impress their potential clients. A curved asymmetrical desk takes pride of place in the centre of the room like a wooden Nike swoosh, and large prints of what look like random shadows hang on the walls. The lighting is orange-hued and there's a small forest of pot plants. Someone in a terrible denim jumpsuit walks from one to the next with a tiny bronze watering can. Bradley looks around, taking it in. All this crap probably appeals to him. He'll have grown up used to people wasting money. But if I was looking for a marketing firm, all this would put me off instantly. I'd want to know that my money was going towards selling more of my product. End of story. Not paying for someone to re-create the entrance of a swanky hotel and employ an indoor fucking gardener.

The receptionist—a woman in her twenties with teeth like a toothpaste commercial—looks up at us and smiles, almost blinding us.

"Welcome to Hunter and Harris," she chirps. "How can I help you this morning?"

I explain that we're from the police, that we're here about Alice Lytton, and her smile freezes.

"Of course," she says. "I'll just let HR know. Please take a seat while you wait." She points towards a cluster of leather beanbags scattered by the window. For fuck's sake. Grow up and stop trying so desperately hard. Beanbags aren't proper chairs. Having beanbags doesn't make you creative. They aren't even comfortable and, once sat in, they're really hard to get up from without looking like a total tool in the process.

I stand in the corner. Bradley sits in a beanbag chair. He's smiling. He looks like he's enjoying this.

Five minutes later a tall woman with ironed hair and a shoulder-padded skirt suit emerges from the lift and strides purposefully towards us. She is smiling intensely. Her whole demeanour reads company fixer. Mafia. Or HR.

"I'm so sorry to have kept you," she says, sticking out a hand. I don't shake it. I get the feeling she likes to control things and I'll get more out of her if I spin her out a bit. She withdraws her hand, the smile still in place but slightly dimmed. "I'm Wendy Cook, head of Human Resources here at Hunter and Harris. Such a terrible time. I was just clearing a meeting out of the conference room so we have somewhere to talk in private. Please follow me."

The conference room is off the main open-plan office floor. The walls are glass so the "in private" thing is rather an exaggeration. As we sit, a man in chinos and a white shirt strolls past and unintentionally meets my eye. Suddenly his walk becomes wooden and he flashes a strange smile that then morphs into a grimace. You get that a lot as police. People are so concerned about looking innocent around you that they act really fake and suspicious. You have to learn to sift out the actual criminals from the cretins.

Tea and coffee are laid out in the centre of the table next to a plate of shortbread biscuits. Wendy asks what we'd like, but we both decline. This isn't a social. This is a murder investigation. She opens her mouth to speak again, but I beat her to it, keeping the power on our side of the table.

"We'd like to talk to everyone who's had contact with Alice. I understand she hadn't been working here long?"

"No. Just two weeks."

"So she joined on the seventh?"

"The sixth, actually."

"Right. And what was her exact role?"

"Junior assistant." She leans forwards—fake conspiratorial. "It's really a glorified secretarial role. She helps—sorry, helped—her senior associate with the administrative side of things."

"And who oversaw her hiring?"

"Well, I conducted the initial interview, but final hiring decisions are made by the relevant senior associate."

"Who's that?" Bradley asks.

She hesitates slightly. Only for a fraction of a second. But it was there.

"Ryan. Ryan Campbell."

I scribble on my pad then take over the questioning again. "We spoke to Alice's sister, who told us Alice dropped out of school at sixteen. I'm curious, what qualifications did she have that made her suitable for the role?"

Wendy's face becomes harder to read.

"She had a very attractive and enthusiastic manner. A real people person." She hesitates again and twists the ring on her finger. "There was some slight confusion over her previous experience at the time."

What is she not saying? Someone screwed up. That was clear body language for someone screwed up.

"She was very pretty," I observe, and watch her squirm again. I've hit a nerve.

"Yes . . . yes, she was."

"Were any other candidates interviewed for the position?"

"Yes."

"Was she your first choice?"

Wendy looks uncomfortable.

". . . It isn't my role to rank candidates. I leave that to the senior associate in question."

"To Mr. Campbell."

"Yes."

Bradley speaks next. His tone is perfectly polite, but there's a darker, colder undercurrent to it. I like it. We're starting to make a good team. It's like in those nature programmes where you see a seal stranded on an iceberg and a couple of killer whales begin circling. It's only a matter of time before the seal is in the water.

"So, to recap. Mr. Campbell selected an assistant with no experience and very few qualifications, based solely on her 'attractive personality'?"

"I don't think I like the implication," Wendy says tightly. "This is a professional firm. We are not afraid to look beyond traditional qualifications for raw talent."

"Let's rewind a minute," I say. "What did you mean about there being some confusion over her previous experience?"

She's properly uncomfortable now. Her right hand picks at a bit of lint on her skirt. Come on. Fall off the ice.

"Well, on her application form, she may have mentioned working in a similar position before."

"May have, or did? We can go through your records ourselves if you prefer? Can't be too hard to find. After all, the interview, as you say, was just a couple of weeks ago."

Wendy swallows. ". . . Did . . . She did mention."

"So 'confusion' doesn't seem quite the right word then, does it? 'Lie.' That's more like it. She lied on the application. Why wasn't she fired as soon as you found out?"

". . . Mr. Campbell, well, he said it would be unfair. They were getting along well. She was an effective assistant. He said we should give her a chance. That ability was more important than a piece of paper."

"How very noble of him." Bradley smiles mockingly.

Wendy picks at the lint again. Pick, pick, pick. Her cheeks are starting to redden.

"Please could you ask Mr. Campbell to come in, and we'll talk to him first."

There's silence. Wendy inhales deeply and pushes down her shoulders as if squaring off for a fight.

"I'm afraid Mr. Campbell isn't in today."

For fuck's sake. She's wasting my time. I hate it when people waste my time.

I slam my fist down on the table, making the empty cups rattle in their saucers.

"I thought, when I called this morning, I specifically asked to speak to everyone who worked with Alice."

"Yes, well. Mr. Campbell hasn't been at work for a couple of days. He's . . . been suspended."

"For what?!"

There's silence. A static humming silence. It makes my brain vibrate.

"OK. Bradley. Get a warrant. We're going through all your personnel files. Every single one of them. We'll shake them till all your dirty little secrets come spilling out."

Bradley stands.

"No," Wendy says quietly. "I'll tell you. I'll tell you everything. I'll need our in-house counsel to join us though."

Great. A lawyer to hide behind. I'm about to push back when Bradley stands.

"A word, please, ma'am?"

I follow him to the corner.

"We need to do this by the book," he says quietly. Of course he bloody does. And he's right. But it still pisses me off. Just when I thought we were starting to gel.

"I know," I hiss. "And you need to bear in mind who's in charge here."

I stick my hands in my pocket to keep them under control, then turn back to Wendy.

"Call your counsel," I say, and she picks up the phone. Minutes later we're joined by John from Legal—a grey man in a grey suit.

He sits next to Wendy as she explains falteringly that on 20th March Alice had come to see her. Alice had alleged that the previous evening, Mr. Campbell had asked her to finish some work at his house and then assaulted her there.

"Assaulted her, how?" I demand. Now's not the time for niceties.

"She said he raped her." Her voice is almost a whisper.

I press the pen down so hard on the pad that the nib snaps.

"A young woman is murdered and it turns out she claimed she was raped the night before. Why the hell are we only hearing about this now?"

Wendy shrinks into her chair. She no longer looks like a tall woman.

"She didn't want to report it. She said she wanted twenty-four hours to think it over before she went to the police."

"And you agreed?"

"Yes. We thought it was her choice."

"And wouldn't it be nice if it all just went away?" I sneer.

Wendy doesn't comment. Her eyes are fixed on the teacups.

"How did she seem when she told you about the rape?"

"Alleged rape," interrupts John. Nasty little weasel of a man. Bradley half smiles. Thought he'd approve. Words like "alleged" probably give him a semi.

I glare at him.

Wendy pauses before she answers, like she's replaying her memories for accuracy. "She seemed . . . nervous."

"Nervous?" I repeat. "Not upset? Distressed?"

"That too. But overall I'd say she seemed nervous."

Wendy meets my eyes. The mask of unflappable competence has completely fallen away and I know that she's telling me the truth.

"Did she have any bruises you could see? Any visible signs of attack?"

"No. But she was wearing a trouser suit and make-up. I don't know if I would have known."

"And did you have any contact with her after she reported it?"

"No," she confirms. "I didn't contact her as I wanted to give her the full twenty-four hours she'd requested, and she didn't call or contact anyone here."

"As far as you're aware," adds Weasel John.

"As far as I'm aware," Wendy repeats flatly.

Bradley clears his throat. Has his semi turned full hard-on? But I let him talk. It'd be petty if I didn't let him do his job.

"How did Mr. Campbell react to his suspension?" Bradley asks.

"He seemed shocked," Wendy replies.

"Was it you who told him?" I ask.

"Yes. Any suspension or investigation falls under HR's remit. I asked him to come into my office. He was smiling. And holding a coffee. He'd just popped out to Starbucks when Sam, my assistant, reached him on his phone, and he brought back a flat white for me. Soya. He was thoughtful like that . . ."

Great, so the HR lady is sweet on the suspect. No wonder she didn't call it in.

"Anyway," Wendy continues, "I explained the situation to Mr. Campbell and he didn't say anything at first. I think he was in shock. His hand just started squeezing the coffee cup until the lid came off and hot coffee was pouring over his hand and on to the carpet. It must have really hurt, burnt even, but he still didn't react."

Her sympathy still lies with him. The alleged rapist. Not the girl. So much for the sisterhood.

"And when he did talk?" Bradley prompts.

"He denied it all. Said he'd invited her back to his to finish some work but he'd never assaulted her."

"And how did his manner seem?" I press.

"Shocked."

"Yes, we've got shocked. Anything else?"

"Angry . . ." she finally admits. "Shocked and angry."

Natalie

"Don't you see? It all makes sense," Ryan says, brandishing the letter in his right hand, creating little air currents that ripple across the living room. He's pacing. Agitated. No, "agitated" is the wrong word. "Excited" captures it better. His words are coming out faster than normal.

"What goes around comes around," he says. "That's what the letter says."

Another flap of the letter. A spin of the heel. I stay out of his path, folded up in the leather wingback chair.

"I know what it says," I say flatly. His reaction grates. He knows how these letters cripple me. He knows I lost time again and woke up in the wardrobe.

"Well, it's a threat, isn't it?" he continues. "Or a boast. It's her. Everything that's happening, she's behind it!"

He pauses expectantly, as if hoping I'm going to leap out the chair and hug him. I don't. His excitement becomes actual agitation. He raises his voice and slows his words, as if it's inaudibility that's impeding my understanding.

"You accused her husband of rape. Now I've been accused of the same thing. It's a set-up. She's set me up. I don't know how, but she has."

I exhale sharply. "Did she force you to have sex with Alice too?"

Ryan swings his cheek away from me as if I've just slapped him.

He perches on the edge of the sofa, his knees pointing away from me. He's plucking up the courage to continue.

When he does, the agitation has left his voice, replaced by a quiet desperation.

"Think about it, Nat. If Fiona Scott's not involved, then how would she know? There's been nothing in the media connecting me to Alice. My firm hasn't even been mentioned. Her first letter, all those years ago, said she'd make you pay. And you always say you get the feeling that she's out there, watching. Well, what if she is? But not just watching. Directing too. Alice doesn't live near here. The only reason she was killed in Sheen Woods was to frame me. Next Tuesday it'll be ten years exactly since the verdict, won't it? That'd be important to her. This whole thing is some warped idea of poetic justice. The ultimate revenge."

I stare at the letter again. At the crudely cut-out letters. Their message. I have to admit there is something gloating about it. Revelling in my misfortune. And what else could it be referring to? Ryan's right. She must know about him and Alice. A little seed of hope begins to germinate. Maybe it *was* all a set-up. Alice as bait. She was beautiful. Too beautiful for Ryan. If she'd paid him attention, he would have been drawn to her. Any man would. Particularly if his wife kept pushing him away. The seed sprouts fully. Tiny shoots and roots emerge. Yes, it all makes sense. Alice lied. The sex was consensual. The murder completely unrelated. The infidelity will be difficult to forgive, but not, perhaps, impossible. I look at Ryan. This time I really look at him. Not as a lawyer. But as his wife. He's aged five years in the last few days. Vitality, youth, sapped out of him. Even his hair seems greyer and his face more lined. How can I have ever thought he might be a predator? A murderer?

"OK," I say softly. "So we go to the police? Get in front of this?"

"No," Ryan replies quickly.

"Why not? You said yourself, they'll find out about the accusation soon enough. This way you stay ahead of the curve. This way you look less guilty."

"I'm not sure they'll believe it. Suddenly there are some anonymous letters, nearly ten years after the first were sent. We can't even prove she sent them."

Before I can say anything else there's a sharp rap at the door, immediately followed by the repeated chime of the bell. My heart rate accelerates as Ryan's face falls. He's thinking the same thing. Could it be? They're here already? It was only a matter of time.

"It might just be a delivery driver," I say, trying to sound reassuring. Ryan doesn't react.

I walk slowly into the hall. Ryan stays rooted to the spot.

A woman in her early forties in a navy trouser suit stands there, flanked by a man in his twenties in dark chinos and a blue striped shirt. He's attractive. She would be too, but her face is hard. She takes a step forward. He doesn't. She's in charge.

"Is this the residence of Ryan Campbell?" Her voice is cold, her accent harsh.

I nod rather than reply.

"I'm Detective Inspector Stratton and this is Detective Sergeant Bradley. May we come in?"

"Nat?" Ryan's voice enters the hall. His body follows. As soon as he sees them he tenses. His whole muscle and bone structure adjusts and becomes taut. Ready.

"Mr. Campbell?" The hard-faced woman's eyes flick over him then travel round the hall.

"Yes." Ryan manages to keep his voice level, but his muscles pull even tighter with it.

"We'd like to ask you a few questions about Alice Lytton. You will probably have heard about her murder on the news."

Ryan manages a nod.

"I understand that she worked for you. Would you mind accompanying us to the station."

Her voice doesn't rise at the end. It's not a question.

"Am . . ." Ryan begins to stammer. "Am I under arrest?"

The DI stares at him, her eyes beady. "Now, why would you say that?"

Ryan's so nervous he can hardly keep it together. And it makes him look so guilty. His hand shakes and he thrusts it inside his pocket to steady it. He looks at me. *Help*, his eyes say. *Help me*. But I don't know what I can do. What his rights are. I specialize in property law. I only did one module of criminal law at uni, and even then the focus was purely philosophical rather than practical. The only essay I remember was on the ethics of R v Brown—something along the lines of whether an adult should be able to legally consent to another adult hammering a nail into their genitals. Nothing about whether you can refuse to help the police with their inquiries. Whether you can refuse to get into their car.

"You worked closely with the victim, so it would really help with our investigation. It could help catch her killer. You do want to catch her killer, don't you, Mr. Campbell?"

Ryan's lips look dry. He runs his tongue over them. "Of course."

"Then if you'll come with us. The car's just outside."

I want to protest. To hold him back, but that will just make him look more suspicious.

Ryan steps forward woodenly and the DI closes in behind him, forming a moving barrier. They begin to walk towards the car. The detective sergeant remains on the doorstep.

He looks at me kindly. He really is very attractive. He reminds me of someone—I rack my brain—yes, a guy I very nearly dated at law school years ago—Charlie Hudson.

I wonder what happened to Charlie Hudson? Over his shoulder I see Ryan duck his head as he climbs into the back of the car. Do they just want to ask him some questions or do they think he killed her? There's no way of telling. I don't trust the hard-faced detective for a moment. She looks like she'd lock him up just for living in a nice house.

The detective sergeant still doesn't move. Instead he speaks, and his voice is surprisingly middle class, posh even. "I know this must be distressing for you, but we just have to ask him a few questions. We're talking to everyone who knew the victim."

"Yes," I say. "Of course."

"If there's anything you think of that might help us, here is my card." He presses a card into my hand and my fingers wrap round it.

His name is printed in the centre in small block capitals together with a mobile number and email address.

"Thank you," I say, my voice wavering. I don't know why he's helping, but I really appreciate it.

Bradley glances back at his boss and then lowers his voice. "In the meantime, the best thing you can do for your husband is to get him a lawyer."

Stratton

I TELL BRADLEY to put Campbell in Interview Room 3 then head to the main floor. Best to let him stew for a while. They're always more communicative that way. Especially the posh ones. It lets their imagination work a bit. They start picturing life without their pretty wife and nice house. They think of prison and the phrase "don't drop the soap" starts bouncing around inside their skull. Then they talk. The innocent tell the truth. The guilty lie through their teeth. But either way you have something to work with. To prove or tear apart. Either way their fate is sealed.

Bradley makes us both a coffee and we stand in the break room to drink it. My phone rings. It's Mum's home. I walk away to answer it, then reconsider and silence it instead. I can't afford to be in two different headspaces at the moment. I go to the ladies to splash water on my face. I feel like I'm flagging. The caffeine hasn't kicked in and I need to be on form.

"So?" I ask, as I return. "What were you saying to the wife?"
"Sorry?" Bradley looks up from his phone. I glance at the screen. He's got the Duolingo app open. Learning Italian. Of course. Every second of his life productively accounted for. Any of the other guys would be playing Fruit Ninja or watching YouTube videos. Not Bradley. Damn, I am starting to like him a bit. Not to hit on. But to have around.

"The wife," I repeat. "What were you telling her?"

"Nothing," he says. "She seemed a bit worried so I was explaining the process."

"How very good of you," I mock. "Thought she'd be your type."

Bradley looks at me curiously but doesn't reply, so I prod a bit more.

"Pretty, very middle-class, slightly weak. You couldn't keep your eyes off her."

Curiosity becomes obvious annoyance. God. I was just kidding. He needs to loosen up if he wants to be part of the team.

"I was just doing my job," he says curtly.

Yeah, right. But I shouldn't be too hard on him. There're times we've all "done our job" that little bit more conscientiously than necessary.

"Just don't get too close to her," I warn. "She might have information we need. She might end up a bloody suspect. Keep your distance till the case is over then take her back to your penthouse and screw her to your heart's content."

Bradley winces. He hates it when I'm crude.

Back on the main floor, Reynolds and Dev are both at their computers. Reynolds is closer so I check in with him first.

"Any movement on the burner or the murder weapon?"

"Sorry, no. The guy at the phone shop had no memory of who bought the burner and they record over their CCTV every week, so there's nothing to check there. No joy on the weapon either. Uniform have done a fine-tooth-comb search of the area and come up empty. The perp must have taken it with them or buried it a hell of a lot better than they did the body."

Bollocks. Murder cases are so much harder to land when the weapon's missing. Especially when there're no witnesses. It gives defence lawyers more wriggle room.

"Where are we on bank statements?" I call over to Dev. I still can't help but feel Alice's sudden ability to pay off Angel must be somehow linked to her murder. It's too much of a coincidence otherwise, and I don't believe in coincidences.

"I've been through the sister's bank details, and it didn't come from her," he says. "No major deposits or withdrawals in the last six months. She's managing, but there's nothing spare to help out someone in need. Definitely not ten K, anyway."

I nod. As I thought.

"What about the friend, Katie?" Bradley asks.

Dev shakes his head. "Sandra tried again, and I also tried her this morning. Still straight to voicemail. We found her on social media, and she hasn't posted for over a week. Looks like she's genuinely turned her phone off, so we probably won't hear anything till she's back."

"Monday?" I check. "Yeah. Monday."

I try not to look despondent. I'm responsible for team morale. People need to feel we're making progress, or everyone slumps.

"We're getting somewhere with CCTV, though," Dev offers.

At last something to smile about. I march over to his computer.

"I managed to track the vic over Hammersmith Bridge," Dev explains, "and then she pops up next at a bus stop on Castlenau—the long road leading into Barnes."

"Good work. Did you see what bus she got on?"

"That's the thing. She didn't get on a bus. She got in a car."

"A car?" My heart starts to speed up. Finally, something to work with.

"A black SUV. Possibly a Nissan. I've only got a partial so far. 'VE'. Then maybe a six or an eight. It's night, so the low light means the footage is too grainy to make out the whole plate. I'm looking for the next appearance of the car now. Hopefully I'll be able to fill in the missing digits and work out the make."

"Any sign of a struggle?"

"No. It looks like she got in voluntarily. The driver stayed in the car. She opened the door herself."

"Front or back door."

"Front."

"So she knew her killer. If the driver's the killer, that is. I'm getting ahead of myself. Maybe it's an Uber."

"You'd normally get in the back of an Uber," Bradley says.

"My sister always sits in the front," Dev counters. "It helps with her car sickness."

It's never simple.

"Either way, excellent work, Dev. Keep on it. See if you can follow where it ends up and get us a full plate."

My phone beeps and I open the email. It's Angie from Mum's home. They want to speak to me again. Mum perked up after my last visit, but then she dipped again. She's not eating. She's asking for me.

Fuck. I can't go every night. I just can't. I reply that I'll call after work. I get an instant reply. An in-person visit might be more beneficial. Fuck. I don't have time. Don't they appreciate what my job is? Don't they want the streets safe?

With anger rising, I pull my jacket back on.

"Come on, Bradley. Time to rip this Mr. Campbell apart."

Natalie

My head is spinning as the detective leaves. I pinch my arm until my eyes water, then dig the nails in deeper and deeper. Beads of blood appear, but it doesn't matter. I'm still here. My vision hasn't started to pixellate. I've caught it in time. I climb the stairs to the bedroom, remove the zip bag I keep in the bedside-table drawer and push a betablocker out of its blister. That leaves just one in the packet. I should call the doctor's for more, but the last prescription was from a few years ago and I doubt they'd issue another over the phone. A face-to-face appointment could take weeks. I swallow the pill with last night's bedside water. It'll take a little time to kick in but then it should slow my heart rate, which might help me get through the next few hours. I can't lose time now, I just can't. Pulling out my phone, I swaddle myself in my duvet and call Rachel. She may be a mergers and acquisitions solicitor but at least she's still fully engaged with the legal world. She has contacts. She'll know a criminal solicitor. Or at least she'll know someone who does.

"What's up?"

Thank God she picks up.

"The police have taken Ryan in for questioning." The words sound ridiculous as I hear them. The police are questioning my husband for murder. I stifle a slightly hysterical laugh.

"Fuck, Nat. Right. Is he under arrest?"

"No."

"Are you sure? Did they caution him?"

"No. They specifically said it wasn't an arrest. Just questions. To help them with their inquiries."

"OK." There's a pause. And a deep breath. I can tell Rachel is psyching herself up for something. "Don't take this the wrong way, Nat . . . Do you want to help him?"

I can't quite believe what I'm hearing.

"What do you mean?" I ask.

Another pause. A longer one this time.

"There's no easy way to say this . . . Do you think he's innocent? You weren't so sure last time we spoke."

"He's innocent," I say firmly. "I think it's all a set-up. There was another letter. Fiona Scott knew, Rach. She knew about Ryan. About Alice. She's behind all of it. I don't know how, but she is. She's waited ten years and is now exacting her revenge."

"If you're sure . . ." She sounds doubtful.

I pretend not to notice.

"I am. I need a lawyer. Or rather Ryan does. A criminal lawyer. A really good one. He's so nervous. If he doesn't have anyone he'll say something stupid."

"Right . . . In that case you need Mallory Cliff. She's the best. I'll WhatsApp you her contact details. She'll say she's too busy, but mention my name and she'll take you on as a favour. She owes me."

"Thanks," I say. "I know you're not Ryan's greatest fan, so this means a lot."

"It's nothing. You're my best friend. Look, I've got a Teams meeting in five, then I'll come over."

I go through the motions of protesting as I know she's snowed under at work and can't afford to take the time out, but I'm so relieved when she waves aside my concerns. I don't know what I'd do if I were on my own tonight. Despite the betablocker, I can feel the stress building up. I don't want to lose time again. I don't know where I might end up.

"I'll make you my special porcini risotto," Rachel says. "And I promise I won't spill the marsala this time."

I laugh. Risotto is her signature dish. Her only dish. When you're a City solicitor you don't get much time in the kitchen. Her last risotto was inedible. It tasted like a cross between a savoury rice pudding and trifle. It feels weird to laugh.

"You'll get through this," she says, more seriously. "I'll make sure of it."

* * *

An hour later Rachel lets herself in, and I don't even hear her until she walks into the kitchen as I have the radio on, loudly, while I'm doing the washing up. It gives my brain something to focus on that's not Ryan. Not Alice.

"Hope you don't mind?" Rachel says, holding up our spare set of keys, and making me jump. "I knocked, but when you didn't answer I thought you might be in the bath and I had visions of you passed out among the bubbles." She does a terrible mime of me flailing about under water and I smile despite everything.

"It's fine," I say. I'd forgotten I'd never asked for the keys back. Rachel kept our plants alive when we were away for a week last month. She was kind enough to offer as she knows how much they mean to me. My substitute offspring. And like mammalian young, newly planted shrubs require a lot of attention in their first year, before the roots are properly established.

Rachel deposits a Waitrose bag on the marble surface and removes a Charlie Bigham Red Thai Curry for Two and a bottle of white, pre-chilled.

"I thought you deserved better than my cooking tonight," she says with a smile.

The curry in the oven, she pours us each a large glass of wine. I shouldn't really drink. I rarely do. My medication has "Avoid alcohol" printed in barely decipherable text on the back. But Rachel's motto has always been, what harm can one glass do? "It's basic back-covering by Big Pharma," she laughs. "The equivalent of writing 'May contain nuts' on every single bakery item."

I take a sip. The wine's fresh with hints of citrus and gooseberry. I take another.

We sit at the table—her at one end, me next to her on her right. Like we're at one of those French pavement cafés. I like it. It's more intimate than sitting across from one another. Rachel's good like that—she lacks that traditional British reserve—but I sense that tonight she's turning it on intentionally, sensing my need for distraction, for closeness. She mentions Meena, a mutual friend from law school who moved out to Bristol but is coming back to London in the next few days for work. She says we should all meet up. I nod and try to force a smile. It'd be good to see Meena. I haven't for years. Not properly since she first had kids. It just got too hard. She offered for me to hold her baby and I just couldn't. I fled in tears. It made everything awkward. We didn't know how to act around each other. Maybe I could try again. But I have no idea what's going to be happening the next few days. It's the present, not the past, that's a foreign country at the moment. Tomorrow my husband might be back home. Tomorrow my husband might have been arrested for rape and murder.

Rachel senses my mood change and drops the entertainer act.

"Nat," she says quietly. "Tell me everything."

I do, every detail, and this time it feels good to share. Not with a therapist, not with someone with quizzical eyes and a notepad, but with a friend.

When I eventually finish, Rachel stands, stretches back her shoulders and rotates her neck until it clicks. Then she exhales and stares down at me, her expression hard to read.

"So, let me check I've got this right . . . You think Fiona Scott—who hates you because she thinks you falsely accused her husband ten years ago—somehow found a very attractive girl, got her employed at Ryan's firm, told her to seduce and then falsely accuse him, and then finally killed the girl herself in order to frame him?"

I take another sip of wine.

"Yes," I say, quietly, my stomach contracting as I glance towards the windowsill and the plants there. I don't want to meet Rachel's eyes. Hearing my theory spoken out loud makes me realize how absurd it all sounds. I don't want to see her incredulity. At the moment I'm like a dandelion head gone to seed. One blow and I'll disintegrate.

"How old would she be now?" Rachel presses.

I do a quick calculation.

"Fifty-seven."

"A fifty-seven-year-old drags a body into Sheen Woods?"

"Alice could have walked in. She could have killed her there."

"But still . . . Fifty-seven?"

"It's not that old."

"It's not that young. And it's you she hates. Not Ryan."

I put the glass down. My hand's trembling now, sending ripples across the wine's meniscus.

"This is how she's getting back at me. Don't you see? She's putting me through what she went through."

"You didn't kill anyone."

"She thinks I did. She thinks he had a heart attack because of me."

"Still, Nat . . . You know there's a simpler explanation."

No. I don't want to hear it. I don't want her to say it.

Rachel leans forwards and takes my hand, tracing her thumb over the knuckles. She lowers her voice.

"I never told you why Ryan and I don't get on."

I don't like her tone. The way she's looking at me. I want to put my hands over my ears and hum.

"He tried it on with me once. Years ago. At Fenn's wedding. Soon after I'd split with Adam. Nothing happened, of course—I rejected him. But that's why he doesn't like me. That's why he doesn't want me to see you. He's worried I'll tell you."

My heart's reverberating in my ears now. My chest is tightening.

"No," I say flatly. "You're mistaken."

It can't be true. Ryan wouldn't. He doesn't even like Rachel. He hates her. And he hates it when I see her.

Rachel doesn't say anything. She just stares at me. Sorrow tinged with sympathy.

"I'm so sorry, Natalie."

And then I think, he didn't use to hate her. He used to like her. They used to get on well and then it all changed. We met Ryan at the same time, Rachel and I. It was at a bar in the City, a year after we'd graduated from law school. I was single, Rachel wasn't. She was seeing some hedge-fund manager. Her relationships never lasted long then. Ryan spoke to us all evening and then at the end he asked for my number. At the time I'd worried that he might have fancied Rachel more. They would have been the pair you'd think to put together. Both shiny and perfect in appearance. The sort of couple that people would talk about admiringly. *They'll have beautiful children.* I even asked him about it early on. Teased him that he'd got the consolation prize. But he'd said, and I remember the words exactly, "Rachel's pretty of course, but in a really obvious way. You're more subtly beautiful. I prefer that." I've cherished those words over the years. A subtle beauty. Like a wild flower. Nuanced, rather than brash and showy. Rachel, the one that guys always flocked to, was obvious.

But now I start thinking, was it all a lie? Something said to placate me, to throw the mousy girl off the scent? Stupid hubris. Naïve fool. Had he wanted Rachel all along? *Obviously pretty.* Who doesn't want obviously pretty? A beauty that's so definite, so inarguable, that it's obvious. Surely that's the pinnacle. What everyone really wants. The achievement prize versus the endeavour cup.

My heart rate starts to surge.

"Nat." Rachel stares at me, forehead creased, her eyebrows nearly touching. I draw myself away, but she grabs my hand.

"I should have told you when it happened," she says. "I'm sorry I didn't. I was worried you wouldn't believe me. Or that you'd think I'd led him on or something and believe me but still resent me for it. Our friendship is precious to me. I didn't want to risk it. I was a coward."

I don't know what to think. She seems so sincere. But it's too much to process. Ryan sleeping with a young pretty thing in a moment of stupid weakness is one thing. His hitting on my best friend years ago quite another. He can be friendly. People like him. Maybe Rachel misconstrued . . .

Rachel increases the pressure on my hand.

"Nat, just answer me one more thing. Who first came up with this theory about Fiona Scott: you or Ryan?"

I don't want to think any more. I just want her to stop talking.

"I'm tired," I say. "I'm going to bed."

Rachel hooks her hand under my elbow.

"I'll help you upstairs," she says. "You look pale."

I allow her to help me up to my room, but then I make my excuses and disappear into the en suite. She offers to stay, but I say I need the quiet. That I have a migraine coming.

By the time I'm out, she's gone, but a couple of Nurofen sit next to a lysine on my bedside table.

I don't take them. Instead I head downstairs and pour myself a shot of whiskey.

* * *

I can't fall asleep. The medication doesn't work its magic. Even with the whiskey starter. My mind is deadened, but it won't fully quieten. Rachel's voice won't quieten.

Ryan hit on Rachel.

Could that be true? How could that be true? He wouldn't do that. Hit on my best friend. If true, it's the bigger betrayal. Worse than sleeping with a beautiful young woman. I can convince myself that Alice lied. The sex was a mistake but consensual. That she was somehow a pawn in Mrs. Scott's game. I can convince myself that Ryan isn't a murderer. But it's so much harder to convince myself that Rachel would lie. Would go out of her way to hurt me like that. And if Ryan had done it. Had hit on Rachel. Then I don't know who he is. I can't trust anything he says.

I end up taking a zopiclone at 1 a.m., knowing that without sleep I'll fall apart.

Stratton

Campbell is slumped at the table, pale, sweaty and slightly wild-eyed. Dark stains spread out from under his armpits. His imagination has clearly been at work. Good.

Bradley pulls out a chair on the other side of the table and there's a squeal of metal against floor tile. I sit myself next to him, two against one, and start the recording.

Campbell confirms he has waived his right to a lawyer being present. "I have nothing to hide," he says with manufactured bravado. Bravado undermined by the fact that his left hand is twitching slightly. Waiving the lawyer was clearly a play on his part. A strategy to make him look trustworthy, innocent. It was a mistake. We're going to make mincemeat of him.

After a few soft identifying preliminaries I bring up Alice.

"Did you find her attractive?" I say.

He flounders. I watch him. Every reaction. Every facial detail. Every hand twitch. It's often not people's words that give them away. It's everything else.

"Err. Of course. She was a very attractive young woman. Everyone thought so. The women too."

"I wasn't asking about everyone. Just you."

"Sure, sorry."

I want to see how quickly he gets angry. The white-collar, middle-aged ones can seem calm. Controlled. Incapable of violence. And then you get under their skin and a switch flicks. The calm is cheap veneer; scratch it and you see the real personality lurking underneath.

But, so far, so passive.

"And you invited her back to your house this Tuesday, nineteenth of March."

"Yes. To finish some work."

"Right," I say, leaning in, deliberately getting in his personal space. "And did you rape her as soon as you got home, or did you do some work first?"

He pushes his chair away from the desk and starts to stand. OK. He can get angry. The question is, how angry?

"Please remain seated, Mr. Campbell," says Bradley calmly.

A muscle is pulsing in his jaw, but he sits down again and manages to make eye contact.

"I did not rape her," he says.

"Right."

"You didn't have sex with her?" Bradley clarifies.

"We . . . we had sex. But it was consensual. She instigated it."

"And where was your wife?"

His face grows even paler, but there's a pink mottling at the base of his neck.

"She was upstairs," he mumbles.

"Sorry. Once again, but louder, for the recording, please."

"She was upstairs in bed."

"So you're saying that this much younger, very attractive young woman seduced you in your house while your wife was upstairs in bed?"

"Yes. That's what happened."

"So why did she tell your work you raped her then?"

He runs his hand through his hair.

"I don't know. She made it up though. I swear she did. She lied." He slams his fist on the table.

"Did her reporting it make you angry, Mr. Campbell? So angry you wanted to silence her?"

"No. No, you're twisting my words. You know you are. Can I have a glass of water? I don't feel well."

I nod to Bradley and he rises to fetch a small plastic bottle from a table in the corner.

I decide to switch tack. "Where were you on the following evening—Wednesday, March the twentieth?"

"At home," he replies.

"All night?"

"All night."

He hesitated. Just for a microsecond. He'll have hoped I didn't see. But I saw. I've trained myself to see.

"Can anyone verify that?" I ask reasonably.

"Yes, my wife."

"The same wife that was upstairs that night?"

His fist clenches so tight I can see the whites of his knuckles as he shifts in his chair. But he remains seated.

My neck is starting to get stiff so I rotate my head to loosen it. Tiny figure-of-eight movements. One direction and then back the other way. I see a shadow cross the window in the door. A face blocks the glass. Dev. He has news.

"Excuse me one moment," I say.

"DI Stratton exits the room at 19:12," Bradley says into the machine.

I close the door behind me. The strip light overhead in the corridor flickers. I was getting somewhere. I had turned up the pressure; he was ready to explode. This had better be good.

"What is it?" I ask impatiently.

Dev is literally bouncing from one foot to the other. He's got something. And, by the look of him, it's big.

"I followed the CCTV. Tracked the car all the way."

"Where did it end up?" I try not to get too excited.

"I got it turning off the South Circular, up Hertford Avenue."

"That leads to the park? And to the woods?"

"Yes."

"And did it leave again?"

"No. I checked all the different exit routes. It doesn't appear again in the next twelve hours."

Yes. I resist an air punch. We have it. Our first concrete piece of the puzzle. We know how Alice got to the woods.

"What about the plate?" I ask quietly, not daring to get my hopes up.

"I've got it," he says, a smile splitting his face open. "The full plate. VE64 TJK. A Nissan Qashqai."

"Brilliant. Great job, Dev. I could kiss you right now."

Dev's smile flickers. I write down the number on my pad. Whenever you see police on TV, they remember everything. Number plates. Phone numbers. How the fuck is that possible? Write it down or get it wrong. That was my first supervisor's motto. He was a dickhead, but it's a good motto and I've stuck with it.

"Have you checked the registered owner?"

Dev nods. He's so excited he can hardly talk. I know that feeling. The thrill of discovery. It's a better high than any drug can deliver.

"It's not an Uber driver."

"Just tell me, Dev. I need to get back in there."

Dev takes a deep breath then the words sort of explode out of his mouth.

"It's him. It's Ryan Campbell."

I clench my fist. *Yes*. Got you, you fucker. You raping, murdering fucker.

I re-enter the interview room. Bradley looks at me. He can sense I have something. I slowly pull out the chair again, deliberately scraping it along the floor to create that nails-on-blackboard sound. I'm almost enjoying myself.

"Mr. Campbell," I say innocently, "would you mind telling us what type of car you drive?"

He looks at me suspiciously.

"Sorry?"

"It's a simple question, Mr. Campbell. Your car."

"Er. A Qashqai. Black. Why? I don't understand."

"And its registration plate?"

He does a goldfish impression before answering.

"Er . . . VE64 TJK. Why is this relevant? What's happened?"

I ignore his question and throw him another.

"And where is your car now?"

"Outside the house, I think. That's where we normally park it. Why? Why are you asking about my car?"

We're interrupted by a sharp rap on the interview-room door. Bollocks. Just when I had him where I wanted him.

"This interrogation needs to cease immediately," comes a sharp voice from outside.

"See who that is," I bark to Bradley, not taking my eyes off Campbell. Enjoy your last moments of freedom.

Bradley opens the door and a woman with coiffed hair and a pencil-skirt suit forces her way inside. I recognize her immediately. Mallory fucking Cliff. Known and hated in police circles. We call her Skeleton Key. She's so bloody thin, and she gets all her clients out of jail. She's the last person we need getting involved in the case.

"Yes?" I say.

"You're interviewing my client without me present."

"He waived his right to a lawyer."

Mallory directs her gaze at Campbell.

"Your wife hired me. She thought you might want a lawyer. Do you want a lawyer, Mr. Campbell?"

"Yes," he says gratefully, nodding with his whole upper body like some stupid sock-puppet toy.

She thrusts a stapled document and a pen in front of him. "Sign here." Hands shaking, he obeys.

"Right," Mallory snaps. "I need a moment alone with my client."

Tiredness suddenly hits me. I can't do any more tonight anyway. We're making progress. We should have enough to get him, even with Mallory Cliff chucking everything she can think of in our path.

"Interview ended at 19:23," I say into the recorder. "We'll continue this in the morning."

"Are you charging my client?" Mallory asks, one perfectly plucked eyebrow raised.

"We have the right to hold him for thirty-six hours. You know that."

"But are you charging him?"

"Goodnight, Mallory."

* * *

There's no food at home. Of course there isn't, I never fucking shop, yet the absence of any obvious dinner always comes as a disappointment. I find a tin of beans at the back of the cupboard, still within date, and heat them up. I've had two missed calls from Mum's home so I call back while I stir.

Angie's off duty so I speak to her less friendly alternative—Agnes. Mum's not doing well. She's asking for Karen. She hit a carer. Daily visits would really help at the moment. I explain that I can't. That I'm on a case and I can't.

Agnes doesn't sound convinced. Fuck. The beans bubble and thicken. I say when the case is over I'll be there more. Agnes starts talking about the "fit". Maybe this home isn't the best "fit" for Mum. It's not a bloody school. They don't get to expel her for bad behaviour. She's an old woman, having difficulties. She's in a care home. Can't they just bloody care for her?

We're not getting anywhere so I say I need to end the call. I'd forgotten to keep stirring the beans so they're burnt; a sticky, charred mess on the bottom of the pan.

SATURDAY, 23 MARCH

Natalie

I WAKE AT six, my tongue woolly and my head fuzzy. I pull on my dressing gown and head downstairs to make some tea. Something to cut through the fog. I drink it looking at that photo of me and Ryan in Florence. Studying it. The way he's staring straight at me. His eyes creased. His lips upturned. It looks like love. It looks like he loves me.

Mallory Cliff calls just after seven. She says she wasn't worried about waking me as she knew I'd doubtless be up all night worrying about Ryan anyway. A flush of guilt passes over me. None of my worries have been about what will happen to Ryan. About what he's been going through.

"I had a long conversation with your husband last night," she says, getting straight down to business. "It seems the police don't have enough evidence to charge him—it's all circumstantial, yet they're drooling to pin this on him. They were asking about your car. Is there anything I need to know there?"

Our car? "No," I say, walking into the kitchen and looking out at the street through the front window. The car is sat on the road outside the house as normal. "No, I don't think so." "Ryan was mentioning some threatening letters," she continues. "I need you to bring them into the station as soon as possible. I was against it at first—introducing this Fiona Scott character seems rather far-fetched and melodramatic, but we do need to throw them another suspect to sink their teeth into before they get complete tunnel vision."

Far-fetched? Melodramatic? She doesn't believe it either. To her, Fiona Scott's a tactical distraction, nothing more. Am I a fool, swept up in the stories Ryan's spinning? Is he a serial liar? A cheater? Are everyone else's eyes open while mine are blind?

No, regardless of who he's slept with, who he's hit on, there's something bigger going on. Mallory doesn't understand. How could she? She wasn't there ten years ago. She didn't live through what we lived through. To be told there is a woman out there who hates someone isn't the same as experiencing it. Seeing that hatred in her eyes. Seeing that hatred cut out and glued on to the page. And that hatred exists independently of whatever Ryan's done.

"Natalie?" Mallory sounds impatient. "The letters?"

"Of course," I mumble.

"And they'll bring you in for questioning, they're bound to. After all, you're his alibi. It's not that strong, obviously, as you're the wife, but it's better than nothing."

I don't understand.

"Alibi?" I ask quietly.

"Yes, you're the only one who can testify that Ryan didn't leave the house that night."

"But—" I'm about to interject that he did leave. He went running. In the woods. Straight past the murder site. But then something in her tone alerts me to the fact that she already knows this. She knows exactly what she's asking.

I swallow. Mallory continues.

"They'll come by to search your home soon. This morning, I'd wager. I think the court will rubber-stamp a warrant; they normally do. So anything you need to tidy up . . . now's the time."

She hangs up. And I'm left reeling.

I retreat into my office room and stare out at the garden, trying to rebalance. Can I really do what she's asking? Lie to the police to protect my husband? A man I'm not sure I know any more. A man who not only admitted to sleeping with a much younger woman but who also may have hit on my best friend.

The alibi issue is one thing. If Fiona Scott is involved, as I feel she must be, and playing us like pawns, then the truth might not be enough to stop her. For me to admit he was out at the scene of the crime is going to make him look as guilty as hell. Particularly if he's lied about not being there. But the other thing—essentially asking me to find and destroy evidence? That's one step too far. If he's innocent, there won't be any evidence. And if there is evidence, if he's done this terrible thing, then I don't want to save him.

I dress. Smarter than normal. Dark denim jeans, a camel rollneck, black blazer. Wearing clothes like armour. Then I open the bottom drawer of Ryan's chest of drawers and pull out the black A4 storage box I know he keeps there. Hands trembling, I remove the lid. I was right. This is where he's put them. The two new letters sit on top. The original six lie beneath. They might not be enough to do anything, but they show there's someone else out there. Someone who wants to do us harm. Maybe that'll be enough. It has to be.

Stratton

Thanks to Mallory fucking Cliff our prime suspect is no longer talking. And without a confession or a murder weapon we don't have enough to nail him. OK, we can show the vic getting into his car, but we don't have an image of him driving. Even if we did, all we could prove was that he gave her a lift to somewhere beyond Hertford Avenue on the night she was killed. The car might even weaken our case. Alice got in voluntarily. Which meant she wasn't scared of the man she accused of assaulting her. Fuck. Cliff would tear us apart in court.

"Any luck with Campbell's bank account?" I ask Dev.

"No." He shakes his head glumly. "Standard pay cheques in from work. Regular expenditure. Bills. Council tax. Waitrose. Coffee shop. Cycle shop. Lots to prove he's a middle-class wanker. But nothing linking him to any payment to Alice. I'm going to keep digging. I've left messages with all the different bank branches in the area to see if he's got any other accounts squirrelled away."

I nod my thanks, but can't hide my disappointment. I was sure he'd be linked to the money. Somehow. But maybe my hunch is wrong. Maybe the money has nothing to do with it. Life's messy. Not everything has to tie up neatly together.

He looks tired. I can't have the team fading so I tell him to take a break from his computer. To get out and try to find the car. Start at the Campbells' house then spread outwards. It's got to be somewhere nearby. The fresh air will perk him up. Dev smiles gratefully.

Reynolds storms into the room, grabs a pad from his desk, removes and then replaces his glasses and starts to stomp back out again.

"What's up?" I ask. He's given to occasional dark moods, but he normally simmers rather than stomps.

"Fucking Forensics," he spits. He also rarely swears. "They lost a piece of evidence I bagged in the Williams case. Fucking lost it. Morons. Without it I have no case. The bastard walks. The bastard fucking walks."

I shoot him a look of sympathy. No wonder he's angry. Another knock-on effect of budget cuts. They think they can fill lower positions—drivers, admin, and so on—with untrained amateurs. It doesn't work like that. Evidence isn't the same as online groceries. You can't substitute a different brand of butter.

We watch him leave and I wrench my mind back to the Lytton case.

"What now?" Bradley asks. He's the only one of the team who still looks fresh.

"We find the car, search the house, and break the wife. She's the alibi. If she admits he went out that evening, it gives us opportunity. We already have motive. Then all we need to throw in is one item of bloodstained clothing and we can nail the son-of-a-bitch."

"OK. Shall I start looking for the car?" Bradley offers.

"No, Dev's already on that. When he's found it, I'll take the car. You bring the wife in."

Bradley looks wary. "Shouldn't we stick together? We're partners."

I roll my eyes. Now's not a time for protocol. We have to keep up the pressure, or this case will slip through our fingers. I have a feeling about it. Cliff's already supplying the grease. And I know it's nothing but stupid superstition, but the voice whispers again at the back of my brain that I have to solve this one. I need to keep my side of the bargain. Every case is important, but this one seems even more so. It feels that if I don't solve it, I'll never get Karen back.

But I don't say any of this. Instead I say, "I get the feeling the wife will be more receptive if it's just you. Bring her in, get her settled. I'll be there for her statement."

I watch him, anxiously. Hopefully the bait of spending time with the "hot" wife will be enough to corrupt him. He pauses then nods. Good. You can lead men anywhere by their dicks.

"Right. We have a plan. Let's time the house search for when you pick up the wife. It'll scare her and then you'll be the white knight, arriving to reassure her."

Bradley loosens his collar. He's not happy.

"Have you got the warrant?" he asks.

I grind my teeth. What does he think I'm going to do? Barge my way in without a warrant and get anything we find thrown out in court?

"Signed off first thing."

Bradley still looks uncomfortable, and I'm not in the mood to take shit from anyone.

"What? What's the problem now? Out with it."

He shakes himself together.

"Nothing. Sorry. It's just the case. It's getting to me."

OK. He's human after all. I nod. I feel it too.

We only have to wait ten minutes for Dev's call. He confirms the car is parked outside the Campbells' house. He's notified Pavarotti, who's already on his way.

"Looks like we are sticking together," Bradley says with a smile.

As we pick up our coats to leave, Dev calls again. His voice has that lit-up quality. Exhaustion banished by the thrill of discovery.

His excitement is contagious.

"Well, spit it out," I say, grinning and putting him on speaker.

"You know I said his personal account was clean?"

"Yes," I say. "Get to the point."

"He also has a joint account he shares with his wife. Different bank. The branch manager just called me. On the eighth of March there was a cash withdrawal."

"Yes?" I try not to get my hopes up.

"He took out £12,000."

Bradley whistles and then grins. I don't know what this proves, but I do know my gut was right—the events are connected. It can't be a coincidence. Campbell takes £12,000 cash out of an account the day before the girl he later rapes miraculously repays ten grand cash to her drug dealer. Could it be he thinks he's buying her? He meets her somewhere. Falls for her. Gets her a job, pays off her debts, and then thinks his noble deeds give him the right to bang her whenever he wants. Some medieval-lord-of-the-manor shit. When she objects, he kills her.

It's all speculation of course, but there's one thing that's certain in my mind.

He's our man.

"Good work, Dev. See you in five."

Me and Bradley take separate cars. We might be going to the same place, but we won't be returning together.

I get there fractionally before him, so he's still parking up when I reach the Campbells' car.

I tell Dev to go and get himself a coffee. He's earned it. I want to look at the car properly before we start on the house. He's got ten minutes.

The car's neatly parked, inches from the pavement, wheels parallel to the kerb. Nothing to suggest it's been abandoned in a hurry by a killer rather than used for a boring suburban Sunday-afternoon trip to the shops. I bend down to examine the driver's door. There's no damage. I stalk round the outside. The left wing mirror is slightly scratched and the right rear brake light glass has a chip out of it, but there's no evidence any door has been jacked open and the windows are all intact.

By the time I've completed my 360-degree tour, Bradley is standing on the pavement.

"What do you think?" he asks.

I think for a moment then answer.

"Whoever drove it had a key."

Natalie

As I reclose the box and shut the drawer, I hear a noise out front. I peer out through the shutters. Two figures are standing on the pavement next to our car, gesturing at it. A woman and a man. They're facing away, but then the woman turns.

God. Her.

The cold detective. And the kind one. What do they want with our car? I want to withdraw, to cocoon myself back into my duvet, but I can't. I can't be left in the dark any more. A creature buffeted by fate, reeling from revelation to revelation. I need to confront this head on.

I head downstairs, slip my feet out of slippers and into the leather boots I left in the hall.

Opening the front door, I steel myself then call out to them, "Can I help you?"

There's no response so I draw myself up, lengthening my spine, and stride down the front path.

Detective Bradley turns towards me. He meets my eye and then looks away. It's not him my anger is directed towards, but her. Standing there, in her trouser suit, not even deigning to look at me.

They're both wearing thin plastic gloves.

"Please can you tell me what's going on?" I ask again, keeping my voice authoritative.

She slowly turns.

"When did you last use your car?" she asks.

"I don't know," I say.

"You don't know?" Her eyebrows are raised as if I've just said the most preposterous thing. But I don't know. Genuinely. Not for a few days, at least. I tend to walk to the shops. Walk or cycle to the gym. We only got the car for daytrips out of town. In the first years of our relationship, Ryan and I were so spontaneous. I think we prided ourselves on it, a little smugly in fact. One Saturday a month we'd each pack an overnight bag and meet at a London station. Then we'd flip a coin to decide which train to take. Sometimes it'd be a night in Bath. Others . . . Slough. But it was always fun. I think Ryan had been trying to recapture this. That he envisaged returning to a life of spontaneous weekends away in the Cotswolds or the Lake District. It just never materialized.

"What about Ryan?" she presses. "When did he last use the car?"

"Ryan?" I rack my brain. He won't have used it for even longer. He cycles to work, unless it's raining and then he takes the train. Drives to golf once a month. Then I remember. "I used it the Tuesday before last," I say. "It was raining so I picked Ryan up from the station after work."

"Tuesday before last," she repeats sceptically, then pulls a notepad and pen from her breast pocket and writes something down. She keeps the pen poised and fixes her beady eyes on me.

"So who was driving it on Wednesday night then?"

Wednesday. The night Alice was killed. No. Surely. No.

I must have looked as faint as I felt as Bradley was suddenly at my arm, supporting my elbow.

"Oh. Thank you," I say.

"Do you feel OK? Do you need to sit down?" he asks.

"No," I say. "I'm fine. Thank you."

But I don't feel fine. It's like the pavement is undulating beneath my feet. Could this be a game they're playing? A fishing expedition? They don't have any idea if the car was used but they're hoping I'll break down and give something away. I glance at the inspector again. She doesn't look like she's fishing. She looks like she's already caught something. The satisfied expression of a predator well fed.

"Would you mind terribly opening the car for us?" she asks mock politely.

I don't answer; I'm trying to weigh all the options. I wish Rachel were here. Or Mallory Cliff. I pull out my phone to call her.

"My asking is only really a courtesy," the inspector continues. "We have a warrant." She removes it from her pocket and thrusts it under my nose. It looks official. Genuine. "You can either unlock it or we can smash a window. It's really up to you." She pulls out a small metal stick and I know she's not joking. Reaching into my pocket, I find the car keys and beep it open.

I peer over her shoulder as she opens the driver's door. What is she looking for? The seats look the same as ever, unsullied from lack of use. There's even still that new-car smell. Then I follow her eyeline down. Past the driver's seat and on to the pedals.

They are streaked with mud.

Before I can try and process this, Detective Bradley's arm is on my elbow again, steering me away from the car.

"Pavarotti's here," he says to his boss.

I turn to see a large man with a black goatee. He's dressed in a white zipped-up bodysuit and is pulling on a pair of thin latex gloves.

My pulse quickens. They're treating our car as a crime scene. Why are they treating our car as a crime scene, and why is there mud on the pedals? There shouldn't be mud on the pedals.

An image invades my mind. Ryan, stood by the utility sink scrubbing at his trainers. The water spiralling reddish brown towards the plughole. No. He didn't take the car. He ran. He ran in the woods.

He says he did . . .

My head starts to throb and my vision's threatening to pixellate when I'm ripped back to reality by the sound of a car on the street grinding its gears. Then a second car approaches. A police car. Three uniformed officers jump out and head towards us.

At the same time, Stratton takes the warrant from her pocket a second time.

Her voice washes over me. I hear the words "search", "house", "questions", but the rest is white noise.

The officers swarm towards the house and in through the still-open front door.

Hands shaking, I call Mallory Cliff. It takes three attempts for me to find her number in my contacts and press my shaking finger on the right spot on the screen.

"They're searching the house," I manage to say when she picks up.

"Of course they are," she snaps back. "Will they find anything?"

I laugh. A hysterical, humourless laugh. I don't know. I have no idea what they'll find.

"Call me if they do," she says, and hangs up.

I stand there, dazed. My mind's trying to process, but it's too much to take in. An onslaught.

"Mrs. Campbell?" There's a movement ahead and I realize that the detective, Bradley, is standing in front of me, looking at me strangely. I don't know how long he's been there. Whether he's been trying to speak to me.

"Mrs. Campbell, please would you accompany me to the station?" he says softly. "It won't take long. We just need to get a statement from you."

He sees me glance back at the house.

"There's nothing you can do here," he says. "I know this must be distressing for you, but we'll go to the station. I'll make you a cup of tea and we can talk."

The box, I think. The letters.

"Please wait a moment," I say. "There's something I need to fetch."

I feel his eyes on my back as I walk up the path.

Stratton

I watch Bradley lead her away. She's carrying a black box, clasping it to her chest like someone might try and wrestle it from her. She's hard to figure out, that one. I had her pinned as pretty but ineffectual. A weak woman, ignorant—intentionally, even—of her husband's faults. But there's something else there too. She hides things. I can sense it. Even her body seems to fold in on itself, like it's wrapping round secrets.

"Stratton," Pavarotti's voice booms behind me and I turn to face him.

"What've you got?" I ask.

"It doesn't look like she was killed in the car. There're no obvious bloodstains, and no strong chemical smell, which I'd expect if the perp had bleached it clean. Nonetheless, I've swabbed the seats and the rest of the interior, so we should pick up any traces of spatter."

I nod. I'd assumed as much. A nice big pool of Alice's blood would have been too easy.

"Anything else?" I ask.

"There's a long blond hair on the passenger headrest. I'll obviously test it against the vic's."

"Good," I say. But it doesn't give us much. He's admitted to an affair. He'll say he gave her a lift once to save her from walking. All totally innocent.

"And I assume you saw the mud?" he adds.

"Yes," I say. The mud gives me more hope.

"We'll try and match it to the mud at the scene."

It'll match. I know it will. But again, I also know Cliff can explain it away. I imagine her enjoying herself in the courtroom. Of course it matches. He lives near the woods. He walks and runs there regularly. Where else would the mud have come from? No, you can't prove a murder case from mud-encrusted pedals. It's circumstantial again. I have to keep going. Find something that takes us out of the realm of reasonable doubt.

I spot Dev. He's back, loitering by the gate. Waiting for me.

"I'm heading inside," I tell Pavarotti. "Let me know if you find anything else."

We nod to the uniformed PC stationed on the gate to deter busybodies then approach the PC guarding the front door. He hands me and Dev each a pair of blue plastic shoe covers and I bend over to put these on before I enter the house. We're not treating it as a crime scene yet, but you never know. Always best not to go traipsing the pavement over the suspect's carpet. You'd just be opening yourself up to the defence crying cross-contamination in court.

The hall is as I remember it. Large brass statement light hanging from a hook in the middle of the ceiling. Parquet flooring, muted blue and grey checked rug, pale grey stained wooden console table tastefully offsetting Scandinavian grey walls. All very minimalist and unimaginative. They've read a magazine and digested what they're supposed to like. Like the pricks who groom their beards into points just because they've had one too many coffees in Hackney. Dev lifts the rug while I snap a photo of the console table then look through it. How many bloody memberships do you need? Fuck.

Off the hall is a downstairs loo. I snap a photo then open the door of the undersink cupboard. Two spare soap dispensers. How horribly organized. But nothing else. I check under the cistern for good measure. Nothing there either.

Dev follows me into the kitchen. For the first time I'm surprised. The tall cupboard is painted a bright, punchy orange. The work's recent. There's still a lingering smell of paint. I quite like the colour, it's so in your face, but it's a completely different feel to the rest of the house. I wonder who chose it—him or her? My bet's on her. I think I'm right. There's something hidden there. A brighter, bolder personality held back.

The kitchen leads through an arch into an open-plan living room with a dark grey sofa, side table and TV unit. How many bloody shades of grey do you need? I tell Dev I'll take the kitchen. He should start in the living area. Dev nods seriously and then goes to squat in front of the TV cabinet. He snaps a "before" photo then starts methodically combing through the contents. Good, he's watching and learning. I don't need to babysit him too closely.

I look through the tall cupboard, which turns out to be a larder. Everything comes out. From the chickpea flour to the emergency "Big Soup" tins at the back. I'd bet he bought those. I line the spice jars up on the floor. Nothing. No sign of a concealed murder weapon. No bloodstained T-shirt.

My hopes rise as I push open the side door off the kitchen and enter a small utility space. It's amazing how many times you find evidence in a utility. Traces of blood in a sink. Something caught in a U-bend. Once, I found a knife soaking in a bucket of bleach, for fuck's sake. Murderers aren't always the sharpest. Although something tells me not to underestimate this one.

Right. No buckets here. Nothing obviously blocking the sink. There's a pair of trainers in the corner that I'll get Dev to bag up. The material's still slightly damp so they've been cleaned, possibly innocently, possibly not. Probably not enough to remove any trace DNA. I'll also get Pavarotti to run some swabs of the sink area and shine his magic UV light when he's finished with the car.

The final stop on the ground floor is a small office room off the living area. The walls are painted a calm deep green and a wooden desk is positioned in front of a set of double doors leading out into the garden. I peer out. The garden's beautiful, I'll give them that. A nice mix of groomed and wild. Such a luxury to have the time to achieve that. Mum always wanted a garden. She had green fingers. Her flower box was the envy of the estate, but there's only so much you can do when your garden measures twenty centimetres by eighty.

There's a laptop on the desk. Pens and Post-its in the drawer. I'll get Dev to bag the laptop. To the left of the desk stands a thin bookcase, painted the same colour as the walls. It's filled with the most boring-looking books imaginable: *Commercial and Residential Service Charges*, *Thompson's Modern Land Law*. So she's a lawyer. Interesting. I don't think I would have guessed that.

Upstairs there're two bedrooms and a bathroom. Both beds are made up and look like they've been slept in recently. Maybe all's not well with the Campbells. Maybe she suspected what he is, saw his darker side and pushed him out. Maybe he felt frustrated. Maybe that's what flipped his switch that night. So many maybes.

Dev follows me upstairs. I tell him to take the spare room and I'll take the master. I start with the husband's bedside table. There's a Shardlake novel, a phone charger and earplugs. Does she snore? I pull the drawer fully out, off its hinges, checking for a secret compartment below. None.

I move on to hers. Another historical fiction novel. Hers has gold embossing and a river running across it. His and hers. Good that they share some interests. The contents of her drawer are more interesting. Some lavender pillow mist and a notebook—just the first page has been filled in. Three dates followed by a time.

- 18/3—9.45 a.m.—Letter—Garden—Roses
- 20/3—11 p.m.—Ryan—Bench
- 22/3—10.25 a.m.—Letter—Wardrobe

The second entry stands out. 20/3: 20 March—the day Alice was killed. What happened at 11 p.m.? "Ryan—Bench". What does that mean?

I take a photo of the page.

I stick my hand further back to check I haven't missed anything. Behind the notebook there's something soft—a small zip bag. Green velvet with an "N" embroidered on the front in gold. Very tasteful. Expensive, no doubt. I open the zip and find three packs of pills. Zopiclone—a prescription sleeping pill. I know it. I've taken it a few times. Mainly around Karen's birthday. It knocks you out, but you wake up feeling groggy, with a dry mouth and woolly tongue. None of the refreshment of real sleep. I look inside the packet: two blisters are open. The date on the prescription label isn't that recent so she doesn't use it that often. Behind that is the next pack of pills. Mirtazapine. There are four empty spaces. I photograph it then look it up. Reduces anxiety. Finally there's a packet of propranolol. I know that. A betablocker. There is only one left. Mum was prescribed it for panic attacks after Karen was taken.

Yes, all isn't right with the Campbells at all.

Natalie

Detective Bradley opens the front passenger door of his car and then steps aside so I can climb in. I appreciate it, his not insisting that I sit in the back. I can feel he's trying to put me at my ease. To show he doesn't suspect me of any wrong-doing. I know it's a calculated move, but it's still working.

"I apologize for the mess," he says with a smile. "I don't normally give lifts."

The car isn't messy at all. There's a jumper in the back, but even that is neatly folded. The car even has a nice smell. A pine air freshener hangs from the rear-view mirror.

"It's far neater than ours," I begin, but then stop midsentence. His familiarity has caught me off guard. I'm not being given a lift by a friend. It's not a situation to joke about how messy our car is. Our car is being swabbed by a pathologist. I'm being driven to a police station. My husband is suspected of murder.

We don't talk for the rest of the journey. I sit and stare ahead, holding the black box, hoping it's what's going to end this nightmare. There's an awkward moment when we stop at a traffic light rather too suddenly and my right knee brushes against his hand on the gear stick. My whole body tenses as I apologize.

"Don't worry about it," he says, and he looks at me intensely. I flush. I think he thinks I did it on purpose.

Bradley parks outside the station and I follow him in, waiting for the panic to hit. The PTSD effect of entering another police station.

It doesn't. My legs don't collapse under me. Maybe it's because it's a different station. The memories, the triggers, somehow tied to particular bricks and mortar. The last building, where I reported the rape, was very much a police station in the traditional mould, virtually unchanged from its Victorian form. An imposing corner building, red brick, high ceilings, a blue lantern hanging outside. The disinterested look in the officers' eyes . . .

No, I drag myself away from the memories before they suffocate me. This building couldn't be more different. It's really unremarkable. A seventies local council build, it could just as easily be the headquarters of town planning or parking permits, a place quiet quitters go to die.

"Right. I'm going to check which room's free," Bradley says gently. "Can I get you anything before we start? Tea, coffee?"

"No, I'm fine, thanks," I reply automatically, and then see a smiling female officer walk past, cradling a steaming mug, and I think how much I would like the same. For comfort as much as anything else. A potable security blanket.

"Actually, a tea would be nice. Thank you."

"Two teas coming up."

As I'm waiting for him to return, my nerves start to build. The building with its low ceilings and long corridors begins to feel claustrophobic. It no longer seems interchangeable with any other council building. A form of transubstantiation has occurred. It is now very definitely a police station that I'm standing in. Alone. Ryan will be here too. In one of the rooms. They've held him for ages now. Why aren't they letting him go? They should have let him go by now. My breathing and pulse increase. The edges of my vision start to pixellate.

"Natalie?"

A sharp voice calls me back to the present.

Mallory Cliff is walking towards me, her heels click-clacking along the corridor. She's come from Ryan, no doubt. Hope germinates. She can stay. She can help.

She acknowledges me with a sharp nod but doesn't look like she's going to stop. I don't understand.

"They're going to ask me some questions," I say. "Shouldn't you be there?"

Her right hand makes a dismissive waving gesture.

"No. Answer carefully. No more information than necessary. But I can't be there. I'm Ryan's lawyer. It'd be a conflict of interest." And with that, she's off, her heels beating a staccato rhythm across the floor.

I try to piece together what she's said. *A conflict of interest.* How can that be? In spite of everything he's done, I'm giving evidence for Ryan. To help Ryan. Her supporting me would be her supporting Ryan. How could it not be?

"We're in Interview Room 1."

Bradley's returned, holding two mugs of tea. He holds one towards me, then I realize I can't take it without putting down the box so there's an awkward moment when he stands, hand outstretched before recognizing the difficulty.

"I'll carry the tea in for you," he says.

The room is small with a tiny window overlooking the South Circular. A functional metal desk sits in the middle, a recording device perched on top. Two chairs have been positioned on either side, facing each other. It doesn't look like the set-up for a chat. It's designed for confrontation. I place the box on the table and he places the tea to its right.

"DI Stratton said she'd be joining us. Let me just give her a ring."

He pulls out a phone, dials and then turns his face away. I can't hear her side of the conversation, but it seems she's caught up. Bradley stands, excuses himself and then returns moments later with the female officer. The smiling one with the curls. I remember when I'd seen her before—outside Alice's flat on the morning after she was murdered. I tense, but she doesn't show any sign of recognizing me.

"Right. Mrs. Campbell, this is FLO Digby. She'll be sitting in on our chat."

That word again. That misnomer. *Chat.*

I stare at the black box. I remember when I gave it to Ryan. Our first anniversary. It was going to be a memory box—full of keepsakes.

Concert-tickets stubs. Restaurant receipts. A Paris Métro map. Before the letters came.

Bradley presses record on the device and then speaks into it.

The first questions are easy. Softening. Like kneading dough to make the cellulose strands more pliable. Then he moves on to her. Alice. And that night.

"Were you aware that your husband was having an affair with the victim, Alice Lytton?"

I nod my head, my stomach starting to constrict.

"For the machine, please."

"Yes," I say quietly. "Ryan told me that they had slept together."

"How many times?"

"One that I'm aware of."

"And are you also aware that the victim reported this one time as a rape?"

I nod my head again then remember and change it to a "Yes." My left eyelid is starting to twitch. "But Ryan wouldn't—"

Would he? He tried it on with Rachel. With my best friend. Why would she lie?

"Just the facts, please, Mrs. Campbell. How did this accusation make your husband feel?"

"Worried. Upset."

"Angry?"

I pause as I remember Ryan's fist hitting the wall. I take a sip of tea.

"Worried and upset," I repeat.

I feel hot. I want to take off my jacket, but the rollneck underneath is tight against my body and I don't want to feel exposed.

"Are you all right, Mrs. Campbell?" Bradley asks, looking at me closely. "Would you like a glass of water?"

"I'm fine, thank you," I manage.

I breathe in through my nose and out through my mouth. Slow, deep rescue breaths.

Detective Bradley moves on to ask about the night Alice was killed. This is the moment I've been dreading.

"Please talk us through Wednesday evening."

"I was home," I say flatly.

"Alone?"

"With Ryan."

"So Ryan was home with you the whole night? Would you be prepared to say that under oath, in a courtroom? You do know that if you're found guilty of perjury you would be struck off the roll? Your career as a solicitor would be over."

He stares at me. He's trying to read me.

I think, what if someone saw him? A neighbour? What if he's already admitted to leaving? It would be worse for him if I lie. It would make him look guilty. I glance down at the box. That's our best way out. Not through lies. But the truth.

"He went for a quick run but was otherwise at home."

"A quick run." Bradley seems to roll the words around his mouth. "How long is a quick run?"

His eyes pierce me.

"Um. I'm not sure exactly. I went to bed early."

"What time did he set out?"

"Just before ten."

"And then you went to bed?"

"Yes."

"Does he normally go out that late?"

"Sometimes." Never. He never runs that late.

"Had you fought?"

"No." Yes, all day. We'd fought all day.

"Did he say where he ran?"

"Just locally."

"Locally as in Sheen Woods?"

I feel the heat rising in my cheeks again. I try to push it away. I visualize a tray of ice cubes. The Norwegian fjords.

"I don't know. The pavements, probably. Possibly the woods. Lots of people run there."

"At night?"

"Yes." My voice tremors.

"Did you ask him where he'd gone?"

"No."

If they don't know he was in the woods, I don't want to be the person to tell them. Even after everything, I feel I owe him that much.

"Even after you found out the girl had been murdered near your house at the very time your husband was out? The same girl who said your husband raped her. You didn't ask him?"

"No," I reply.

"And you went to bed early."

"Yes."

I should tell him about blacking out. Waking up on the pavement. I know I should. But he didn't specifically ask if I was in all night. It's an omission. Not a lie. My blackouts aren't relevant. And they won't help Ryan. Bradley is less likely to take what I have to say next seriously if he thinks I'm unstable.

Bradley ends his questions and I take a deep breath before reaching towards the box. Tentatively I lift the lid.

"There's something else you need to know," I say, as calmly as I can. "I believe that someone from my past is trying to frame my husband."

Bradley places his hands on the table, palms down, and looks at me curiously.

"Please explain," he says.

I recite the history of the letters. The court case that triggered them. The fact that next Tuesday is the ten-year anniversary of the verdict. As I talk I put my right hand under the table and dig my fingernails into my thigh. I feel them tear skin. Liberate blood. The pain pricks at the corner of my eyes but I manage to remain present, in the room. It helps that he's there. That I'm not alone. I show him the letters as I talk. The first ones, the ones at the bottom of the box, have yellowed slightly and give off a musty aroma. The lettering is still as clear as ever though.

LIAR.

WHORE.

KILLER.

I'm worried that he's going to laugh at me. That he won't let me finish. But he doesn't. He's gravely serious. He listens attentively, never taking his eyes off me, even when I leave history behind and embark on my theory—Ryan's theory—that Fiona Scott is now somehow involved with Alice. That it's all a set-up. I don't know if he believes me, but he's listening. He's open. I'm so pleased that the other detective isn't here. His boss. I know she'd have laughed. She'd have looked at me with her cold blue eyes and laughed.

At the end he asks if I could leave the letters here, with him. He says he'll look into it. Find out where Fiona Scott is now.

I agree. I trust him. I think he might somehow be the one who can put a stop to it all. I push the box towards him.

"Just one more thing," he says. "I need to take your finger-prints for elimination purposes."

Stratton

I FINISH SEARCHING behind the curtains and under the bed. It's amazing how often you find things under a bed. It seems that the early childhood hide-and-seek mentality is hard to shake. If it worked when you were four . . .

This time though: nothing.

Pavarotti's voice booms up the stairs. He needs to go. Another case. He's finished swabbing. He'll call with results. I should bag anything else I find and a driver from Forensics will pick it up when I'm ready.

I acknowledge him and then turn back to the room.

Only one more place to search—the wardrobe.

I open the doors. It's neatly divided. Her stuff on the left—dresses, the odd blouse, a couple of mid-length skirts. All very uninspired suburban-housewife stuff. His is on the right—pressed shirts and trousers. A couple of blazers. The marketing firm is clearly too cool for traditional suits. Maybe they'd get creased on the bloody beanbags.

The wardrobe is deep so I crouch down on hands and knees to explore further, snapping photos as I go. It's dark towards the back so I flip my phone on to torch mode. I explore his side first. There's a line of smart shoes, polished, shoe horns in place. Behind them comes a jumble of trainers. Most hardly worn. I pick them up and examine them. They are dry, the soles clean. They haven't seen pavements for a while, if ever.

Further behind the trainers are a couple of bags. One creased tan leather gym-style holdall. Empty. The price tag still attached. Fuck me. Seems you pay extra for something to be fakely aged. These people. Next to it, one small wheelie case. The sort people use as hand luggage on aeroplanes to avoid the baggage queues. God, it's been a long time since I went on an aeroplane. Last time was Spain two years ago. I went by myself. Waste of money. Ended up sitting on the beach, alone, far too hot, surrounded by total idiots, having shelled out £600 for the privilege. I don't even like chorizo.

I sweep the torch in an arc again. There's something behind the holdall right at the back. A flash of colour. I crawl towards it, hanging trousers brushing over my back as I go. Hands reaching forward, I grab hold and pull it towards me. The end of a blanket. Wool. Blue and orange checks. My heart accelerates. I remember the blue and orange fibres found in the vic's wound. I tell myself not to get too excited. It could be a coincidence. But it's an unusual colour combination. Adrenaline spiking, I lean over the holdall and lift out the whole blanket. It's been wrapped into a ball. And it's heavy. There's something inside.

Holding it, I shuffle backwards into the light of the room. I photograph the bundle and then begin to unwrap it, peeling back the layers like it's Christmas. When I get to the end, there's a flash of silver. I throw back the final layer of blanket and there it sits: a chrome dumbbell, approximately 25 centimetres long. Pavarotti's words from the autopsy ring in my ears. *A heavy, curved surface, probably metallic or stone.*

I pick the weight up and turn it round slowly, examining it in the light. There's a word stamped across the middle bar: Sparta. But that's not what catches my eye. No, it's the end of the weight that does it. The curved surface that's etched with "4kg" is encrusted in a dried, reddy-brown residue.

I've got him. I've bloody got him.

"Dev, in here!" I yell.

There's the sound of running and then Dev, ever keen, enters, tripping over himself in enthusiasm.

"What is it?" he pants excitedly.

I gesture towards the weight.

"We have ourselves a murder weapon."

A grin splits open Dev's face.

He comes over to peer at it.

"Do you know what Sparta is?" I ask, pointing at the central lettering. "A brand?"

"No. It's a gym," he says. "A small chain. I think one of my mates is a member. Let me check."

Dev's immediately on Google. He's right. It's a niche southwest London gym chain. Smaller membership at inflated rates to appeal to entitled suburbanites. There are only five of them. The closest is just a mile and a half away. Their website is littered with photos of impossibly ripped young bodies. Lifting weights, plunging into pools, rowing on the spot.

"Check their sales page," I instruct. "See if their weights can be bought online."

He checks. The sales page is for gift cards. A friend's birthday? Why not insult them with a month's overpriced gym trial? I scroll down. Their weights aren't for sale. They pride themselves on designing their own equipment for maximizing results. You have to be a member if you want to use them. Right. I have to cross all the "t"s—establish how Ryan Campbell had access to a Sparta dumbbell or Mallory will claim we've planted evidence.

Dev puts the phone on speaker and dials the number.

Someone picks up. It's a woman. Young, chirpy. She answers on the fifth ring.

"Sparta, Richmond. How can I help you?"

I gesture to Dev that he can lead this one and he explains who he is and what we need.

She sounds wary. Cites data protection. I'm about to intervene when Dev turns on the charm. Pours molten honey down the phone as he explains how much it would help us. It's a side of him I haven't seen. It's impressive, and soon she's putty in his hands.

"What was the name again?"

"Ryan Campbell. C-A-M-P-B-E-L-L."

We wait as she types it into the system.

"Yes, he is a member."

Dev checks the address. It's a match.

"When did he last use the gym?"

There's a pause as she pulls up the records, an annoying tapping sound of nail extensions hitting keys as she types.

"Ryan Campbell last swiped in at 7.12 a.m. this Tuesday."

Dev thanks her profusely and she giggles flirtatiously before hanging up.

He looks at me embarrassed. "About that . . ."

"Whatever it takes," I say with a smile. "Whatever it takes."

Right, Ryan swiped in on Tuesday. The day before the murder. Maybe he was working out and then had the idea and slipped it into his bag. An impulse thing. Or maybe he'd planned it for ages. The workout was an excuse. We'll probably never know. Either way, we'll check the security tapes. Maybe we'll even get footage of him stashing it. The cherry on top.

With an almost smug feeling, I supervise Dev bagging the dumbbell and the blanket and dictate a detailed recording of exactly how I found them and everything that I may have disturbed in the process.

As we're about to head down I get a call. Bradley.

"Stratton."

"I don't know if I should be telling you this, but I got a call from a colleague based out near Windsor. I'd put the word out. Not mentioning your name, of course."

He's whispering into the phone. I can hardly hear what he's saying, let alone understand what he means.

"Get to the point, Bradley."

". . . A woman's body's been found."

There's a clenching feeling in my chest. I walk away from Dev and shut myself in the bathroom.

"Go on."

"Pulled out of Virginia Water just now. Currently unidentified. Estimated as late forties. And . . ."

"Yes?" I snap.

"There was a tattoo of a butterfly on her shoulder."

Fuck. The clenching tightens. I think of the deal I made. I found the weapon. I found the murderer. God or the universe or whatever is giving me back my sister.

"I'm heading over."

"I thought you might."

"Cover for me if Parker asks."

"Sure."

My head's swirling. I need to get it in order. To focus. I can't tell Dev what I'm up to. I don't know him well enough to trust him with the truth so I tell him I'm off to check out a different lead.

He looks confused. "Shall I come?" he asks.

"No. Wait here for the driver from Forensics."

"Can't I get Uniform to do it?"

I shake my head. I think of Reynolds. His crucial evidence lost. I can't let that happen here. The stakes are too high. I need it to be someone I trust. And I trust Dev.

"And go with Forensics," I say. "Watch them log it in. The whole chain of custody. Only leave when you see it sitting in Pavarotti's hands. They won't like it, but it's too important not to."

Natalie

B RADLEY OFFERS TO drive me home.
I'm about to decline when I think of the journey. The sky's slate grey and it's raining steadily. I don't have a coat with me, let alone an umbrella, and at this time I'd probably have to wait at least fifteen minutes for a bus.

"It really wouldn't be a problem," he says kindly. "I do appreciate this is a very difficult time for you."

I hesitate, then thank him and accept.

We don't talk in the car, but I feel his presence there and notice his gaze flit over me when we stop at the lights. If I weren't so exhausted I might be flattered by his concern. He's going beyond the call of duty. I can feel it. He's young, attractive. He doesn't need to pay me such attention.

I can feel his eyes on my back again as I walk up the front path.

"Will you be all right?" he says. "Do you need me to come in with you? It can be a bit of a shock seeing your home after it's been searched. They don't always put things back."

I thank him but say I want to be alone.

I put the key in the lock and turn.

He tried to prepare me. But there are some things you can't be prepared for. The hall rug's been rolled back. The console table drawer yawns open. In the kitchen the larder cupboard is a mess. They clearly took everything out and then just bundled it back in again. No thought. Jars on the wrong shelf, bags of flour, spilling out their contents in snowdrifts. The cumin packet is on its side, scenting the air. The utility room smells strange. Traces of chemicals outside my normal olfactory range. Ryan's trainers no longer sit on the draining board. In the living area the TV cabinet has been opened, DVDs and spare wires tipped out in a jumble. I head upstairs. Our wardrobe doors stand wide open. Even my side-table drawer sits ajar. My heart hammers. My diary. My medication. It's private. That's private. But their probing fingers have been through everything. Have pulled my house apart. Violated it. Me.

There's a sound from downstairs and I stiffen.

"Hello?" Ryan's voice.

He's back. I don't know whether to feel relief or fear. They've let him go. They haven't charged him. Does this mean they've worked out he didn't do it? That he's innocent? Bradley won't have had time to tell anyone about the letters yet, let alone look into them himself. They must have found a different suspect altogether. Ryan must have been wrong. The letters had nothing to do with it. So where's the wave of relief I expected to feel?

The stairs creak as he ascends.

"Nat?"

He pushes open the door. He sees me and his brows knit together with hurt. "Oh. I thought you must be out. I called for you."

He walks towards me. He looks exhausted. Dark circles orbit his eyes and he smells sour, stale. Involuntarily, I flinch away.

"Aren't you pleased to see me?" he asks incredulously. "Aren't you pleased I'm back? That they let me go?"

I stare at him.

What do I feel? Am I pleased he's back? I want his face to give him away. His eyes to tell me the truth. Show me his soul. All the questions I have. All the doubts. They rise to the surface and I can't suppress them any more.

"Did you hit on Rachel?" I ask quietly.

Ryan stares at me strangely and then balls his hands into fists. He taps one against the bedroom wall. A dull, repeated beat. The muscle in his neck tells me it's taking everything for him not to slam it.

"Seriously? I've just been held in a bloody police station worrying I'm being framed for murder and you ask me this? Of course I haven't hit on Rachel. I can't stand Rachel, you know that."

"You used to like her."

"Did she say something?" he snaps. "Rachel?" His eyebrows are high and raised at the centre like speech marks. "What the fuck did she say?"

I don't reply.

This time his fist does slam the wall.

"That bitch. That fucking, fucking bitch."

I shrink further away from him. His whole body is wired. He sees the fear in my eyes and then tries to calm himself, palm now flat against the wall, as if he's stroking it.

"Nat, listen. I didn't want to ever have to tell you this . . ."

I feel the bile rise up my throat.

"No," he says, catching my expression. "It's not true. That's not it. It's the opposite." He takes another deep breath then continues. "Remember Fenn's wedding? You left early. You had a migraine. Well . . . Rachel . . . she made a pass at me."

I can't believe what he's saying.

"She was drunk, but not so drunk she didn't know what she was doing. I turned her down. Not too politely . . . That's why she doesn't like me. You know how she has to get her way. Has to have all the men fawn over her. She gets such a kick out of it. But to go after the husband of her supposed best friend. To try and hurt you. That's why I can't stand her."

Anger radiates off him. He seems so believable.

"Why didn't you tell me?" I ask.

"I know how important she is to you. I know there are not many people you're close to. I didn't want to take one of them away."

I feel the truth in what he's saying. Having no family leaves you vulnerable. Friends assume greater importance. They can't be disposed of with the same disregard. And Rachel's my only really close friend left.

Ryan takes another step towards me.

I don't know what to think, now. I don't know.

"I need to be alone," I say.

He starts to take another step then thinks better of it and exhales angrily. "Fine."

The door shuts and I hear him stomp his way downstairs. My nerves are on edge. I need to quieten them. I close the shutters, trying to block out stimuli from the street, and sit at the end of the bed. My thoughts rise up and spiral.

Either my husband or my best friend is lying to me. The two people I'm closest to in the world. The stress, the pressure of the last few days—the police station, my house being defiled, my belongings poured out over the floor and examined—all of it builds and builds till the edges of my vision start to pixellate once more. I'm floating. *No*, I want to shout, but I can't access my voice. I can't control my hands. I can't make my teeth bite my cheek.

I'm—

Blackness.

Stratton

I THINK ABOUT calling Parker as I drive. To boast that we've found the murder weapon. But I don't. I couldn't account for why I'm not coming straight back in. He wouldn't approve of my going to Virginia Water. Chasing a ghost. Especially when I'm lead detective on a live case. But it can't wait.

She can't wait.

It starts to rain. Proper soaking rain that blurs the wind-screen and sends spray off the road on to any poor fucker who happens to be traipsing the pavement.

I turn the car radio on and up. And sing along. I never sing in the car. An activity for self-indulgent wannabes who think that the only reason they don't already have a record deal is that Simon Cowell hasn't heard them yet. Maybe they're hoping he'll be driving past and hear them and then thrust a contract in through their window at the next set of traffic lights. Morons. But today I sing. Every stupid little track that comes on. Just to stop my mind thinking about what I might be about to see.

But it doesn't work. All I think is that Karen liked to sing. Karen was a good singer. I might be about to see Karen's body.

I park in the visitors' car park by the lake. It's officially closed, but I flash my badge at the young officer in charge of guarding the entrance and he lets me through and tells me where to go.

I've never been to Virginia Water before, even though it's not really that far away. I don't think I'll be back. It's a weird place. There's neither the wild beauty of the countryside nor the manicured beauty of a city park. Just a slightly crap halfway house of semi-nature with a soundtrack of traffic noise.

I duck under the police tape and follow the tarmacked path round to the right of the lake to where I see a tent and a cluster of officers and someone from Forensics suited up in their white all-in-one.

The body's in the tent.

I force myself forward. A detective spots me and starts waving his arms, trying to get rid of me like some house fly. I increase my speed. His face reddens.

"Crime scene. Please disperse."

Disperse? Am I a fucking crowd?

I flash my badge again and explain that this might overlap with one of my cases. That I'm looking for a female. Aged forty-six. Straight brown hair. Possibly dyed. Tattoo on her right shoulder.

I don't mention the personal connection. I don't say the word "sister".

He looks me up and down and then seems to calculate he has no good reason to keep me away so introduces me to the first responder instead, and I get suited up.

"The body's been in the water a while so might be hard to identify," the detective explains. "Throat cut. Tied down with a weight, but the rope came loose. Either that or was eaten by fish." He laughs. I stare daggers at him.

He opens the tent flap and I duck and enter.

I've seen bodies fished from water before. Rivers. Lakes. Ponds. Barrels. But never when the body might belong to my sister. I fight the impulse to gag and force myself not to look away.

The body's hideously swollen from the water. Facial features distorted. Eyes closed. The hair's brown. Shoulder length. Could it be you, Karen? The build seems bigger, but people change. It's been thirty years. Tears prick at my eyes. I don't know. I just don't know.

"Where's the tattoo?" I ask.

"Round here," the pathologist answers. He lifts a section of hair covering the body's right shoulder.

Heart in mouth, I step forward to look.

There's a small tattoo, blue and black ink, wings rising from a body . . . but it's not of a butterfly. It's of a bird. A fucking humming bird.

I start crying.

The detective looks at me with a stupid fucking smile on his face. "All right, love?"

I resist the urge to punch him, and storm out of the tent and retch into the lake.

Then I just stand there. I don't know for how long, staring at the heavens.

But I found the murderer, I think. I found him. Keep your fucking side of the deal.

* * *

It's 3 p.m. when I return to the station. I've decided not to explain my absence. Not to apologize for it. I found the murder weapon. It's my case. It's on track. And I'm not in the mood to take shit from anyone.

Reynolds is on the phone but throws a worried glance in my direction and mouths a sorry. I smile thinly. He thinks my long absence is a mark of failure. That I'm returning empty-handed. He doesn't know. He doesn't know that we have him. And then my spirits start to rise. Maybe the deal's only complete when Campbell's behind bars. I'll get Karen back. Just not yet.

I scan the floor for Dev, but I can't see him. Maybe he's still with Pavarotti. I walk over to Parker's office and knock. He beckons me in.

He looks slightly sheepish. I ignore it and launch into my prepared speech.

"Do you want to come with me?" I say.

Parker looks confused.

"To whatever room Campbell's in. We're arresting the bastard."

There's that annoying sheepish look again, followed by anger as he recognizes his own weakness. His fear of me.

"What's going on?" I ask.

He puffs up his chest.

"We had to let him go."

"You did what?" I can't quite believe what I'm hearing. I'm gone for a couple of hours and the prime suspect walks?

"It was all circumstantial. Nothing tied him to the actual murder. He was guilty of an affair. That's not a crime."

"What did she do?" I bark.

"Who?"

"You know who. Mallory fucking Cliff. What did she pull?"

"I don't appreciate your tone, Detective."

"She used her connections to the superintendent, didn't she?"

"The evidence was circumstantial."

He's too gutless to admit he's been walked over by upstairs.

"I've found the murder weapon. In his wardrobe. It has blood on it, for God's sake. Pavarotti's testing it now."

Parker's eyes narrow. "Why didn't you call it in immediately?"

I should have done. Fuck. I should have done. I sidestep, answering a question with a question.

"When did you let him go?"

"An hour ago."

Fuck. If I hadn't gone to the lake I'd have been back in time.

"I'm going to go and bring him back in now."

Before he runs, I think. If he has any sense, he'll be out of here. Driving. On the train. Sitting in the departure lounge to God knows where, but he'll be running.

"No. You can't bring him in again without arresting him. You have one shot at this. You need to make sure it's watertight. Wait for the tests to come back. Wait for Pavarotti."

I know he's right, but it doesn't make it any less frustrating.

My anger at myself fuels my anger at him.

His door rattles in its frame as I slam it.

Dev gets back. He'd started to get on Pavarotti's nerves, so Pavarotti sent him away. Promised to prioritize the dumb-bell. We'll get the results as fast as he can deliver them.

I can't do anything other than stare at the clock on my monitor. Minutes tick by. Hours. How long does it take to check some blood? Run some fingerprints? Dev tries to make small talk but I brush him away. I'm not in the mood.

I think about calling Pavarotti. Chasing for an update. But I know it wouldn't change anything and would just piss him off. He'll be working as fast as he can.

At some point Bradley stands at my shoulder.

"Any luck?" he says quietly. I know he's not talking about the Campbell case.

"No," I reply. "It wasn't her."

"I'm so sorry," he says. "I shouldn't have told you. I knew the chances were slim."

"No," I reply. "You had my back. I appreciate it."

"I've made you a coffee," he says, placing a mug down next to me. "Extra strong. Just the slightest trace of milk."

I thank him and take a sip. It's perfect. Fast-Track's turning out to be a decent partner after all. A shadow falls over my screen. He's still there, hovering.

"We've broken Campbell's alibi," he says.

I perk up. I've been so caught up in my frustration and anger at Parker that I realize I haven't spoken to Bradley since he interviewed the wife.

"What did she say?"

"He went out for a run. Tennish. Then she went to bed. She doesn't know when he came back."

"Good work. That lying fuck. He should be here, now. Locked up. Fucking Parker."

Bradley shoots me a strange look. I've gone too far. Shocked him. He doesn't want to be associated with someone slagging off the top brass.

But then he says sorry with his face as much as his words.

"I was driving Mrs. Campbell home, then I had the bank paperwork to complete. I only just found out. If I'd been there I would have said something. Urged Parker to keep him here longer."

I almost smile. As if the request of a late-twenties fast-tracker would have made any difference. Bradley's egotistical, but he means well. And I'm grateful for the sentiment. He goes back to his desk.

There's a call from Mum's home. I reject it. Five minutes later there's an email. They're bloody persistent, I'll give them that.

Mrs. Stratton would benefit from a visit, they say. She's having another dip... they're becoming more frequent... this might not be the best place for her. I tell them I'll come as soon as I can. They're not going to pass her on like some bloody relay baton. They don't get to do that.

I'm so worked up that I head up to the smokers' terrace to escape. It's there that I get the call from Pavarotti. His voice sounds disappointed. Mr. Campbell's fingerprints weren't on the weight. Fuck. Still, means nothing. He could have worn gloves. And I know there's something better to come. He's overplaying the disappointment. It's his love of melodrama. We've worked together long enough for me to be able to read him. "However..." he continues. "I also tested the dried blood at the end of the dumbbell against the victim's, and..." he says, drawing it out like a bloody game-show host, "... it was a match."

Yes. Gotcha.

I thank Pavarotti, and then I'm pounding back down the stairs to Parker's office and pushing open his door.

"Stratton—" He starts to have a go at me for barging in, but I talk over him.

"The blood's a match. Ryan Campbell's our guy. I'm going to arrest him now, unless of course you have any more objections?"

"No. Proceed, Detective," Parker replies, trying to remain dignified and managerial.

I march out, calling over to Bradley as I go, "Get your coat. We're bringing him in again."

A cheer goes up across the floor.

Natalie

Wooden surface. Worn smooth beneath my hands. Chequered green shapes ahead. More solid to the side. Light above. Muted. The world slowly focuses itself. I'm in my office room. Sat at my desk. Facing the French windows. The ceiling spots are on but dimmed. A couple of law books lie open on pages I don't recognize. I've changed my jumper to a thick purple polo neck. I must have been cold. I glance at the wall clock. I've been out for just over an hour. I dredge my memory. As always, there's nothing.

I fight back the wave of anxiety that threatens to overwhelm me. At least I didn't fall this time. At least I haven't hurt myself.

"Ryan?" I call. There's no reply. I hate myself for needing him.

I force myself to stand and walk through the living area and into the kitchen. A cup of tea might help revive me. Camomile or lavender. Then I see it. On the work surface next to the sink sits the blender and a cup with the dregs of a chocolate protein shake in it. No attempt has been made to even rinse it. Disproportionate anger rises up in me. I'm not going to clean up his mess any more.

Ryan. Where the hell is Ryan?

I call his name again, but there's no reply. Maybe he's gone out, or maybe he's simply in a different room, sulking. Could he even have walked past the office and seen me there but ignored me? Would he even have known anything was wrong? I have no idea how I seem to the outside world when I lose time.

Even with the thicker jumper on I'm cold. The whole house feels cold, so I head towards the hall and then upstairs to adjust the thermostat. As I reach the landing, I hear something. *Drip. Drip. Drip*. The door to the bathroom sits ajar in front of me. The scent of lavender intermingled with rosemary drifts out. I recognize it immediately. The expensive bath foam Ryan got me at Christmas—"potent herbal wellbeing", or so the packaging claimed. Ryan must have had a bath; the sound's a dripping tap. He won't have turned the handle tightly enough. He often doesn't. I used to think of it as one of his faults. Before I knew how big faults could be.

Drip. Drip. Drip.

The sound is starting to unnerve me so I edge towards the bathroom to turn off the tap.

Pushing the door open, I enter, and everything changes.

Red.

Red water.

Red pools on the floor.

Ryan.

My brain registers then flickers then tries to reprocess. To unsee. My knees fold under me and I'm on the floor. Crawling. Crawling towards the bath, a soft mewling sound escaping my lips. A primitive language unlearnt as one grows.

No.

Red.

Ryan.

His eyes are open. Staring. One of his arms hangs out of the bath, a red gash vertically along the length of the wrist. The rest of his body lies in the bath, the foam flecked pink. The water underneath red. Crimson. Scarlet. My head chases synonyms. Anything to escape here. Now.

A razor blade sits on the side next to him. Seemingly innocuous. It's neatly lined up against the wall. The bath tap drips. *Drips. Drips.*

I force myself closer and put a hand to his neck, checking for a pulse. I can't feel one, but I don't know if I'm even checking the right place. I've never felt for a pulse before. They ran a first-aid course once at work, a couple of years before I left. I meant to sign up. I should have signed up. I place my cheek over his mouth. I saw someone do that in a TV show once. I wait to feel the soft whisper of air. Breath. Nothing.

His eyes keep staring. I want to close them.

I need to call the police . . . or the ambulance. I don't know which. I'm so useless I don't even know who to call. Ryan was always the one who was good in an emergency. He'd stay calm, logical. I'd always panic. I'm panting now. My breath short and shallow. Swallowing diminishing increments of air. My vision threatens to pixellate once more, but I can't let it. I slap my face. Harder. And harder. It works. I'm still here. I need my phone.

Think.

I was in the bedroom before I lost time. My phone must be there. Using the edge of the bath, I pull myself up. My hand brushes against Ryan's. It's not yet cold, but already there's something wrong about the skin, something reptilian. My lizard brain recognizes it and recoils.

I stumble down the corridor and into the bedroom. My phone is there. On the bed, cushioned on a mound of duvet.

I pick it up. I'm about to dial when there's a hammering at the door.

Stratton

I TELL BRADLEY to knock again, harder this time. Fuck. Has Campbell already run? He's had time to. Taking a couple of steps back, I run my eyes over the house. The lights are on downstairs, but there's no sign of movement, no shadows crossing walls. Upstairs, the shutters are closed, but there's the faint glow of light through the gaps on the side. Maybe he's upstairs. Napping. Or maybe no one's home. The lights are a decoy to throw us off the scent. Has he taken the wife with him? Or is she left behind? Mourning or celebrating. God knows which.

Bradley's raps shake the door.

"What do you think?" he says. "Should we break it down?"

I'm mulling it over when there's the sound of footsteps clattering down the stairs. An irregular rhythm. Someone tripping over themselves in their urgency.

The door starts to open.

"Mr. Campbell?" I call.

The door opens fully. It's not him. It's the wife. And she looks completely mad. Her eyes wide and wild, the irises surrounded by white. Her face white too. Apart from her left cheek. That has a livid red patch across it.

"Is your husband home?" I demand.

Her face crumples and then she makes a strange yelping sound. I roll my eyes. Last thing I need is a bloody hysterical woman.

"We're here to arrest him for the murder of Alice Lytton. If you try to conceal his person, then we shall have to charge you as an accomplice."

That sort of threat normally works. Loyalty only lasts so long when the spectre of prison rears its ugly head. A ring versus a cage. No contest. She stares at me again and then starts laughing. A strange high-pitched laugh. Fuck. She's clearly cracked.

Bradley steps forward and places a hand on her shoulder. Any excuse. He says softly, "Is everything all right, Mrs. Campbell?"

Look at her, I think. Of course she's not bloody all right. Her husband's clearly done a runner. Cheated on her, killed someone then disappeared. I expect her to throw his stupid question back in his face, but she doesn't. She stops laughing, at least. And then just looks at him. Then at me. But I get the feeling she is looking through me. Through the front door. And out. Out beyond this world. She gives me the creeps. Eventually she speaks.

"You're too late," she says. "You're too late."

She holds her hands to her face, and that's when I notice the cuffs of her jumper. They're soaked. Her jeans are wet too, from the knees down, and there's a reddish stain on her left thigh.

"What's happened, Mrs. Campbell?" Bradley asks quietly. I let him do the talking. She responds better to him.

She doesn't say anything but just points weakly up the stairs.

She leads the way. I go next, and Bradley brings up the rear. My throat is tight as I climb. I know what to expect, but I don't want it to be true. The air is hazy outside the bathroom—a wall of warm air meeting cool. Mrs. Campbell stands back, her body rigid. She doesn't want to enter again. I push the door with my elbow. It's not a crime scene, but I don't have gloves on and habits die hard.

Fuck.

She's right.

We're too late.

He's killed himself. The fucking coward killed himself. His eyes are open. The bathwater bright red. A razor blade on the side. I look at his exposed wrist. Then pull the other arm out of the water too. It's the same. This was no cry for help. The incisions are vertical. It's the quickest way to bleed out.

Bradley's on the phone back to the station. Pavarotti will be on his way. Not that there's anything for him to do here. It's a simple coroner's case. A run-of-the-mill suicide.

I walk out. She's standing on the landing, back against the wall, snivelling. A rush of anger rises in me.

"Don't cry over him," I say. "He's not worth it. If you have to cry, cry for his victim. Cry for Alice. Cry for Alice's family."

She slowly lifts her head, stares questioningly at me.

"He didn't do it," she says. "You wouldn't have let him go if he did it."

Her naïve lamb thing is too much.

"We found the murder weapon in your wardrobe," I say. "He did it."

She seems to shrink in on herself and I step away before I lose it altogether with her.

Bradley keeps his calm though. 'Course he does, with his little schoolboy crush.

"Is there anybody you'd like us to call?" he says.

She stares at him, blinks, then stares again.

Bradley's right. Procedure dictates she shouldn't be left alone.

"Would you like us to send a liaison officer round?" I ask with a veneer of sympathy.

That seems to jolt some sense into her.

"An officer? No. No. I'll call someone. You can go. Please go."

I don't believe her, but we've done our part.

I'm on autopilot as we head back to the station. The floor is empty apart from Parker in his office. Dev and Reynolds have already gone home. Sandra too, by the looks of it. The place has never felt so bleak. So depressing. Bradley asks if I'd like him to write up the report and I nod, numbly. Then he has the sense to leave me alone.

Parker has less sense. He sidles over, hands outstretched in some biblical fucking gesture of peace.

"Well, at least he got the ultimate justice," he says smugly.

I turn round to face him. What did I ever see in this man?

"No, he didn't," I snap. "He got to choose. He took the easy way out. That's not justice. Justice would be him in court, aware that all his friends, his colleagues, his family knew what he'd done. Justice would be him led away in handcuffs, convicted, shamed. Justice would be him in prison. Suffering. Regretting and reliving. Day after day. That's what Alice's sister will have to do. She doesn't get to check out. She has to live with what he did to her sister. Don't talk to me about fucking justice."

"Detective," he says sharply, looking around to see if anyone else is in hearing distance. They're not.

"I want to press charges anyway," I say, staring him straight in the eye. Defiant.

"Helen," he says, more gently this time. "You know we can't. The CPS won't make a charging decision in respect of a dead person."

I know he's right. I know I'm being irrational. I read the Court of Appeal's decision in Turk v R in 2017. We all did. "The death of a defendant brings any criminal prosecution of that defendant to an end." They said it was important for the "consistent and even-handed" operation of the criminal justice system. But what about the victims? What about denying them a verdict? Doesn't a murderer deserve to be buried with the word "guilty" chiselled into people's memories?

Parker touches my arm in an awkward and slightly frightened gesture of comfort and then scuttles back into his office.

I wait and watch as he picks up his coat and bag, turns off the light and leaves.

Natalie

HE DID IT. They found the murder weapon. In our wardrobe.
I feel hot and cold and sick.
He did it. He killed Alice. He probably raped her too.
I sit at the bottom of the stairs, staring at the front door.
I don't think I ever really believed he was guilty. Not really. Or I wouldn't feel like someone had just stabbed me in the chest now.

Could the detective be lying? She didn't look like she was lying. She looked at me with such contempt. Like I was the world's biggest fool for not knowing. Am I?

They could have planted it, I think. Police plant things all the time. So many are corrupt. You read it in the papers. London ones, particularly. There was a recent inquiry published. A lot should never have been police. They should have failed the background checks. You can't trust them.

But then I think of Bradley. He seems respectable. To have integrity. He wouldn't let her plant evidence, would he?

And if Ryan didn't do it, why did he kill himself? The pressure of it all was clearly getting to him, I knew that. And it didn't help that I kept pushing him away. But still, if he didn't kill her, rape her, he wouldn't have taken his own life, would he? That's the act of a guilty man. If it was me he now hated. If he felt I'd let him down, he could have divorced me and walked away. It doesn't make sense.

So how am I meant to feel now? My husband is lying dead in the bath upstairs and I don't know how I'm supposed to feel. If I mourn him and he's a murderer, does that make me a monster too? How do you delete fourteen years of feelings?

There's the sound of footsteps up the front path and talking outside the door and then a knock.

I stand and open it, worried that it's the DI back again. To taunt me.

It's not. Two men in white coveralls stand there instead. One's young; his moustache still has a wispy quality. The other's older, larger, his beard badger-striped with grey. They say they're here to take the body. The young one holds a stretcher, almost apologetically. They pull masks over their faces and head up the stairs. I don't know what's expected of me so I stay in the hall, pressed against the wall, making sure they have space to pass. I hear movement upstairs. Straining. I cover my ears. I start thinking the most inane thoughts. He's been in the water for hours. Will his skin be completely wrinkled? They say bodies go stiff after death. Does water counteract that? Will they close his eyes or is it too late? Are they now permanently stuck open? I hope they manage to close his eyes.

Moments later they're coming down the stairs. The stretcher between them. There's a shape on the stretcher, covered by a white sheet. Shrouded, that's the term. There are patches of pink on the edges of the sheet. Water mixed with blood.

They take him away.

And I'm left. All alone.

SUNDAY, 24 MARCH

Stratton

P<small>ARKER TELLS ME</small> not to go in.
"Take the day off," he texts. "It's Sunday. The case is over."
But I can't. It's never over. Not until I find Karen.

The office floor is empty when I arrive at lunchtime. I open up the database search engines and input my usual parameters. Dead female. Thirty to sixty. If the body has no ID it's best to set the age limits widely.

There are two new hits. I scroll through them. Stare at the photos. Neither is Karen. A crushing sense of hopelessness presses down on me. I've failed.

It starts to rain again outside. Drops forming on the windows and then chasing themselves down the glass. I used to play that with Karen. We'd each pick a drop. Bet on ours to win. She always used to win. We said she was lucky. Lucky Karen.

Bradley walks in. Seems like I'm not the only one who can't stay away. He says he wants to get the final case details written up. Then asks if I'm OK. If I want to get a drink or something.

"Thought you didn't drink?" I say.
"I don't. But you look like you could do with one."
He catches sight of the screen.
"Any luck?"
His concern is genuine.

"No," I reply flatly.

He's still there.

"Why did you join?" I ask quietly. "Why spend your life doing this?"

He takes his time before he answers.

"For justice," he says seriously. "People deserve justice. I know my reputation"—he smiles—"that I'm a Boy Scout. That I do things by the book. Report abuses of power. But I genuinely believe, if you chase every lead, if you interrogate every piece of information, pick apart every witness, then the guilty go down and the innocent walk free."

He says it all with a quiet intensity. It's personal for him. Like it's personal for me.

I squeeze his shoulder, shake myself together and pick up my coat. I don't want to go for a drink with Bradley, as nice as he's being. I don't want to go home. So I go to Mum's instead. Angie's on duty and she looks pleased to see me.

"It's good you came," she says. "Your visits really do lift her spirits."

I don't see how. She doesn't speak to me. She normally doesn't even know who I am.

Mum's asleep—her "siesta", they call it—so I just sit on a chair by the bed.

"Just speak to her," Angie coaxes. "She'll still hear you. It'll still help."

Angie leaves. I try to talk, but the words feel too large for my mouth and I can't get the volume right. I feel like a total idiot. Talking to a sleeping person. Playing a game.

Instead I stare round the room, eyes coming to rest on the crucifix on the wall. The Jesus's eyes are closed. It's like he's deliberately not helping. Blind to my need.

"Please," I end up whispering. "I tried everything I could. I found the killer. I kept my end of the bargain. Please now show me where Karen is. Please."

The silence in the room is deafening.

Natalie

I SLEPT ON the sofa. In spite of everything. Of what happened on it. Ryan. Alice. I couldn't face being upstairs. It's like that is his territory now. He marked it when he hid the murder weapon in our wardrobe. He marked it with his blood. It's all his. Even though he's not coming back to claim it. I make myself a cup of camomile tea, inhaling the scented steam, reaching out for calm and finding none. Then I fetch the bucket of cleaning products from the utility. I follow the trail of footprints up the stairs. I couldn't deal with it last night. I couldn't re-enter that room. I force myself to deal with it now.

They didn't even empty the bath. Anger rises in me. There are puddles on the floor and they didn't even empty the bath. I have to roll up my sleeve and then put my arm into a mixture of cold water and my husband's blood to pull out the plug. That's not right. That's cruel.

I watch the red water spiral away.

Then I open the bleach.

And I scrub, scrub, scrub.

Eventually I finish and return to the kitchen. The blender is still sitting on the side. I open up the bin and throw it in. As I do, something catches my eye. Stuck to the edge of the bin liner is a yellow Post-it note. A heart drawn in biro on it.

Was that meant for me? A final goodbye?

MONDAY, 25 MARCH

Stratton

I GET INTO work late. I hardly slept so I have that so-tired-that-you're-wired feeling.

A coffee from the machine doesn't help and my left eyelid starts to twitch.

There's hardly anything to do, which makes it worse. A final bit of paperwork to fill in on the Campbell case before the file is closed and placed in storage. It doesn't even need to be done really. It's over. His death means it's over. No one will ever ask to see the file. Or check we followed procedure.

It's over.

Parker won't put me on another case yet. He says I need time to process and reset. He doesn't learn. He doesn't listen. He didn't even think to send someone to tell Alice's sister.

Let her know she won't get her day in court. That she won't get to look Alice's killer in the eye and curse him to hell.

Useless man.

I say I'll do it. I'll go over at lunchtime. I got Sandra to check her shifts with the hospital, and she worked last night, so I don't want to risk waking her. Sleep, if she manages it, is all she has left. A few precious hours to escape reality.

Reynolds lets me look over some surveillance footage for a new case he's leading. It's something to focus on. Otherwise, there's nothing. A sea of pointless nothingness. In which I'll never make a difference. I'll never find Karen. I'll never help Mum.

"Stratton?"

I don't register my name the first time. It's just a two-syllable noise that washes over me.

"Stratton?" It's clearer the second time.

I turn round. It's Bradley. There's a glint in his eye.

"What is it?" I ask.

He holds up a USB stick.

"There's something you need to see."

"What?" I ask. I'm in no mood for guessing games.

"On the Alice Lytton case."

"Didn't you get the memo?" I say sarcastically. "There is no case. You can't try a dead man."

"I know." He smiles this time, tips of white teeth showing under his top lip. "You need to watch this," he says again.

I hold out my hand and he passes over the stick. I insert it into my computer drive.

An image appears. A video of the inside of a gym. It looks expensive. The paintwork clean, the equipment new and shiny. The camera is pointed towards various weight machines. In the foreground there's an area of blue floor mats next to two racks of freestanding weights. Various people in gym wear cross the screen. A man with bright red hair and even brighter red cheeks struggles at a rowing machine before stopping and leaning over in discomfort. He reminds me of Cooper.

"What am I watching?" I ask impatiently.

"This is taken from the Richmond Sparta the day before Alice was murdered."

"And?"

"Keep watching."

I roll my eyes so I miss her walk on to the screen. When I next focus, she's there. Natalie Campbell. She's in black leggings and a baggy T-shirt. The other women are in tight-fitting vests. I flick my eyes over to Bradley. He stares at the screen. I copy him.

She stands by one of the racks of dumbbells and then selects one. I can't see the details at this resolution but I can tell it's chrome and of a similar size to the one we found in their wardrobe.

I keep watching. Her face seems to harden. She stares straight ahead and starts lifting the weight. Again and again and again. Her scared-mouse persona has gone. She looks strong. Fierce. Angry.

Bradley presses stop and the footage freezes on the screen.

"Well?" he says, expectantly.

I think. I want it to mean something, but does it?

"It doesn't prove anything," I say. "So she was a member too. So she used the dumbbells. That just shows she's another bored wife, living her best suburban life."

"Her card wasn't used that day," Bradley says. "Only his was swiped. She must have used his. He doesn't appear at all on their security feed. Not for that day, nor the previous two."

God, he must have been up all night watching the feed. How doesn't he look exhausted? The stamina of youth.

I feel a tiny spark of excitement form. The numb feeling starts to go and it's like my cells start to vibrate instead.

"Can we zoom in on the footage at all?" I ask. "Find out which weight she was using?"

"I can ask the IT team," he says.

"Who've you shown this to?" I ask.

"No one," he says. "Just you, now."

"Keep it that way," I say, glancing involuntarily towards Parker's office. "It's probably nothing, so we don't want to get the brass involved yet. Ask IT if they can blow up the image, but tell them to put it under the code for general. Don't tell them it's for the Lytton case."

I start running scenarios in my head. Lining up all the evidence we had against the husband. We were so sure. I was so sure.

"The bank-account withdrawal," I say. "You said his personal accounts were clean?"

"Yes. The twelve K came out of their joint account."

The vibration turns to a hum. My cells are dancing.

"Pull the bank's security feed. Find out which Campbell withdrew the cash."

Bradley nods, and he's off. I turn back to my computer and open up the police database. I input two words into the search engine.

Natalie Campbell.

Natalie

I SLEPT ON the sofa again. Fitfully. When morning finally arrives and I get up, my muscles hurt, my arms especially. Standing in front of the mirror, I am shocked by the version of me that returns my stare. My hair sticks to my face in strands and my face has a red crease diagonally across the right cheek from the piping round the edge of the sofa cushion. My eyes are red-rimmed and hollow. My hands and arms still smell faintly of bleach.

My phone vibrates on the coffee table. Rachel. I had five missed calls from her yesterday and it's the third time she's called this morning. I think about letting it ring out again, but I know she'll just try again in half an hour so I pick it up reluctantly.

"Hello," I say. My voice sounds like it's trapped behind glass.

"Thank God!" she says. "I was about to drive over. I was worried you'd done something stupid."

There's a levity to her voice. I think about her comments last time I saw her. Her joking I'd killed myself in the bath. I used to think she knew me better than other people. That she didn't tread on eggshells because she cared. I used to think she was fun, edgy. Now I'm not so sure. And a little voice says maybe she doesn't adjust her behaviour because she can't be bothered to.

"Is Ryan there?" she asks in a stage whisper.

Ryan.

Wrist open.

Eyes open.

I try to speak, but the words stick. I cough then retch to dislodge them.

"Nat?"

Finally I manage to speak, but the glass is even thicker now. Hardly any sound gets through.

"Ryan's dead," I whisper. "He killed himself."

". . . Oh God . . . Oh Nat! I'm so sorry. God, how awful! Did you . . . were you the one who found him?"

I nod. Then murmur a "yes".

There's a pause.

"Well," she says quietly. "At least you know now."

I don't understand.

"That he did it, I mean," she explains matter-of-factly. "He raped her and killed her. And he couldn't live with what he'd done. It's awful, but you can move on."

Move on? How does someone move on?

And she's so certain. Definitive. She doesn't even know about the murder weapon being found, yet there's no doubt in her mind that he did it. No admission that possibly the stress could have got to him. That the investigation itself pushed him over the edge.

Her reaction drives me to defend him, throws me into a role I'm not quite ready for.

"It could be a set-up," I say, "by the police . . . Or by Fiona Scott."

She cuts me off with a laugh.

"Nat, stop. The police don't set people up. The Fiona Scott theory never held water. It's absurd. Imagining that some fifty-odd-year-old woman is puppet-mastering all of this. That was Ryan's theory, not yours. You must see that it's nonsense. He was deflecting your attention. It was him all along. He's a liar, Nat. Or rather he was. He did it. And he killed himself. It sounds harsh, but there's no other way of looking at it."

She's pleased he's dead. I can feel it in her tone. Her words. A revelling, gloating schadenfreude. If he hit on her, I understand why she doesn't like him. But to be pleased . . .

It doesn't make sense. It's too strong a response. There must be something else going on. I hold the phone away from my ear and hang up.

She tries to call back but I reject the call and put my phone on silent.

Maybe I'm being paranoid. Maybe I'm reading too much into a tone. I need confirmation.

Then I remember. Meena. Meena was at Fenn's wedding. If anything happened between Ryan and Rachel, she might have seen it.

She might be better friends with Rachel than with me now, but it used to be the other way round. Meena's and my personalities are more naturally aligned. Quieter, less extrovert. Rachel pulled us both into her orbit, dazzling us with her sun.

I should have tried harder to be around her. Should have worked out how to function around a young family.

Rachel said Meena was in town on business. I'll arrange to meet her and then ask her directly to her face. She won't lie to me. She's one of those people who has integrity fused into their bones.

And I'll know.

I scroll through my contacts then press dial.

Stratton

I HAVE TO reassess everything I ever thought about Natalie Campbell. The search engine revealed one entry. She was the alleged victim in a rape case brought ten years ago against a Mr. Gavin Scott, her then boss. She claimed he assaulted her at work. He denied it and was found not guilty.

It explains the secretiveness. The way of holding herself. The loose T-shirt in the gym.

I feel guilt at having dismissed her as mousy. A suburban wife. Stuck at home. Shuttling to and fro between her home and Waitrose. No wonder she hid herself away. Seemed guarded. But then I think of her in the gym, lifting the weight. Her strength. Her anger. The two halves don't fit together.

I head up to the smokers' balcony to call Bradley. I want to share what I've found without being overheard. He answers and the sound distortion tells me he's driving and on speaker phone through the car's info system. It's starting to drizzle so I pull my jacket over my head to keep the worst of it off.

"Any luck?" I ask.

"They've given me a copy of the footage for the right time period. I thought we could watch it together."

"Good."

"Anything your end?"

"She was involved in a rape case before. Around ten years ago. Accuser rather than defendant. The guy was found not guilty."

"So you're thinking we can't trust her word. She lied in the past, she'll lie again?"

What? That's clearly not what I'm thinking at all.

"You're police," I say, exasperated. "Stay here long enough and you'll learn a not-guilty verdict isn't the same as a declaration of innocence. It just means they didn't have enough to prove he did it."

He's silent. I sense I've pissed him off. If so, I don't care. He might have his idealistic views of justice. He might think if you work hard, follow the rules, fill in the paperwork, then the guilty will go down and the innocent will walk free. If so, he's got a lot to learn.

There's the *swish, swish* as his windscreen wipers fight drops of rain.

"Well, if you're right, it strengthens motive," he says at last.

"Go on," I say. I've been thinking the same thing, but I want to see if his reasoning matches mine.

"She finds out her husband cheated on her. So we have jealousy, which is motive enough already in most cases. The whole 'woman scorned' thing."

I sigh. It's not a female thing. Anyone "scorned" can erupt. It's not like men have a special safety valve.

He goes on: "Then, on top of that, she finds out that her husband is accused of rape. The very thing that she claims was done to her. It triggers something. She kills the girl and frames the husband for her murder."

I nod along. It's extreme but it's not impossible.

"It's her who was driving the car," Bradley continues, "her mud on the pedals. The husband went out that night, as she said, but he just went on a jog. She drove to Barnes, picked Alice up, took her to the woods and killed her. She has no alibi. No one to vouch she stayed in alone all night."

I mull it over.

"How did she arrange to meet Alice?" I ask.

"It was her burner. She got Alice's number from her husband's phone."

"Why would Alice get in the car?"

"Maybe she wanted to warn Mrs. Campbell about her husband's true character?"

"But why kill Alice?" I say. "Wouldn't she feel sympathy for the girl?"

This is where the theory hits a rock.

"I don't know," he answers. "She may have pitied her and hated her at the same time. Or seen her as a necessary pawn to be sacrificed to bring her husband down."

True. Feelings are never simple.

The rain gets heavier and I have to head back inside. Bradley gets back twenty minutes later. He walks over to my desk. I scan the room. Reynolds is out. Sandra too. Parker has his door closed.

"Coast is clear," I say. Bradley wordlessly inserts the USB stick into the computer drive. We fast-forward the footage to the time stamp we're looking for: 11.35 a.m.—the time when someone withdrew £12,000 from the Campbells' joint account.

The camera faces away from the cashier's desk. An elderly man stands waiting. He's hunched over and wears a tweed flat cap. He starts to pat his pocket, flustered, then shuffles off. He must have forgotten his bank card or chequebook. The next customer steps forward to the front of the queue. My breath quickens. It's her. Unmistakeably her. Natalie Campbell. She looks around her calmly. There's no suggestion she's there under coercion. She speaks to the cashier then inserts her card into the machine. A moment later she shows the cashier something—ID, no doubt. Then she waits as he counts out the notes.

Twelve grand in cash. What did Natalie Campbell need £12,000 cash for? And why would she give £10,000 of it to Alice?

There's no reason she would have for paying off Alice's debts. Is the money just a red herring? Something unconnected to the case after all? Fuck. One thing's for sure though—the case against Ryan Campbell is growing weaker and weaker. I should have demanded the footage earlier. Looked more closely. I think I just wanted it to be him too much and lost my edge. Idiot.

"Call Alice's work," I say to Bradley. "See if there's something we're missing. Find out if anyone witnessed any contact between

Mrs. Campbell and Alice. Ask the sister too. And try the friend again. See if she's turned her phone back on and will actually talk to us now."

"What are you going to do?" he asks.

I line up my thoughts. "Well," I say slowly, "if we're going down this route—looking into whether Mrs. Campbell could have killed Alice, then we need to take it to its logical conclusion."

"Which is?"

"That she also killed her husband. We didn't question it as a suicide because it made sense. He'd killed Alice. It was an admission of guilt. An evasion of justice. But if he didn't kill her . . ."

Bradley swallows. "She killed him and dressed it as a suicide?"

"Exactly."

Thinking back, there was something about the murder then suicide explanation that felt wrong. Mr. Campbell didn't know we were still on to him. He'd just been let go. If he had killed Alice, then as far as he knew he'd got away with it. He should have been celebrating. And men who want to top themselves usually hang themselves or use a gun, if they can get their hands on one. They don't normally slit their wrists in the bath. That's typically a woman's way out. But he wouldn't have just lain there. Climbed in and held his wrists steady . . .

Bradley leaves, and I'm about to call Pavarotti when Reynolds reappears. He tries to involve me in something, a pity ask rather than a genuine need for help, but I make up some excuse and brave the smokers' balcony once more.

The rain has stopped, but it's damp and miserable. Luckily Pavarotti answers quickly.

"Stratton?" he says, surprised. "Another case already?"

"No, same case. Different theory."

I explain that we're looking into a different angle. That I need him to run some tests.

"Do I detect you're flying solo on this?"

He's perceptive. Sees things you think he won't. The jolly, round persona is deceiving.

"I'd appreciate it if you didn't tell Parker yet. The case is officially closed."

"I see."
He hasn't said no.
"I need a tox report on the deceased."
"We've run it. It's one of the first things we did."
"No, sorry, I'm not being clear enough. Not for Alice. For Ryan Campbell."

Natalie

Meena meets me in the café at the bottom of the road. She offered to come round, but I want to spend as little time as possible at "home". It's just bricks and mortar now. Bricks and mortar and ghosts. I'll put it on the market soon.

Meena is there when I arrive and stands to hug me. She's dressed head to foot in Boden and looks every inch the off-duty City solicitor. She may have swapped London for Bristol, but nothing else has changed. Her smile lights up her face as she wraps her arms around me.

"It's so good to see you, Nat. It's been forever."

I hug her back, eyes welling with tears.

Meena notices immediately and swaps her smile for a sombre expression as she remembers the circumstances surrounding our reunion.

She's always been more serious than Rachel, more sensible. In that way she's more similar to me. I think that's why we both ended up gravitating more towards Rachel. The "fun", "edgy" person we wanted to be.

But now I'm glad she's how she is.

I try to make small talk. How's Bristol? How are Ravi and the kids? I tell her I'd love to see them. That I think I could cope with it now. That at least I'd like to try.

"I'd like that," she says. "We all would."

Then she leans in and squeezes my hand.

"How are you?" she says, her eyes fixing on mine. "I can't imagine what you've been through."

I don't want to dredge it all up again. Not here. Not now. I don't want to sit in the window of a café bawling my eyes out. So I ignore her question, take a deep breath, and ask one of my own. The question that I most need answers to.

"Meena, do you remember Fenn's wedding?"

She's surprised. Taken off guard. But there's something else too. A flash of worry in her eyes.

"Yes," she says warily.

"I left early. I had a migraine."

"I remember."

"Did . . . did Rachel ever mention that evening to you?"

Meena swallows.

"No . . ."

She's being evasive.

"Meena, just tell me what happened."

Meena takes a sip of coffee—a delaying tactic—then swallows, pauses again, and begins to talk.

She'd seen me leave. I'd been off form all evening. Ravi was dancing and she went to call home. Their youngest was just thirteen months old and it was the first time she'd left him so she was worried. She found a quiet place, away from the band, to make the call and she'd been surprised to see Ryan arguing with a girl behind the marquee. Even more surprised to see that it was Rachel.

"Did you hear what they were saying?"

"Enough," Meena replies, then takes my hand in hers and stares at me. "Nat, are you sure you want to go into this now?"

"Yes," I say firmly.

". . . Ryan told Rachel that she was drunk and that she should go to bed. Rachel slapped him. Said that he was a fool. That he should be grateful. That he'd never get a better offer. Then Ryan really laid into her. Told her that she was the worst possible friend. Rachel started crying and begged him not to tell you. I'm sorry—I should have told you back then. Years ago. I don't know why I didn't tell you."

Because you think I'm fragile. Everyone thinks I'm fragile.

I shakily stand. I knew. I think I already knew. But "knowing" and having your knowledge confirmed are surprisingly different things.

I tell Meena that I need to be alone, and I can feel her eyes on my back as I weave out of the café and up the road. Guilt stabs at me for having misjudged Ryan. For having believed Rachel's word over his.

I try to examine everything with fresh eyes. Clearly. Dispassionately. He didn't hit on Rachel. He told the truth about that. Does that mean he didn't rape Alice? Didn't kill her? If so, who did? Someone who knew about the affair. Someone who had access to our car. Someone who could plant the murder weapon in our wardrobe.

Suddenly a horrible image invades my mind. Rachel standing in the kitchen, holding up the pair of keys I'd forgotten she had. There's not a car key on it, but she knows the spare is on the key rack in the understairs coat cupboard. She's always upstairs. She knows our house inside and out. She knew about Alice. She was the only one I'd told about the affair.

Stratton

Time drags as I wait for Pavarotti to call back. Minutes register as hours. Hours as days.

I can't sit and wait any more so I decide to pay the sister, Ms. Lytton, a visit. She'll be up by now. Bradley insists on coming too.

"Let me lead with the questioning," I tell him. "We've got to play this carefully. The case is still officially closed. I don't want it getting back to Parker."

Bradley nods.

Ms Lytton opens the door with bloodshot eyes. Anyone who's worked nights knows that day sleep doesn't work in the same way as night sleep does. It's like the body knows you're cheating nature and makes you pay for it. Ms. Lytton doesn't look like she's slept at all. Unsurprising, of course.

She looks confused to see us.

"Has he been charged now?" she asks.

How to handle this . . .

"Can we come in?" I say.

She opens the door fully and stands aside to let us enter. We walk in. We don't sit down and she doesn't offer. Instead we stand, an awkward triangle, next to the settee.

"Mr. Campbell was found dead on Saturday afternoon," I say quietly.

She throws me a look of disbelief. How did I let this happen?

"How?"

"It looks like a suicide," I say carefully.

She blinks away tears.

"Too good for him," she sniffs. "Why does he get to die in peace? He doesn't deserve it."

I wait a moment to give her a chance to vent. When she seems calmer I speak again.

"We just have one more question to ask," I say.

"Why? What's the point? He's dead, isn't he? It's over."

"Just for the paperwork," I say. She's a nurse, part of a bureaucracy. Hopefully the demands of paperwork are something she can understand.

She sniffs again then nods.

I produce a photo of Natalie Campbell.

"Have you ever seen this woman?"

She gives the photo a cursory glance. It's not enough.

"Do you know if she knew Alice?"

She starts to shake her head. Damn. She hasn't looked properly. She hasn't tried.

"Would you mind having another look?" I say. "Please, it's important."

Ms Lytton looks at me as if trying to work something out, then turns her eyes back to the photo. This time she studies it carefully.

"Actually . . . I think I did see her. Once. The morning . . . the morning you lot told me about Alice. She was here. Yes, I'm sure that was her. She came here, looking for Alice. Said she needed to speak to her. Said she was a friend."

This is not what I'm expecting. It doesn't make sense.

"So she didn't know Alice was dead?"

"No, she seemed shocked. She had no idea."

I try not to let the confusion show on my face.

We thank her then start to leave.

"If something new comes up, you'll let me know, won't you?" she says as we head down the path. "Anything relevant to Alice. I need to know."

She knows that something's up. That the case isn't as closed as it's meant to be. She can feel it. Intuition. Gut instinct. Call it what you want. I reassure her that we will. Knowing is better. Whatever the information. It's better to know.

As we head back to the car I try to process what we've just heard. Natalie Campbell knew where Alice lived. She came to see her. Said she was a friend. This all points to her being involved. Yet, on the other hand, Ms. Lytton was adamant that Natalie Campbell seemed shocked that Alice was dead. If she'd killed her she wouldn't have gone to her flat. She'd have had no reason to. She'd have stayed as far away from Alice's flat as possible. And certainly not have talked to the sister.

It doesn't make sense.

"What do you make of it?" I ask Bradley.

He shrugs. "Maybe the sister was confused. It wasn't her. If you think about the timing, she'd have just heard that her sister was dead. Her memories could easily be confused. You made it clear that the photo was important so she probably wanted to recognize her. Thinking that it might help in some way."

There's some sense to what he's saying. People can be desperate to help. They can want to have seen someone. Misremember things. Pick someone out of a line-up just to be able to act. But I don't think that's what's happening here. Ms. Lytton seemed so sure.

I don't know. I just don't. Maybe this time we're the desperate ones. Looking for evidence that isn't there. Maybe the husband did kill her. Maybe Parker's right. We got our guy. The case is closed.

The wind is picking up and sending leaves and old crisp packets spiralling down the pavement. Bradley ducks into a newsagent's to buy a Diet Coke. I tell him to make it two and then go and sit in the car to wait. I'm starting to feel down when my pocket starts vibrating. It's Pavarotti.

"Stratton," I bark. I can't keep the excitement out of my voice.

"Hello to you too." Pavarotti's laugh rumbles down the phone. "I have some results you may be interested in."

"Yes?"

"I ran a full blood tox spectrum on Ryan Campbell as requested, and—"

"Yes?"

"Patience, Stratton, is a virtue. Imagine trying to sit through *Giulio Cesare in Egitto* with that attitude." I roll my eyes but bite my tongue and wait for him to continue. "As I was saying, I ran a full tox spectrum and there was a hit. Strong traces of zopiclone—a prescription sleeping pill."

Zopiclone. Natalie Campbell's velvet zip bag. The one tucked away in her bedside table.

"What quantities are we talking?" I ask.

"Significant," he replies.

My heartbeat quickens. Did she drug him? Is that how she managed to get him into the bath? To keep him still while she slit his wrists?

Slow down. I jumped to conclusions with the husband. Saw links because I wanted them to exist. I can't make the same mistake again. At the moment all I have is a lot of coincidences. Natalie Campbell withdrew £12,000. Alice received £10,000. Natalie Campbell held a dumbbell in a gym. The same make of dumbbell was used to kill Alice and found in the Campbells' wardrobe. It doesn't prove she's the killer. It could still be the husband. I know I want to take someone down for Alice's murder. I want to put someone away. But it has to be the right person.

"Could he have self-administered?" I ask.

"Yes."

Damn. That gets us nowhere. He would have known where she kept her medication and could have swallowed the pills voluntarily to knock himself out.

"But—"

"Yes?" I want to stay calm, neutral, but hope bubbles up anyway.

"The dosage was considerable. Higher than I'd expect to see if someone was planning a second step, so to speak."

"What do you mean?"

"The pills themselves could have sufficed. Slitting the wrists too might have been overkill, pardon the phrasing."

So it's possible she forcibly drugged him to make him compliant. Then added the cuts to make it look more like suicide. Possible, if not probable.

"Was there any bruising around the mouth or neck?" I ask. "Anything to suggest he was forced to swallow them?" I try to picture Natalie Campbell standing on tiptoes, pushing pills in then clamping her hand over her husband's mouth, forcing them down. I can't make the picture look anything but ridiculous. He'd have been able to swat her away like a fly.

"No," Pavarotti confirms.

"What about the rest of the stomach contents? Anything else we can work with?"

"He hadn't eaten a proper meal in the final hours before his death. However, there were high levels of whey protein."

"As in protein powder?"

"Exactly."

"Could that disguise the taste of the zopiclone?"

"Beyond my realm of expertise, and you know it," laughs Pavarotti.

I turn my memory back to when I first started on the force. We had to do regular circuits workouts and the instructor encouraged us to drink protein shakes afterwards to build muscle. I remember the taste of the powder. Bitter. Overpowering. It could cover a lot . . .

"There is one more thing though," Pavarotti continues. "I rechecked the dumbbell for fingerprints. I still didn't find any for Ryan Campbell, but there was a clear print." He pauses, trying to tempt me into interrupting. I manage to resist. "The print belongs to a Mrs. Natalie Campbell."

Natalie

THE HOUSE IS too quiet. My footsteps echo. I can hear my breathing. In. Out. In. Out. Feel the air being sucked in and then expelled.

His body cannot be released yet. How can that be? This morning I finally summoned up the courage to call an undertaker's. The man there sounded kind, a Mr. Williams of Williams and Daughters. The right level of sombre. A voice that said the end would be dignified for all parties involved. The right voice. He said he'd liaise with the coroners. Make all the necessary arrangements. When the cause of death is straightforward, he reassured me, the release of the body is timely. That's what he'd said.

But now it's early afternoon and he's calling back and saying that they won't release the body. I needn't fret, he says. He'll get to the bottom of it. In the meantime, could he trouble me with a few more questions?

"Of course," I say. I can't say I want him to get off the phone. That I don't want to talk about this. That I don't want to organize my husband's funeral.

"What were the wishes of the deceased with regard to burial or cremation?"

I don't say anything. I don't know. And I feel inadequate. I should know, shouldn't I? Aren't those the sort of things a wife is supposed to know? But we'd never had those discussions. Death was something that happened to other people. To old people. We were meant to have years to have those discussions.

I'm failing him. I didn't believe him when he was alive. Now I'm failing him in death.

"I'll leave you in peace to reflect on this," the undertaker says tactfully. "And I'll email you some headstone and coffin options."

He hangs up. Leaving me in the promised peace. But the quiet isn't peaceful, it's oppressive.

I turn on the radio to fill the silence. A song draws to an end. It's bland, instantly forgettable. A combination of synths and autotune. No heart. No soul. Disposable music for a disposable world. Then the distinctive beeps start, signalling the news. I tense, ready to retreat into my tortoise shell, waiting to hear Ryan's name. But it isn't mentioned. The one positive of a disposable world—news, like anything else, is churned out, each new day a reset. The lead story is the Manchester Strangler. I remember hearing about him months ago, when they found the body of that poor girl, strangled. Ryan wouldn't let me walk anywhere by myself for a week afterwards. As if his capture might trigger a wave of copycat murders. As if there were hordes of people who had the potential to kill but just lacked the seed of an idea as to how.

I hadn't registered his being sentenced. It must have happened in the midst of everything. There could have been a political coup in the last few days and I wouldn't have known. Anyway, he's talking now. The girl in the car park wasn't his first victim. He's telling the police about others. They've dug up the remains of two more girls already. He says he's talking now because he's found God in prison. I don't believe it. He's only been locked up for a couple of days. God isn't as easy to find as that. I searched for him after the attack. I searched again when I first found out I was infertile. I searched hard, and I couldn't find him. No, he's telling people because he wants them to know. To appreciate how clever he is. "Look what I did," he's gloating. "Look what I got away with, and you only know now because I'm telling you." He's not a repentant sinner. He hasn't found God, he's playing God.

The news isn't helping. I need peace. I need to order my thoughts. Decide what to do about Rachel. An article I once read pops into my head—"The Power of Walking Barefoot on Grass". It's supposed to have immeasurable health benefits. The green is soothing and it's meant to ground you as free electrons from the earth are absorbed by the body and negatively charged electrons from the body are neutralized by the earth. It's probably rubbish—the new pseudoscience that's the rabbit's foot and crystal charms of its time. Still, anything is worth a try.

I take off my shoes and step out via the French windows and on to the lawn. The grass is longer than usual. It hasn't been mown for two weeks and the blades flatten under the pressure of my feet. It's cold. Slightly damp. Do I feel anything?

I need grounding. I feel like I'm floating, tethered to this world by a fraying rope. My best friend lied to me. My best friend. The person I thought of as my family. Said my husband had tried to cheat on me with her, when it was her who wanted it. Her who tried to cheat on me.

Could she have gone further? Could she have somehow convinced Alice to lie about Ryan? And then killed her to frame him? Surely not. It's psychotic. But who tries to seduce their best friend's husband and then claims he did the very same thing?

She could be a sociopath. She wants to be in control. Apparently doesn't care if she hurts others. Is manipulative and deceitful.

How big a jump is it from sociopath to psychopath?

She knows where Ryan works. She could have gone there. Met Alice. Convinced her. Paid her. Alice's flat looked so run-down. Maybe she needed the money?

God, she even knew where Alice lived. She was checking my location when I was on the phone to her outside Alice's flat . . .

Thoughts tumble on top of each other and jumble. The cold is starting to spread up my feet and into my legs. The green isn't calming me. No endorphins are being generated. I turn and go back inside, leaving a trail of damp footprints in my wake.

Rachel could have killed Alice.

And driven Ryan to suicide.

I need to tell someone.

Stratton

I START TO thank Pavarotti when there's a rap on the car window. It's Bradley, trying to catch my attention. He's on the phone. Flips it to mute.

"What is it?" I ask him as he opens the door and climbs in.

"The friend—Katie. She's back and she wants to talk."

"Put her on speaker."

"In person."

"Then tell her to come in immediately."

Bradley shakes his head. "It'll scare her. I'm developing a rapport. I think I should go myself."

"No," I say firmly. It's one thing sending Bradley solo to drive someone home or bring them in. A bit of eye candy to soften up the ladies. It's quite another to have him questioning key witnesses without me. We've waited long enough to hear what this one has to say. I want to be there when she says it.

He's right about one thing though—we want her chatty. We want her spilling her dead friend's secrets. And she's more likely to do that somewhere she feels safe.

"Get an address," I say. "Tell her we're on our way." He seems annoyed. His ego again. He probably thinks he should lead. That he can solve this all by himself.

* * *

Forty minutes later we're sitting in her flat, me and Bradley squeezed next to each other on a small two-seater navy settee while she sits across from us, legs curled under her, in an old leather armchair. We quickly cover the preliminaries.

She's Katie Roberts. Aged twenty-four. A friend of Alice's from school who did well for herself. When Alice chose modelling, Katie chose studying instead and ended up going to Nottingham uni and studying physiology. She's started work for a sports physio team attached to a leading football club. She's polite, smartly presented, sensible haircut, looks older than her years. She's renting a nice two-bed with a friend in a smartish area of Ealing. Just returned from a holiday in Vietnam. No wonder Alice's sister approves of her.

"I'm sorry I didn't call back immediately," she says. "But I didn't get your message till I landed this morning. I turned my phone off while I was away, you see. I've never been somewhere like that. I've hardly left the country before, to be honest. I had two weeks. And I wanted to really feel it—to be there. Sorry if that sounds really poncy."

It does, but it also doesn't. If I ever get to go somewhere like Vietnam, my phone won't be coming with me.

"We understand," I say. "And we're very sorry for your loss."

"Thank you," she says, suddenly looking her actual age. "I don't think I've processed it yet."

"How close were you?"

"At school we were really close. Then, as I said, we . . . lost touch."

It doesn't take a detective to see the heartache in those words. "Lost touch" was code for rejection, for pain, for seeing a friend throw their life away.

"When did you get in touch again?" Bradley asks.

"A few months ago. When Alice got clean. Her sister reached out. I think she thought I'd be a good influence. Alice didn't have many friends from before and was trying to keep away from her newer ones."

I nod.

"And did you feel that Alice was sorting her life out?"

Katie becomes quite animated. She gestures with her hands and her facial expressions intensify. "Oh yes, absolutely. She was back to her old self. She was clean. There was no doubt about it. And ambitious. She had plans. A future."

Then she stops suddenly, as if realizing for the first time the extent of what had been taken from Alice. The potential. A future to redress past mistakes.

"But she was in trouble too, wasn't she?" I probe gently. "She owed a dealer called Angel a lot of money. How did she pay him back? Did you lend her the money?"

Katie shakes her head and a muscle tightens in her jaw.

"I would have done. I have around £3,000 in savings. I said she could have that. Try and buy herself some more time—but she wouldn't take my money. She said it had to be the full amount. If she didn't pay it all back, he was going to take her eyes. Can you believe that? He was going to blind her."

I shake my head in disgust. That sick fuck.

Final avenue closed. The money came from the Campbells. Withdrawn by the wife. It had to.

"Are you aware if Alice was seeing anyone?" I ask. "A man. Anyone new. She met in a bar, or out, or at work maybe?"

She hesitates. I press her.

"Did she talk about her new job with you?"

"Yes," Katie says. "She liked it. She'd only just started when I saw her but she said she liked being there."

Bradley's knee's tapping. He's itching to get involved. He's right. He's not going to learn if I monopolize the questioning. I nod at him to have a go.

"What about her boss, Mr. Campbell?" he asks.

Her lips become a firm thin line. Bradley doesn't go for the jugular so I press her further. We need momentum. Bradley can learn later.

"Alice claimed that he raped her. Did she talk to you about this?"

She stares at the floor.

"Katie," I say, "if you don't tell us everything, then we can't catch her killer. We can't give her justice. We know she was a good person. We're not trying to catch you out. We're not trying to put her on trial. She's the victim. We know that."

She sighs then buries her head in her hands.

"It happened after I left for Vietnam," she says.

"Did she mention that she was scared of him? That he was pressurizing her?"

She doesn't say anything, just buries her face deeper. I need to change tack.

"Did she ever mention his wife, Natalie Campbell? Could they have met at a work function? Or when she visited her husband?"

Katie raises her head and stares at me, the tears preparing to return.

"What is it, Katie?"

Her eyes tell me she wants to speak.

"I promised I'd never tell."

"Katie, Alice is dead. If you can help us catch her killer, you have to."

She looks at me as if for absolution and I give it to her. "She would want you to talk. You owe it to Alice."

Katie doesn't look at us as she talks, preferring instead to focus on the lamp sitting on the side table. She tells the lamp about an evening. About the last time she'd met up with Alice. Alice was excited. Everything was going to be all right, she'd said. She'd be able to pay off Angel and she was working somewhere fancy for a bit.

"I was worried for her, of course. I mean, how do you suddenly get £10,000 if it's not for something bad? But Alice was convinced. She said she was going to do a moral thing. Make society safer."

"What was she going to do, Katie?" I feel the tension rise in my body. The anticipation.

"Someone was going to pay her . . ." She starts to falter. Bradley and I have subconsciously moved forward. Both literally on the edge of our seats.

"Pay her to do what?"

"Say that a man had raped her. Say that her new boss had raped her."

The room suddenly feels very quiet. I can feel the prickle on my skin as hairs stand on end, one after the other.

"Who, Katie? Who was going to pay her?"

She swallows.

"Natalie Campbell. The wife."

Natalie

I THINK ABOUT calling the lead detective, Stratton, but then I imagine her eyes raking over me, judging me. Her questions, shredding me. She'll have already closed the case. She thinks Ryan did it. I won't be able to change her mind. Instead I rummage through the drawer of the console table. It's still there, at the back. DS Bradley's card. I pick it up and call.

He doesn't answer, so I leave a message asking him to come round. Tell him that I don't think Ryan did it. That I have an idea who might have. Ask him to look into Rachel Conway. Age thirty-five. Works at Greene & Stokes.

I go to make myself a cup of tea while I wait. My mind starts leaping from image to image. It speeds up, the colours intensifying. I need something to do. A task to focus on. The bright orange of the larder cupboard catches my eye. The shelves have been a mess since the police search.

Humans aren't meant to live in chaos. We're meant to live in small communities. Know a hundred people. Mate with one. There'd be no space to tolerate predators and liars in a village. They'd be discovered and hounded out. The current world is too enormous. It swallows you. Half your time is spent trying not to be subsumed.

Order tethers.

I'm about to start on the pasta-and-rice shelf when there's a noise from the hall. The rattle of the letterbox.

Annoyed at the interruption, I pad, still barefoot, into the hall, leaving wet, grass-embroidered footprints in my wake. A single letter sits on the doormat. A white A5 envelope with my name and address typed on a label stuck symmetrically in the centre. There's no stamp this time. It's been hand-delivered.

No. No. My fingers start to tingle as I open the door, trying to see if she's out there. But I don't see her. I think I can make out the figure of a young child fleeing down the pavement, but I'm not sure. Is it just in my imagination?

My heart's accelerating as I close the door again. I'd forgotten about the letters. In the midst of everything else, the letters had faded. She had faded. Part of a theory that had been laughed at and discarded. It had become Ryan's theory, not mine, and died with him. The letters had become unreal. Replaced by a husband as killer. Then a friend. Now I'm holding one, the threat is real again. Very real.

Biting my lip, I tear open the envelope and pull out the letter. The parchment is thick like before. Crudely cut-out letters claim the centre.

Just two words this time.

THE END

The tingling spreads to my hands and then my feet.

It's her. It's all her.

I've been so blind.

I can't shake the feeling that the letter is laughing at me. That somewhere out there she is laughing at me. Fiona Scott. She's been leading me this way and that, toying with my emotions, playing with me, with my reality. She made me doubt my husband. Believe my friend capable of murder. Now she wants to finish it. She wants to finish me. I slap my face. Nothing. The edges of my vision are starting to pixellate. I stagger to the stairs and manage to crawl up, focusing on the feeling of the rough wool runner on my kneecaps. I slap my face again halfway up. I need to get to the bedroom. To my washbag. If I can take the last betablocker I might not pass out. I might not lose time. I drag myself along the landing, my vision and hearing dipping in and out. The bedroom door is open and I pull myself through. My right hand reaches for the bedside-table drawer handle . . .

Then blackness.

Stratton

I TRY NOT to let my shock show as my heart rate accelerates. We're getting somewhere. Finally, we're getting to some kernel of truth.

"Natalie Campbell was going to pay Alice to say that her husband raped her?"

I need to make sure I understand.

Katie nods mutely, then buries her head in her hands.

I wait for her to re-emerge. We can't rush this.

"I told Alice not to do it," Katie continues eventually. "I begged her not to. You can't make false accusations like that. No matter what. It hurts women. All women. I said there had to be another way to get the money. But she wouldn't change her mind. She said it wasn't like that. She said the husband was a serial abuser. He'd sexually assaulted women before. And not just once. This was the only way the wife could think to stop him. To keep other women safe. Alice believed her. Who would lie about something like that? And it struck a chord with her. You have to realize, Alice was on the streets for a year. She met her fair share of predators. She knew what they were capable of. She knew how hard it was to stop them."

I have to try and piece this together. Make sense of it all.

"So she met Alice at her husband's work?"

"No. No, it was before that, don't you see? The wife arranged the job interview. She organized all of it."

Everything becomes clearer. I'd never understood how someone like Alice would have applied to the marketing firm. How she'd have known how to game the system. Natalie Campbell engineered it all. She could have written the CV. Made up the sort of relevant experience that she'd known would guarantee Alice an interview.

"And Mr. Campbell didn't rape her?" I clarify.

"No."

"But she did sleep with him?"

Katie looks from the lamp to the floor.

"Alice said it was going to be OK. She'd had sex for far less before. And at least this time it was to stop a predator."

I try to understand. Alice needed the money. She convinced herself she was doing a good thing in accusing him. But did she really understand what she was letting herself in for? The trial. A defence attorney ripping her to shreds. Her whole sordid past being put on display. Was she really prepared to lie on the stand and send someone to prison for something they hadn't done, even if they'd done as bad in the past?

I put this to Katie.

"Oh no," she says. "Alice said she just needed to accuse him. That was the agreement. Threaten to go to the police but not go through with it. It was meant to be a wake-up call. That was all. No police statements. No trial. She said there's no way she would have agreed to it if there'd been a trial. She wouldn't have perjured herself in court. She was meant to scare him into stopping his behaviour then walk away. Start again."

But she didn't. She didn't have the chance. She wasn't going to have to go through with it because she was going to be dead. That was the plan all along, wasn't it? I feel a chill run through me.

"Did you talk to her afterwards?" I ask.

"No." Katie shakes her head. "As I said, I'd already left for Vietnam. I left before it happened."

Then Katie completely breaks down. She's sobbing and sobbing.

"Please don't tell her sister," she says. "I promised Alice that I'd never say a word to her sister. She wouldn't understand. I don't want her to think badly of Alice. She's dead. Isn't that enough?"

I have more questions—how did Natalie Campbell first meet Alice? How did she know Alice could be manipulated?—but Bradley touches my elbow and nods towards the door. He's right. We have everything we need for now. I'll send Sandra round later to follow up.

Natalie Campbell. To think I'd thought of her as weak. A victim. A fly caught in a web.

But she's not.

She's the spider.

In the centre of it all.

Spinning.

Natalie

I COME TO. I'm kneeling, this time. The floor is brown... wooden. Something bright stands in front. Shapes morph, then solidify. The larder cupboard. I'm in the kitchen. Upstairs bedroom to kitchen—I came down the stairs, but at least I didn't leave the house. How long have I been out? The oven clock reads 4.11p.m. I'd check my phone to see when I called the detective, but it's not in my pocket. I must have left it upstairs. I look around, trying to fully orientate myself before I stand.

What's changed?

Everything looks the same as when I left it. No. Not quite. The larder door is closed. I ease myself to standing, checking my limbs for damage. My right foot is sore and I wince as I try to get it to bear weight.

I limp towards the larder door, then open it.

My breath stops. Everything is neatly arranged. The packets of flour. The pasta. The rice. A separate shelf for the sweet ingredients: the sugar, the raisins, the custard powder. Packets in parallel lines. Labels facing front.

Even the spice trays in the doors are filled.

I did this. I have no memory of doing this.

If I can do this, what else can I do?

There's a noise.

Someone's in the house.

Stratton

Parker sits across from me. I don't let him interrupt. He tries to, but I just speak louder and faster and block his words. Mine are like tanks: they crush his. Finally, I finish and he breathes out loudly. Not a sigh. More like a long, angry exhale. He doesn't say anything. Then he hooks his fingers through his belt and stretches his shoulders back. He's trying to physically intimidate me. Dickhead. I don't take my eyes off him.

He blinks first.

"So what do you want to do?" he asks.

"Reopen the case," I say. I manage to not add the words *you moron*.

"And your prime suspect is now the wife?"

I nod.

He sighs. A proper sigh this time. He doesn't want me here. He'd prefer not to know we cocked up. He'd prefer us not to catch the killer than to have to perform a humiliating u-turn. To put his fingers in his ears and hum. But he knows he can't say that. He knows he has to let me have my way.

"Well, make sure you get it right this time. Mistakes like this don't reflect well on our department."

Pompous idiot.

He tells me to get another search warrant. Different suspect, different warrant. We might have missed something last time. We were focusing on the husband, not the wife.

"I can interview her without."

"You can talk to her, but don't touch anything else in the house till the warrant's signed off."

I grab my coat. Dev's at his terminal, so I tell him to sort out the warrant and call me when it's done. He wants to ask questions. I tell him there's no time. Then I tap Bradley's shoulder and tell him to come with me.

"Did Parker clear it?" Bradley asks.

"Yup."

"Right."

Bradley sounds guarded. There's something else.

"What's up?"

Bradley fidgets. "Natalie Campbell left me a message."

For Christ's sake. Are they at love-note stage already?

"What did she say?"

"That she thinks she knows who killed Alice."

It takes me a second to process.

"What the fuck?"

"She asked me to look into a Rachel Conway. What should I do?"

I want to laugh. Laugh it off as a complete joke. We have a friend of the vic's saying the wife set it all up. We have her fingerprint on the weapon, the weapon in her wardrobe, footage of her taking the money out of the bank. But then again, there's the part that doesn't fit. The sister saying that Mrs. Campbell was there the next morning looking for Alice. Shocked that she was dead. I don't want to be blindsided again.

I call over to Reynolds.

"Can you look into someone for me? Rachel Conway."

I look at Bradley. "Anything else to go on?"

"Thirty-five," he supplies. "Works at Greene & Stokes. It's a law firm."

"Find out if she has an alibi for the night of the 20th," I say.

Reynolds looks puzzled. "Sure. Didn't you solve that one?"

* * *

Traffic is light, so we reach the Campbells' house in under fifteen minutes. I ring the bell. Nothing. Then I hammer on the door. The car's outside, the lights are on. I have a sudden vision of her copying her husband. Bleeding out in the bath. Taking the easy way out. I'm not going to let that happen.

"Any news on the warrant yet?" Bradley asks.

"No, nothing."

I hammer on the door again.

"We need to force the door down," I say to Bradley.

"On what cause?"

Fuck. I don't need the Boy Scout routine right now.

"I'm worried something's happened," I say. "That she might be taking her own life."

"OK. We need to go in," he says.

At last. He's understanding the job. He's becoming a police officer rather than a lawyer.

"I think I hear a disturbance," he says. "I have reasonable belief that a crime is being committed."

I smile him a thanks and he backs away and then takes a run at the door, throwing his whole weight through his right shoulder and into the wood. It shudders then caves in and comes off its hinges, hitting the floor with a crash.

"Check the bathroom!" I yell. Bradley leaps over the fallen door and pounds up the stairs.

I start to search the downstairs.

"All clear," he shouts from the landing.

"Check the bedrooms," I instruct. I picture her hanging from the ceiling from a makeshift noose.

I race through the rooms. Hall. Living room. Kitchen. She's in the kitchen. I stop in the doorway. She's kneeling but slightly unsteady. Slowly, she pushes herself up to standing.

"Mrs. Campbell," I say. She doesn't seem to hear me.

She opens the doors of the food cupboard then stands and stares, as if she's scared of something. Her feet are wet and bits of grass are sticking to the soles.

"Mrs. Campbell," I say again.

She turns to face me but doesn't seem to register me fully. Her eyes have a glassy quality. Has she taken something? OD'd? Then her eyelids flicker and her breathing becomes more noticeable, her nostrils flaring, and it seems she can suddenly see me, is suddenly aware of her surroundings.

I offer my arm and lead her over to the kitchen table. Her gait is uneven, like she's hurt one of her legs. I pull out one of the wooden benches and carefully lower her on to it, checking that she can maintain balance without her back supported.

"Have you taken something, Mrs. Campbell?"

I feel her pulse in her wrist. It's slow. She shakes her head, eyes blinking rapidly. A stroke? A heart attack?

"Did you have a seizure? Do you need a doctor?"

Another head shake.

"What happened then?"

She takes a deep breath, and I can see she's deciding whether or not to tell me something. Something important. I crouch down next to her, making myself look as unthreatening as possible. Adopting prey-animal body language. And it's not all an act. I find myself actually wanting to help her. Doubt is creeping in. I can't reconcile this version of Natalie Campbell with the puppet master I've built up in my head.

"Please tell me," I say. "I can help you."

She closes her eyes in one long blink. Then starts to speak.

"I . . . lose time sometimes. In stressful situations, I can black out."

"I see." Do I? It sounds far-fetched, but I don't think she's faking it. When I found her, her eyes were open but she wasn't registering me.

"What happens when you lose time?" I ask gently. Using my most soothing voice. A vocal tiptoe.

"I . . . I don't know. It can just be for a few minutes. Or for . . . longer. I can end up places. I do things."

What do you do, Natalie?

"And do you remember things from these moments?"

She hesitates before replying.

". . . No," she says.

I need to get her assessed by a psychiatrist. I ask her whether she thinks she might have broken or strained anything. No. She shakes her head. She sits on the chair, skin pale, head bowed.

I hear a movement from behind me and see him standing in the doorframe. At least he had the tact to keep his distance. Two against one would have seemed like too obvious an interrogation rather than concern.

"Let me get you a glass of water," I say, catching Bradley's eye and signalling towards the sink. We need to talk.

"Did you look around upstairs?"

"We don't have a warrant," he warns.

I check my phone to see if there's any status update from Dev. Nothing. Fuck. The court's running slow, so we might not have a warrant until the morning.

"So we bring her in now and come back and search the place tomorrow."

Bradley doesn't look happy. He swivels his neck to look at her then turns back to me.

"Look at her. She's not going anywhere. We should let her spend the night here. Bring her in tomorrow when we've got the warrant."

So much for following the rules. For justice. But I follow his gaze and see her sitting there. Slumped. He's right. If we bring her in now she'll be in a cell overnight. There'd be no harm waiting a few hours longer. She doesn't know we suspect her. It's not like she poses a danger to anyone else.

"OK," I say.

We head back over.

"Is there anyone you'd like us to call?" I ask. "Family? A friend?"

There's a pause, then a quiet, "No."

"Right. I have some questions," I say. "But they can wait till tomorrow. Rest for now. We'll send someone over to sort out the front door."

She's no longer looking at me. She's looking past me and at Bradley.

"There's been another letter," she says, trying to stand but then wincing from pain. "I need to show you the letter."

"Show me tomorrow," he says.

"Thank you," she says. "Thank you for coming."

I almost feel guilty.

Natalie

I THINK I misjudged Stratton. She seemed different this time. Kinder. Maybe the harshness is a front. A mask to get ahead at work and keep the world out. I know all about masks.

I called Bradley and they came. They believed me when I said I didn't think Ryan did it. Or they believed me enough to come and see.

Then it strikes me. I didn't tell them I was wrong about Rachel. That she's a bad person but not a murderer.

I should have insisted they stayed. Should have made them listen about the letters. They need to find Fiona Scott now. Before she hurts anyone else.

Anyone else.

It hits me like a sledgehammer. Ryan. First I'd assumed he'd killed himself from guilt. Then I thought he'd killed himself from stress. Because the world hadn't believed him. Because I hadn't believed him. But I haven't acknowledged that there might be a third option. That he didn't kill himself. That it wasn't suicide. It was murder. Could she have done it? Slit his wrists for him. Do the police suspect foul play? Is this why they're not releasing the body?

The more I think about it, the more convinced I am that I'm right. When I last spoke to Ryan he wasn't despondent, he was angry. He'd been sent home from the station. He thought he was a free man.

He didn't know about them finding the murder weapon. He thought the case against him had been dropped. He wouldn't have killed himself.

It was her. I don't know how, but she killed him. She killed him because she thinks I killed her husband. An eye for an eye. A warped, biblical version of justice.

And now the final letter. The two words.

"THE END."

She's coming for me.

I can feel it.

Stratton

I WAIT TILL we're back in the car before I talk to Bradley. You never know if there's a neighbour on the street. Some busybody eavesdropping.

The doors shut, windows up, I ask him.

"What's this about some letters?"

"Didn't I tell you?"

No, I think I'd remember that. I let rip.

"For fuck's sake, Bradley. We're in the middle of a murder investigation that has already gone tits up. I can't have my partner forgetting to share potentially important evidence with me!"

He flushes red and apologizes. He explains that when he brought her in, she produced a box of letters. The next time he saw me we were dealing with the aftermath of Ryan's release. They hadn't seemed that important.

"That's for me to judge," I snap. "What sort of letters?"

"Anonymous ones. Messages made from letters cut out of newspapers and glued on to paper. That sort of thing."

"Threatening?"

"Of a kind."

He says that some were from around ten years ago, straight after the court case. The widow was angry. Blamed Mrs. Campbell for her husband's death. There was a restraining order placed on her.

I digest the information. Even more annoyed now that this is the first I've heard of it. It seems significant. Bradley should have brought it to my attention.

"OK. And the more recent ones?"

"Started a week ago."

"From the widow again?"

Bradley shrugs.

"This is where it gets interesting," he says. "The newer ones are superficially the same. Same style, same layout."

"But . . ."

"The postmarks on the originals were all from the same place—a village in Surrey. But all the postmarks are local this time."

"The widow could have moved. Or travelled to post them."

"I ran them for fingerprints. You weren't there, so Reynolds signed it off. The only ones we found belonged to Natalie and Ryan Campbell."

Again. It's not definitive. It's usual for senders of anonymous hate mail to wear gloves. I have to remember to keep each segment of information separate. The human brain wants patterns. It wants links. It's tuned to seek out confirmation bias.

We sit in silence for the rest of the drive.

"What do you make of the blackouts?" Bradley asks as we turn into the station car park.

"We need to get a psychiatrist to assess her," I say. "Can you put a call in?"

"Sure," he agrees.

The blackouts. The blackouts change everything. If everything she's done has been in a blacked-out state, a sort of split-personality disorder, then it all comes together. Her own rape could have traumatized her. Broken her brain in some way. Created a shield between certain negative thoughts and her everyday experience. A protective barrier. Stress could bring that barrier crashing down so that the negative thoughts took over entirely. Her everyday brain would register the takeover as a blackout. Maybe her husband was a cheat. Maybe he was a predator. Subjected countless women to what she herself had endured. She could have bottled up all this hatred and then dissociated and killed the woman who slept with her husband, even though she paid her to. She could have framed her husband and then killed him to stop him hurting anyone else ever again. And yet been completely unaware of it. It explains how she could have turned up at the sister's door, asking about Alice. It explains how she could have been genuinely shocked at the news of Alice's death.

Back at the station, Reynolds accosts me.

"I looked into Rachel Conway," he says.

"Thanks. And?"

"She was at a fundraising dinner all night on the 20th. Ten people who sat at a table with her and paid £250 a head for the privilege can attest to it."

Right. So that rules her out, not that we'd ever taken her seriously in the first place.

I settle down at my desk and start to write up what we'd witnessed this afternoon. Coming upon Mrs. Campbell with her unnerving open, glazed-over eyes. Her account of "losing time". If only we had a way of knowing exactly when these blackouts had happened. Then I have a sudden thought and pull up the photos from the house search. There are hundreds. I move through them quickly till I get to the ones of the bedroom. The ones from the bedside table. There are six of the velvet zip bag. I keep swiping till I reach the ones I'm interested in. The diary. Open at the relevant page. Three dates and times.

All within the last week.

I hadn't understood what they were at the time. What their significance could be.

But then I hadn't known about the blackouts.

It makes sense she kept a list. "Losing time" would be frightening and disorientating. She'd want a record.

My eyes move down the list again and pause on the second entry.

20/3 11 p.m.

The night Alice was killed.

Natalie

Someone comes to fix the door. I thought they'd forget, but they don't and he comes: Clive. Not police, but security staff from a contractor the police use. I make him tea and he keeps up a gentle patter of conversation as he works. The traffic; the South Circular's getting worse and worse—I blame that Sadiq Khan. The weather; it's been mild recently, hasn't it? It feels both surreal and mundane at the same time. He says they'd normally just board the gap, but the door's still largely intact, just off its hinges. It'd be just as easy for him to reattach it and cover over the splintered section with ply. I thank him as he screws it back on the wall and tests the lock. I offer to pay; I don't know what the etiquette is. The man laughs away my offer. When the police break a door down they have a duty to make it safe afterwards, he explains. He hands me a form when he's finished. It details what he's done and there's a phone number to contact for further information.

I almost miss him when he leaves.

Dark begins to steal in through the open curtains. I manage to hobble over to the light switch. I turn all the lights on, twisting the dimmer so that they are at maximum brightness. Then, putting as little weight on my right foot as I can, I do a lap of the downstairs, closing all the curtains, testing all the windows, the French doors. Checking that all are shut and that she can't get in.

I finally approach the front door, and then it hits me.

She has a key. It's the only way everything makes sense. The day I found the downstairs window open. The time I couldn't find my keys in my bag. She must have broken in through the open window and taken my house and car keys to copy. It's how she could have picked Alice up in our car. It's how she could have planted the murder weapon. It's how she could have killed Ryan.

I start laughing. A weird, high laugh that I don't recognize.

All these precautions, they're pointless. It doesn't matter how well Clive reattached the front door, she can still just walk straight in. One turn of the key and she's inside.

I fetch one of Ryan's golf clubs from the understairs cupboard and sit on the sofa and wait.

Wait to see if she comes. Tomorrow's Tuesday. The anniversary of the verdict.

She's going to try and kill me, I can feel it.

TUESDAY, 26 MARCH

Stratton

I KNOCK AT the door, the search warrant in my pocket. Bradley stands next to me. We drove separately as we each came straight from home, but still managed to arrive at pretty much the same time. Our cars are parked side by side outside.

Natalie Campbell looks grateful to see us when she opens the door, and that annoying feeling of guilt returns.

She's looking even wilder than yesterday. Her hair, unbrushed, is pulled back in a makeshift ponytail and she's still wearing the same clothes. There's a mania to her too, and in her left hand she clutches a golf club like a weapon. I don't trust her not to whack us one.

Bradley seems to read my thoughts.

"Let me take that from you," he says calmly, putting his hand round the bottom of the club's shaft. She lets him and he stashes it in the corner, away from her. She leads us into the living room.

"It was for protection," she says. "The club, that is. In case she came in the night."

"In case who came, Mrs. Campbell?" I ask. "Your friend Rachel? We checked her out. She didn't kill Ryan."

She frowns and makes a waving gesture with her hand.

"No, not her. I meant to tell you. It wasn't Rachel. I know that now."

Another suspect? Really? She's starting to become completely unhinged. I humour her.

"Then who?"

"Fiona Scott, of course. The person who sent the letters."

"Of course," I say.

I steer her towards the settee, giving Bradley the signal. He says he needs to re-examine the upstairs bathroom. To look for evidence of foul play. We have a search warrant if she wants to see it?

She looks pleased. "No need. Please look. Look everywhere. She's clever, but she might have slipped up. Left something behind."

Bradley leaves and I wait for Mrs. Campbell to sit. She doesn't. I begin to worry that she'll follow him upstairs, but she doesn't. She stops in front of the side table. "I'll show you the letter, the new one," she says, placing her left hand on the handle. The drawer judders then opens and she pulls out a white envelope. She hobbles back and holds it out to me. I ask her to wait as I put latex gloves on. She nods her approval. "There's no stamp on the envelope," I comment as I examine it. "And no postmark. I thought the ones before had been posted?"

"They were," she replies. "She wants me to know that she delivered this one herself. That she's been here."

I nod non-committally. The letter comes out of the envelope easily. Thick parchment. Letters stuck on, just above the central crease. "THE END". There is something unsettling about it, I can see that. I'd be scared if I received it. Particularly if it was one of many. A campaign of hate.

"And what do you think it means?" I ask.

Her shoulders rise higher.

"That it's soon going to be over," she says quietly. "That she's going to kill me like she killed Alice and Ryan. It's ten years today since the court hearing. My death will be her finale."

She walks over to the high-backed leather armchair and crumples into it.

I want to understand her theory. To see how she's created this delusion. Maybe if I can highlight enough holes in it, she'll be forced to reject it herself and confront the inevitable truth.

"And how did Mrs. Scott know Alice?" I ask.

Mrs. Campbell's forehead creases.

"I don't know."

"And how did she kill Ryan?"

Natalie Campbell becomes more animated. "She broke in. Ryan left a window open. She must have taken a key and had it copied. That's how she planted the murder weapon. That's how she got in and killed Ryan. Don't you see?"

"Mrs. Campbell, I saw that you were holding the letter in your left hand. Are you left-handed?"

"Yes," she replies brusquely, waving it away as an irrelevance. She hasn't seen Pavarotti's report. Doesn't know the killer struck with their left hand.

"Why didn't you come to the police sooner about the letters?" I ask. "You came to us after the first ones ten years ago. Why not now?"

She hesitates. A rabbit in the headlights.

"I . . . have bad associations with the police," she says. "I thought going to them, to you, might retrigger the blackouts."

"But they're happening anyway, aren't they?" I say calmly.

She doesn't say anything. Her eyes lower. I understand, though. Her aversion to the police. After Karen was taken, I hated the police. If I hadn't joined them, I wouldn't have ever gone to them for help. I still have difficulty sometimes being part of the "them" rather than the "us".

There's a creak on the stairs. Bradley's descending. He walks through the kitchen towards us, gloves on too, carrying something.

It's a box. A4 in size. Dark green. The velvet zip bag is balanced on top.

He puts the box down on the settee and then picks up the bag. I watch as he removes the strip of zopiclone from its packet. There are now thirteen empty blisters where there had been only two before. I was right. It was her drugs that had been used on her husband.

"That's private," she says. "Why are you snooping round my private things?"

"We have a search warrant and your permission, remember?" I say.

"I found the box under the spare bed," Bradley continues.

Mrs. Campbell's eyes flick over it.

"What's that?" she says. "I've never seen that before."

Bradley puts the box down on the coffee table in front of me.

"Open it," he says simply.

Mrs. Campbell slumps back in the settee, looking suspiciously at the box.

Curious, I lift the lid.

Inside is a collection of magazines and newspapers. Last month's *Grazia* sitting on top.

Mrs. Campbell leans forwards. "They're not mine. I don't read magazines."

I ignore her.

Without speaking, Bradley bends down and removes the top magazine then takes out and unfolds the newspaper sitting underneath. A copy of *The Times*, dated a month ago. He opens it to the second page and then holds it up to the light. Small squares have been cut from the page, light filtering through the holes in diagonal shafts.

Impatiently, I take the paper off him. The characters in the missing squares match the ones in the letters. Some from headlines, some from subheadings. Different sizes, different fonts.

Dev missed it in the original search. Or maybe he saw it but dismissed it. We didn't know about the letters then. A box of magazines and papers would have seemed an irrelevance. Either way, it doesn't matter. It's over. It's her. She sent the letters to herself.

I turn to face Mrs. Campbell. She's gone even paler, blinking in disbelief. Her finger is paused, midair, pointing at the paper.

"It's not what it looks like," she says. "She's done it. Fiona Scott. She's planted this too. Don't you see? She's playing you. She's framing me."

I ignore her as I have another thought. A long shot. The burner. I take out my notebook and flick through to where I noted the number. I carefully type it into my phone and press dial. Then wait with bated breath. There's a buzzing sound from upstairs. Faint, but it's there. I tell Bradley to follow it. To bag what he finds. Moments later, he's back. A small black phone lies in a plastic bag.

"In her chest of drawers," he says.

"No. What's that? I've never seen that before," Natalie protests again.

I don't respond. Instead I tell Bradley to take the box and the phone to Pavarotti. I want both tested for fingerprints and added to evidence immediately.

"Shouldn't I stay here?" he questions.

I steer him out into the hall. "There's nothing more to do here. We have all the evidence we need. All that remains is for a psychiatrist to judge to what extent she was aware of her actions. I'll read her her rights. I'll take her into the station."

Bradley leaves with the box. I can tell he's not happy about it, but it'll do him good to remember who's in charge. He's still at the bottom of the ladder. Needs to work his way up.

Mrs. Campbell has gone completely still. She's drawn her legs up and put her hands round them. She then starts rocking, slowly. It freaks me out. It reminds me of Mum after Karen left. She went nuts for a few days. Social services were even talking about having her committed.

"Shall I get you a glass of water?" I say.

She stops rocking, raises her head and stares at me, tilting her head to one side.

I know I shouldn't engage. I should wait till she's at the station on the record before I talk to her. But this case isn't going to trial. It'll be an insanity plea. Her defence will make her see there's no other option. We won't contest it. And I want to know. It's eating away at me, the not knowing. What drove her to do what she did? A few questions can't do any harm.

"I didn't do this," she says. "I know how it looks, but I didn't do this."

Natalie

STRATTON STARES AT me. Her stare has changed. It used to be sharp and tinged with ridicule. Disdain. Now it's filled with pity, and somehow this is worse.

She thinks I'm mad. She thinks I did it and I belong in a padded cell somewhere.

"Mrs. Campbell," Stratton says calmly, as if talking to a child, "we know everything. A friend of the victim told us that you paid Alice. You paid her to say that your husband raped her."

It's like a trapdoor opens beneath my feet and I'm falling. There's not even a noose to break my descent. I can hear laughing. I feel my body shake. The sound's coming from me.

"I paid her?" I say. "I paid her to lie about my husband? Why? Why the hell would I do that? Do you know what happened to me? Of course you do. You'll have run my name through your database. Do you really think I could let someone lie about a rape?"

I'm angry now. The fear's gone, and anger's taken its place. I paid Alice? I didn't know Alice. Where the hell is this coming from?

"Mrs. Campbell, did your husband assault women? Had he attacked women in the past? Is that why you did what you did?"

Ryan? They're trying to paint him as a predator. He isn't. Wasn't. I know that now. He shouldn't have slept with her. With Alice. He was weak. I don't know if I could have forgiven him with time. But the idea I needed him taken down. For womankind? It's just so preposterous.

"Why pay her then?" she says. "We saw the bank security cameras. The bank records. You withdrew £12,000 in cash."

I think, drag my memory. When did I withdraw cash? Then I remember.

"To pay for the kitchen. Workmen like cash. Didn't you know? You can still smell the paint, for God's sake."

She wavers slightly. I've made her think.

"Do you have proof?" she asks.

"I can show you a builder's invoice. He didn't give me a receipt."

"Mrs. Campbell, how did you meet Alice?"

"Through Ryan, of course. That night he brought her back. Here. How else am I supposed to have met her? What do you presume? That I found her on the street? That I took out an advert? *Crazy lady seeks whore?* Is that how you do it? Please tell me, because I don't know. I live at home. I work from home. How am I supposed to have met her?"

The pity has gone from her gaze. She's looking at me more carefully now. She's less sure of herself.

"Mrs. Campbell, you've admitted that you suffer from blackouts. You said that you're not aware of what you do when you lose time."

I should never have told her. That was a mistake.

"I black out," I say. "I travel short distances. I prune roses. I tidy cupboards. I fall over. I don't arrange secret deals. I don't drive cars. I don't kill people."

Just as quickly as it came, the anger seems to leave me, like I've exhausted my final reserves of energy.

"Please," I say with a quiet desperation. "Please look into her. Fiona Scott. Late fifties. Widow of Gavin Scott. She lives in Ambleshere. Or at least she used to. I didn't do this. At least I don't think I did. Please. Please. You have to believe me."

Stratton

I'M TRANSPORTED BACK to Mum again. Mum standing at the door of our flat. Mum literally on her knees in front of the arrogant policeman. Begging him to take Karen's disappearance seriously. "Please," she'd said. "Please. You have to believe me."

Mrs. Campbell's staring at me. Begging me.

It goes against all the evidence.

It's a waste of police time.

I should cuff her and read her her rights.

But I don't.

I say yes. I'll look into it.

I need to go now. I have to find and interview this woman today. If it's the dead end it's bound to be, I can still take Mrs. Campbell into the station before lunchtime and Parker will be none the wiser. But if he hears about it, he'll take me off the case. Say I've lost my focus. My judgement.

And he'll be right.

I call Sandra. She's completely trustworthy. Won't rat me out. I ask her to come over and watch Mrs. Campbell while I'm gone. I can't take her to the station or Parker will want to know why I'm not there too and what I'm up to.

Then I call Reynolds. I ask him for the most recent address of a Mrs. Fiona Scott. Used to live in Ambleshere. Maybe still does.

"Do I want to ask why?" he says.

"Nope," I reply.

"OK."

There's a sound of keys tapping. Muffled conversations in the background. Then the phone's back to his ear.

"Ready?"

"Yes." My pen hovers over the notebook.

He reads out an address. Fox Corner, South Lane, Ambleshere. Seems she hasn't moved.

I wait for Sandra to arrive then jump in the car. The satnav says forty-two minutes. I should be there and back in under two hours. And then there'll be no doubt. I'll know I haven't made another mistake. I'll know who Alice's killer is. *And maybe I'll find Karen at last*, the little voice whispers.

As I reach the M25, the clouds start to make way for blue sky. The traffic's not too bad and I get that feeling of escape I always get when I leave London. As I turn off the motorway, the A-road cuts through green fields and there's even a fucking horse sticking its neck over a fence. The villages are film-level pretty. Duck ponds, light stone cottages, that sort of thing. I almost expect to see Bill Nighy sipping a pint at the pub I pass. Maybe it would suit me—the quiet life. The countryside. Fewer crimes. Fresher air . . . No. Who am I kidding? I don't know what the hell I'd do with myself out here. There'd be vicarage tea parties. Vegetable-fucking-growing competitions. Neighbours who'd want to know every aspect of your life, as gossip's the currency. Small minds living small lives. I'd never fit in.

I follow the satnav down a lane that's far too small for a car. Thank fuck I don't meet anyone coming the other way. Then, at last, I'm on a bigger lane and round the bend there's the house—Fox Corner—visible behind a high and smartly trimmed yew hedge. It's grand. Stone. Wooden windows painted a tasteful grey/green. A gravel driveway, double garage attached. I can't believe just one person could live here. Maybe she remarried. Had kids.

OK, Mrs. Scott. Let's do this. I park on the lane and crunch up the drive.

There's a car parked outside—a smart new Mini—the SUV variety. I don't get the appeal. Minis were small. That was the whole point. It's in the fucking name. Supersize one and all you have is a normal car.

I rehearse my opening questions, but then, before I have a chance to ring it, the front door opens and a vicar emerges. I suppress a laugh. A genuine bloody vicar. And one who's watched too many episodes of *Rev*, his white collar contrasting with a pair of jeans. The ecclesiastical equivalent of mutton dressed as lamb. He greets me with a smile and a, "Hullo," then waddles off down the drive to the rest of his flock.

Mrs. Scott spies me through the still-open door.

"Hello, can I help you?" she says curiously.

She's late fifties, five seven—same height as me—with grey-streaked shoulder-length brown hair and strong cheek-bones that protrude from her gaunt face. Her skin's pale, too pale, and her eye sockets sit deep. She's ill. It's written all over her. The vicar's visit is suddenly less amusing. I doubt she'd have the strength to lift a weight, let alone kill someone with it. And the idea of her lifting a sleeping Ryan into the bath. Absurd.

I regret coming. She doesn't need this. Doesn't deserve this visit. I consider leaving, but then I've come all this way. And, selfish as it is, I need to know. For sure this time. The little voice whispers in my ear: *If I'm going to get Karen back.*

I take my ID out of my pocket and hold it facing her. "DI Stratton," I say. "Mrs. Scott, do you mind if I come in and ask you some questions?"

I notice I've unintentionally poshed up my pronunciation. Rich people can sometimes have that effect on me. Well, they push in one of two ways—I either RP it up to impress them or, if they piss me off, I go the other way. Full south London. Either way, I'm annoyed at myself. They don't change for me, so why do I feel the need?

She pauses for a moment, as if disorientated, and then recovers herself.

"Of course," she says. "Please come in. And do call me Fiona. What is it? Has someone been hurt?" Concern flashes across her face.

She guides me through to the kitchen, where a recently boiled old-fashioned copper kettle sits on a hob beneath a cloud of steam. Who the hell gets a hob kettle? Plug the fucker in—it'll save you so much time. The whole place is like something out of a fancy home-and-garden magazine. Huge square marble-topped island, brass taps, flagstone tiles and a massive fireplace that looks like it's still used, as the charred remains of a log sit in the basket. A large wooden farmhouse table sits behind the island in a classy conservatory-style extension.

"Tea?" she offers.

"Yes, please," I say. She makes me a mug and I take it with a smile. We sit at the table. The tea's Earl Grey—I can smell it—and the weakest beige. I'll just be leaving it on the coaster then.

She adjusts her position, as if finding it hard to get comfortable.

"You wanted to ask something?" she prompts. OK. Just leap right in.

"Mrs. Sc—Fiona," I begin. "I apologize if this is distressing, but I need to ask you about your husband. The trial. And what happened after his death."

Her whole body tenses, her back becoming ram-rod straight. I've hit a nerve. Of course I have. Her husband was accused of rape and then died. Her reaction is perfectly normal.

Her finger traces a knot in the wooden table.

"Fiona, did you blame Natalie Campbell for his death?"

The finger pauses then retraces the loop. Slowly, she lifts her eyes.

"At the time I did, yes."

"But not now?"

She stands and then moves towards the glass panels to look out over the garden. She stares, as if fascinated by a pair of pigeons pecking at the lawn.

"Poor girl," she says quietly.

I don't know what to think. Mrs. Campbell had prepared me for vitriol. For hatred. Not pity.

"So you think she was telling the truth?"

Her eyes flick to the right, to where a cat stalks along the foot of a hedgerow.

"Undoubtably. My husband was not a good man, Detective. He hid it well. I only found out after the trial. After his death. Other friends came forward. With stories. Terrible stories. I feel responsible. I should have known."

I don't understand. If she found out so quickly, then why send the letters, the first ones? I ask her.

Her body goes rigid again, legs straightening, elbows locking. She stares at the sky, closes her eyes. Then she opens them again and turns to look at me.

"Knowing you're going to die is a strange feeling," she says. "You have to prepare. For the great unknown. Father Paul's been helping me."

I make a sympathetic noise. I don't know where this is going.

"'Unburdening', he calls it."

I make another noise. She seems to expect it.

"One must meet one's maker with a clear conscience," she says.

She lapses into silence.

"The letters?" I prompt. "If you forgave her, why did you send the letters?"

She swallows.

"I didn't send them," she says.

Natalie

THE FLO MAKES me a second cup of tea and then, sensing that I'm still not in the mood to talk, retakes her seat a discreet distance away. She can keep an eye on me from her perch in a non-intrusive manner. She catches me looking at her and smiles back warmly. I turn my head away. I don't want her reading my face. Seeing the fear and doubt consume me. I put on the radio at a low volume. It doesn't help. Stratton's allegations are spinning round in my head. I paid Alice. I instructed her to lie about my husband. I killed her. I wrote the new letters to myself. God, she probably even thinks I killed Ryan.

It isn't true. It can't be true.

But then a little voice in my ear whispers, *What if it is?* I don't know what happens when I lose time. I wake up minutes, sometimes hours, later. I've travelled. My body has worked. Muscles pulled on bone. The places I end up are usually significant so I must have been guided there by my brain. It's switched on, thinking in those moments, yet I remember nothing. Is there really such a big leap from tidying a cupboard to driving? From pruning roses to hitting a girl over the head? What if I do do terrible things? What if I am actually mad? A psychopath? A killer?

Soldiers can lose their minds after combat. After seeing their comrades blown to pieces. Is that what happened to me after the rape? Have I lost my mind too?

I was meant to be seeing Dr. Browning this afternoon. He was going to help me with coping strategies. Should I call him? Ask him if I could have done this? Do I want to hear his answer?

A memory flashes before my eyes. Alice sitting at our kitchen table. "What do you want me to do?" she says. The words struck me as strange at the time. And the way she was looking at me. As if for instruction. My palms grow sweaty. Another image. I'm accosting Alice outside Ryan's work. "Did he rape you?" I'm asking. She's looking at me, confused. "I don't understand," she says. Which doesn't make sense. Unless I'd told her to accuse him. Then it makes a hell of a lot of sense . . .

I dig my fingernails into my palms.

No. I refuse to accept it.

The first letters were real. No one contests that. And she hated me. I saw that with my own eyes. I saw her face in court. And outside the courthouse, when she confronted me on the steps. Mrs. Scott hated me. She blamed me for destroying her life. Her family. She hated me. Hates me.

Stratton will be there soon. Questioning her.

I need to know what she says.

I'm terrified to know what she says.

The doorbell rings and I stand to answer it, but Sandra tells me to stay comfortable. She'll get it.

There are voices in the hall, then the sound of the door closing. Two pairs of footsteps walk this way.

Stratton

"Fiona, who sent the letters?" I try not to let my frustration show.

She tucks her hair behind her ears as if playing for time, then glances out through the glass again.

"Fiona."

She sighs and then turns and looks me straight in the eye.

"My son," she says flatly.

A son. I wasn't aware of a son. This adds a whole new dimension.

"Do you have children, Detective?" she asks.

"No," I admit.

"If you did, you'd understand. Any parent would try to protect their children. It's hardwired into us. An evolutionary trait. I told the police I sent the letters. It was better that way."

"Why did your son send hate letters?" I ask, trying to keep my voice level. Softly, softly. If I sound like I'm too interested in him, she'll close up or scratch.

"Simple," she says, with an opening of her palms. "He loved his father. It was more than love, in fact. It was a sort of hero worship. Boys can be like that. When they're little they want their mothers. But as they grow up they want to be men. With men." Her hair escapes from behind her ear and she pushes it back again.

"How old was he at the time of the trial?" I ask.

"Seventeen. They were spending so much time together. Camping. Fishing trips. Everyone said I was lucky to have a husband who was such a good father. So involved. Gavin, my husband, told him that he didn't do it. That he was innocent and the girl was lying. My son believed him. He took his father's death very badly."

Seventeen then, twenty-seven now . . .

"Where's your son now?"

A look of sadness crosses her face.

"He moved out at eighteen. Went to university and never came back. He doesn't stay in touch. He hasn't forgiven me for losing faith in his father."

I need to find him. See if there's any way he could be involved in the case.

"Do you know anyone who is in contact with him?"

She suddenly looks worried, as if she's said too much.

"Oh. Oh no. You don't need to worry about him. Is that what this is about? I shouldn't have said anything. It was a short act of teenage rage. Nothing more. He grew out of it. I forgot you're police. I have terrible brain fog these days. He's sorted his life out. I hear from old friends of his. He's doing well. Working hard. And he's one of you now. A detective."

Out of nowhere, I have a horrible feeling. A creeping sense of dread.

"When I first got here," I say, "you reacted strangely when I called you Mrs. Scott. Can I ask you why that was?"

"It's a name I haven't used for a while," she says. "After my husband's death, after I found out his true nature, I reverted to my maiden name. For myself and my son."

"Fiona," I ask, hiding my hands in my lap so she doesn't see them tremble. "What's your maiden name?"

"Bradley," she says.

My heart starts hammering, blood rushing to my ears.

"I'm sorry," I say, forcing my voice to stay level, "but do you have a photo of your son?"

She looks surprised but stands nonetheless and walks over to the mantelpiece that surrounds the huge fireplace. She returns with a frame in her hands and passes it to me. A tall broad man stands on the left; Fiona, younger, beautiful, stands on the right. In the middle of them both a teenage boy smiles for the camera. He takes after his mother rather than his father. The same perfect cheekbones. Brown hair. Hazel eyes. Bradley. Fuck. Bradley.

I stand abruptly, knees colliding with the underside of the table as they straighten. I need to leave. It can't be a coincidence, it can't. It all starts to make sense. Bradley's insistence on protecting the rights of defendants. His penchant for rules. *Family is the most important thing*. He thought his dad was wrongly prosecuted, that the system conspired against him. He blamed Natalie Campbell. He hated her. Hates her. The feeling hasn't gone away. It's festered. Become an obsession. His staring at her, his fascination with her, I mistook for lust. It wasn't. It was a different kind of hunger. He could have gained access. Taken their car. Planted the murder weapon. Planted the box of newspapers and magazines. Planted the burner. He knew about the zopiclone in her velvet bag. He could have drugged Ryan Campbell. He's strong enough to have easily lifted his body into the bath. Slit his wrists.

I stumble over a doorstop in the hall like I'm drunk. I need to get it together.

He used me. He sent me on a wild-goose chase to Virginia Water. He played on my need to find my sister to get me out the way so he could kill the husband. He probably knew the dead woman's tattoo was of a hummingbird. Not a butterfly.

I can't believe I was starting to like him. That I was pleased he was my partner. The betrayal cuts, burns.

There's just one thing I don't know. How did he set it up? How did he find Alice? And why did the friend, Katie, lie?

I start the engine, then, as soon as I'm off the smaller lanes, I dial hands free.

"Katie Roberts," the voice answers. It's hard to make out against the background hum. She's somewhere busy.

I swerve to overtake the car in front.

"Katie, hi, this is DI Stratton. We need to talk."

She sounds surprised to hear from me. I hear her excusing herself and a door open and close. The background noise lessens and I can hear her more clearly.

"Katie, I need to ask you a couple of questions." I stare at the satnav. Right. Then left. The traffic's light, I'm making good progress.

"You said the wife paid Alice to lie about her husband. Are you sure about that?"

"It's what Alice told me." She sounds defensive, annoyed. I'm not handling this well. Another right on to the A-road.

"How did the wife first find Alice?" As I ask the question, I realize this is what's been niggling away at me. The thing I've always glossed over.

"Someone put them in touch. Someone Alice trusted."

"Who, Katie, who?"

There's a pause. I can hear her breathing. I can almost hear the *tick tick tick* of her mind, as she's deciding whether or not to speak. I have no time for this.

"Refusing to cooperate with the police is a very serious offence, Ms. Roberts." I make my tone as threatening as I can.

Another pause. Then she finally speaks.

". . . A policeman. He'd come across Alice before. Caught her with a . . . customer and let her go. He acted as go-between, swore it was all above board. He said the husband was known to his team, that multiple allegations of sexual assault had been levelled against him, but they lacked the evidence to put him away. It's the main reason Alice agreed to go along with it. How could what she was doing be wrong, she reasoned, if a policeman suggested she do it?"

Bradley admitted having dealings with the Latimer Road team on a case. He must have run into Alice while in the area. Maybe that's what gave him the idea. Or maybe the idea had been brewing for years. This was just his first chance to execute it.

It's all falling into place. Natalie Campbell never had any contact with Alice. It was all Bradley. Pretending to be go-between. I should have seen it sooner. No woman would think to weaponize rape in this way. But Bradley... how clever he must have thought he was. Arranging for her husband to be falsely accused in the same way he thought his father was. How much he must have enjoyed watching her suffer. Thinking he was dispensing the ultimate justice.

I feel a sudden flare of anger towards Katie. "Why didn't you tell me this before?"

"I'm sorry," Katie says quietly. "Alice said I could never mention it. That the detective could lose his job. She really liked him. Said he was one of the few good guys left. Said we needed policemen like him."

Bet she did. The fucking irony. Everyone likes Bradley.

Where's he now? At least Sandra's with Mrs. Campbell. She'll keep her safe. I'll just give her a quick call. Tell her to make sure she's always got eyes on her.

The satnav says I'll be there in nineteen minutes.

Natalie

Bradley enters behind Sandra and looks at me intensely.
"Are you OK?" he asks, concerned.

I nod. It's nice to feel cared about.

Sandra tells me that she's needed on another case. That Bradley will stay with me.

"Don't worry," she says. "DI Stratton will be back soon."

She says it like it's reassuring. It's not. It's like I'm waiting for a verdict again. Only this time it's me in the dock.

Bradley walks Sandra to the door, then I hear the sound of it shutting. He comes back through the kitchen and into the living area. He's carrying a bag. He looks different. His face looks different. He's no longer smiling, but it's more than that. His eyes have hardened. Deadened. His lips look cruel rather than generous. He starts to remind me of someone.

He puts the bag down and crouches next to it. He unzips it and takes out a pair of thin latex gloves, which he proceeds to put on.

"What are you doing?" I ask quietly.

He stares at me but doesn't answer. Instead he removes two long lengths of rope from the bag.

Fear begins to stud my skin.

"What's going on?" I ask, my voice trembling.

"You genuinely thought I liked you, didn't you?" he says, looking at me with detachment, like I'm a butterfly he's about to pin to a frame. "I thought I might be overdoing it, but no, you expected the flattery. Expected the concern. Is that why you turned on him? Lied? Because he didn't worship you enough?"

I feel like I've switched realities, slid sideways into a dark, parallel world. Who is this man? Where's the kind detective gone?

"Who?" I ask. "Who did I turn on? When did I lie?"

He laughs. A harsh mocking sound.

"The stress got to you," he says, turning his attention to the rope, tugging at a section, testing its strength. "The stress and the guilt. You couldn't live with what you'd done. Killing Alice, killing your husband, so you decided to take your own life."

What's he planning? To kill me? God, he's planning to kill me.

"I don't understand," I say. "Why are you acting like this?"

"Whores need to pay," he says. He moves position and the light hits his face at a different angle. All the air is knocked out of my lungs. I can't believe I didn't see it before. It was hidden by the smile, rendered fuzzy by the mask of concern. I thought he reminded me of someone. I thought he looked like a guy from law school. How was I so blind? The shape of the eyes. The curve of the mouth. Traces of Gavin Scott's features.

No. No . . . My mind flashes back to the trial. I'd always focused on the wife sitting there, staring at me. Never on the teenage boy sat at her side.

"You're his son, aren't you?" The words come out in gasps.

"You lied about him. You killed him. You destroyed our family."

He starts to loop one of the ends of the rope round.

"No! No. I didn't lie. He raped me. Please. Believe me." I stare pleadingly at him, willing him to look into my eyes, to see my soul. Instead his eyes graze my face then return to the rope.

"No, you're a whore. You spread your legs for him. I saw you in the car. Touching my leg. Pretending it was an accident. Flirting. You would have spread them for me too. I know it."

"You sent the letters, didn't you?" I'm playing for time. My phone's on the side in the kitchen. Could I get there before him? Call the police?

He's the police.

"Of course I did," he answers. "My mother's weak. She believed you, you see. Not at the time. In the end, though. She listened to your lies and believed you. She didn't deserve my father."

I stand and try to run to the kitchen. I'm past him, through the arch. Hand reaching for the phone. Then his arm's round my waist and he's pulling me backwards. I struggle and scratch but he has me held too tight.

He starts to tie one of the ropes around me, pinning my arms to my sides. I struggle, resist, but it's futile. He's too strong for me.

"It's all over," he says. "'The end', remember?" He smiles, but it's not the same smile as before. There's such a bitterness to it. The teeth are lupine.

"Why kill Alice?" I ask. "She did nothing to you."

"She could have given me away. People always say they won't talk, but they do. At some point, they all do. Besides, she was a whore too. Had sex for money. You, Alice. You're all the same."

He throws me on to the sofa, looming over me as he finishes tying the second rope into a noose.

"And it is you, Natalie, who killed her. Not me. If you hadn't lied, none of this would have had to happen. You killed her. You killed your husband too."

"You'll never get away with this," I say.

He smiles again. That same dark, bitter smile. He takes his phone out of his pocket, then sits next to me, hand clamped over my mouth.

He dials and it goes to voicemail. I hear Sandra's bubbly voice on the other end. I try to scream, but his hand clamps my jaw closed.

"Hi, Sandra," he says. "Bradley here. I have to go out of the house a moment. There's a disturbance across the street. I won't be ten minutes. Mrs. Campbell's promised not to let anyone in."

I press my jaw forward, teeth scrabbling for purchase, and manage to bite his finger. I clamp down tighter, tasting blood. He moves his hand and I scream, but it's too late. He's already hung up. She won't have heard me.

He shakes his bitten finger and stares at me. "I left, and you seized the window of opportunity. How was I to know what you'd do?"

He grabs the back of my neck and steers me out of the living room and into the kitchen. On the way he stops at the radio and turns up the volume, R.E.M's "Shiny Happy People" filling the house. He pauses at the end of the dining table to wrap his other hand round the back of the green chair and then pushes me into the hall, dragging the chair behind him. I try to headbutt him, to kick him, but his grip on my neck is too tight. I can't twist my body round.

He stops directly beneath the hall light then kicks me to the ground. My brain's leaping, looking for exits, but there aren't any. He's blocking the front door. I'd only trap myself if I went upstairs. It's as if he reads my thoughts though, as suddenly he's straddling me, retying the rope so that my legs are trussed too. I can't move. I can't run. Instead I writhe on the floor, watching as he stands on the chair and unhooks the heavy brass lantern. He sits it on the floor next to me, the glass diffracting rainbows of lights.

"No one will question it," he says. "I've watched you. Followed you. At the gym. In cafés. In shops. To the therapist. You have few friends. You have a history of anxiety and depression. You're unstable. It'll be written off as sad but inevitable, given the circumstances."

He threads the second rope through the hook in the ceiling, tying the other end to the stair banister, then tests its weight. A satisfied smile spreads over his face. I watch him.

The noose dangles.

I identify all his vulnerable spots. Eyes. Balls. Kidneys. But it's no use. My hands are tied.

He grabs me and pulls me roughly to standing, left hand wrapping round my waist so that I'm clamped to his body. I scream again.

"Your blackouts, 'losing time'—whatever you want to call them—were the icing on the cake. I could have managed without them of course, but it did make my life so much easier."

He lifts me on to the chair then forces the noose over my head and around my neck. No. No. It can't end like this. I scream again, but know that it's pointless. The neighbours will be at work. The radio drowns me out.

He yanks up the rope so that I have to stand on tiptoes, then reties it to the banister. Calmly, he unties the ropes from my legs—of course, I can't be found tied up if it's supposed to be a suicide—then my arms. I flex my fingers, preparing to lunge . . .

"Goodbye, Natalie," he says.

And then he kicks the chair away.

My vision is pixellating. My body is falling.

Neck squeezing.

Lungs cracking.

Tongue swelling.

Fear.

Fear.

Fear.

Then blackness.

Stratton

Sandra doesn't answer the first time I call. Sweat beads on my forehead and starts to drip down my face.

I wait two minutes then try again.

"FLO Digby," she says.

Thank God.

"Sandra. It's Stratton. Have you got eyes on Natalie Campbell?"

There's a pause.

"Sorry, no. I got called away on another case."

"Fuck, Sandra, I said it was important. She wasn't to be left alone."

Sandra rushes to reassure me.

"Oh, don't worry. She's not alone. Bradley took over babysitting duty. He'll be there with her now."

Fuck. Fuck.

I look at the satnav. Eight minutes back to Sheen. If I take the back roads I could skip a section of the South Circular and be at her address in five.

Will that be quick enough?

Fuck.

I call Reynolds. Tell him to get Uniform to Mrs. Campbell's. An all-units call-out.

"I thought Bradley was there?" he says.

"He is," I reply. "He's to be treated as hostile. I'll fill you in later."

Pressing down on the accelerator, I increase speed, weaving in and out of the other cars.

A driver beeps me. Then another. And another.

Tyres screeching, I turn off up Hertford Avenue, the suspension hitting against the top of the speed humps as I take them far too fast.

Along Vicarage Road then right down Sheen Lane. Left into Sheen Common Road.

There's no police car outside; I'm first on the scene. I abandon my car in the middle of the road and then race the last few steps to the house. The door is locked. I take a run at it, slamming my shoulder against the door. It doesn't budge. Pain stabs in my shoulder from the impact. Fuck. I try again. The door teeters this time, then comes off its hinges.

I'm inside.

I don't need to look for her. She's right there in front of me. Hanging from a rope tied to the banister. Body swaying. Eyes bulging. She hasn't been hanging long if she's still moving. There's a chance. I run forward and grab her legs, lifting her higher so the rope is no longer taking her weight and throttling her. Is she breathing? I can't tell. I can't cut her down while I'm supporting her. Fuck.

Then there's the wail of sirens from the street and the strobing of blue light. Uniform. A young policewoman and her partner enter the property and take in the scene. They don't panic. They've been trained well.

"Cut her down," I instruct. The policewoman immediately acts. She's up the stairs, and takes a penknife from her zip pocket and starts to saw at the rope. The policeman steps forward and helps take the weight of the body. The rope snaps and we stagger as she changes position. Carefully we lay her down and loosen the noose. A purple welt circles her neck. I put my cheek next to her lips to check for breath. It's more reliable than a pulse. Nothing. She could be dead. Or she could be unconscious. I kneel by her chest, start CPR. One rescue breath then thirty chest compressions—the heel of my hand on her sternum, arms straight, fingers interlocked. One rescue breath. Thirty pumps. One rescue breath. Thirty pumps.

Then suddenly she's coughing. She's alive and she's coughing. Tears form at the edge of my eyes. The policewoman hugs me.

She's alive.

We're alive.

Suddenly the mere act of living seems the greatest gift.

With the PO's help I move her into the recovery position.

Then I'm aware of another presence behind me.

I turn slowly.

It's Bradley. He's walked in through the front door. He's plastered on a look of concern. He's good. He's really good.

"What happened? Oh no. I was only gone ten minutes. Is she . . . Oh God, is she . . ."

"Hold him," I say to the policeman. He looks at me, as if I've made a mistake. "Hold him," I repeat.

Bradley struggles, but the policeman manages to restrain him. I circle round and cuff him.

"Hugh Bradley, or should I say Scott? You are under arrest for the murders of Alice Lytton and Ryan Campbell and the attempted murder of Natalie Campbell."

I read him his rights.

I spit on the ground as I leave.

APRIL

Natalie

I TAKE ONE day at a time. The house is on the market. I've decided to move somewhere smaller. Somewhere else. I'm thinking Bath, maybe. It's beautiful there, and I'd be nearer to Meena. It'd be good to get to know her family properly.

There's a course at Bath Uni I might enrol in. Garden design. I could still write legal articles part time, but it might be good to throw myself into my hobbies.

Dr Browning has recommended a therapist there. He's also given me the name of the clinic in the Netherlands that uses psilocybin during PTSD therapy. I might contact them. It scares me, but I also like the idea that something as simple as a fungus might provide a cure. Of nature healing me.

This time, choosing to move house doesn't feel like I'm running away.

It's something I want to do.

For me.

Stratton

Bradley confesses to it all. The worst part is that, at first, he thinks I'll understand. That we're the same. We bend rules for our family. Family's the most important thing. I have to leave the room at that point. I'm nothing like him. Never will be. The only thing he shows any remorse for is for lying to me. He said he knew the body they pulled out of Virginia Water wasn't Karen. He knew the tattoo was of a humming bird and not a butterfly, but he needed me out of the way. I hope they lock him away for the rest of his life.

As soon as the interview is over I walk into Parker's office. He looks up at me. His skin's grey, eyes tinged red from lack of sleep. No doubt worrying about how he's going to spin it. How he's going to explain we had a predator in our midst and didn't know. How the public shouldn't feel alarmed. How we can all trust the boys in blue.

"Did he confess?" he asks slowly.

I nod.

"Right." I can't tell if he's pleased or not. I think he's neither. Just tired.

I reach into my blazer pocket and retrieve the warrant card that sits there. I lay it down on Parker's desk, facing him.

He looks confused.

"What's this?"

I wait till he meets my eyes then I tell him that I'm done. I can't serve in a force that lets people like that in.

Parker tries to talk me out of it, but I don't listen. I stand and leave, shutting the door on his words. His platitudes.

Reynolds, Dev and Sandra all watch me remove my things from my desk and head out. I ignore their questions. I'm too numb to say goodbye.

Natalie

We buried Ryan yesterday. I hadn't expected grief to hit me like it has. I thought his infidelity was a barrier. A dam. But the dam's broken and it's come. A piercing, disabling grief. I've lost my life partner. The one person who always believed me. He was flawed, of course, but then, aren't we all? And I think he really did love me.

Rachel didn't come to the funeral. I didn't ask her. I won't be asking her to anything again. I thought she was my crutch, but she wasn't. She was more like a parasite. She liked the way I looked up to her. Relied on her. But even that wasn't enough. She had to also try and take what was mine.

Stratton came by to check on me. I didn't think she was the sort. She told me Bradley had confessed to it all. He'd been planning it for years. Looking for his moment to act. He'd broken in, taken the keys, driven the car that night, planted the murder weapon and the newspapers. He'd put the sleeping pills in a protein shake. Left it on the side for Ryan with a Post-it note of a hand-drawn heart stuck on it so Ryan would think I'd made it for him. He'd brought a rope and a syringe of animal tranquillizer in case he'd had to tie me up or knock me out. He hadn't had to, of course. The last letter, he'd paid a kid to deliver.

I shiver at it all. The coldness. The planning. The obsession.

He's proof of the dangers of holding on to the past. Of how it can eat you up.

I'm not going to let that happen to me.

I need to move forward.

It's time to finally leave the past behind.

To live.

Stratton

I DESCEND INTO a dark place. Days are filled with mindless television—overly shiny people sitting on overly bright settees spouting crap. I don't shower. I rarely go outside. To the corner shop and back, nothing more. Pat there asks if I'm OK. I force a smile. I'm fine. Everything's fine. Parker keeps ringing. Sandra and Reynolds did too, at first, but now they've stopped. Parker's the most persistent. I'm surprised. I didn't think that's the way it would play out. I don't answer though. What is there to say? In the end I just turn off my phone.

* * *

The detectives come four days later. They wear black suits and serious expressions. I show them into the lounge and clear an old ready meal from the settee so they have somewhere to sit. I'm not used to visitors. I see their noses wrinkle and open a window. It must smell fucking awful in here. I've just got too used to it to notice.

The taller, thinner one, Detective Sivyer, does all the talking. They're sorry to turn up unannounced. They tried to call in advance but they couldn't get through. They've found another of the Manchester Strangler's victims. Female. Forensics put the body at around age sixteen when killed. She'd been in the ground for thirty years. Buried in Epping Forest.

I become very aware of my heart beat. My breathing.

"Did you find any ID on her?" I ask.

They shake their heads.

"What about clothing?" I ask.

Again. No. Everything's decomposed. They found bones. Nothing more. They're waiting on dental records checks.

Then I'm confused.

"Why come to me?"

"The Strangler said something when he gave us the location of the grave."

"What? What did he say?"

"He called her his little butterfly."

It's her. It's Karen.

"We scoured the missing persons reports. We saw the one your mother filed."

I knew she was dead; it's the only thing that made sense. I knew I was looking for a body, but it still hurts. It really hurts. And the fact that she was strangled. Left the world in that way.

I thank the detectives and walk them to the door.

* * *

The dental records match.

Mum comes to the funeral. I chose a crematorium close to the nursing home. I decided on cremation. Karen's spent too long buried under ground already.

I help Mum into a black dress and then Angie and another nurse help lift her into the minibus and then out into a wheelchair.

The crematorium chapel is only half full. Me, Mum and Angie sit in the front. A couple of the other more with-it residents from the home are there too. At the back sit Sandra, Reynolds and Dev. Sandra shoots me a sad smile and I nod an acknowledgement. Just before the service starts, Parker enters too, his leather-soled shoes loud against the stone floor. He bobs his head apologetically. I didn't invite them. Word must have filtered through the force. But they came. All of them.

And I'm grateful. They never knew Karen, of course, but they know me. They're my second family. I don't know how I think I could have walked away from them.

I give a eulogy. I keep it short. Manage not to choke. Mum looks at me when I return to the pew.

"You're a good girl, Helen," she says. Then I do choke and I can't stop the tears from coming.

The vicar starts a final prayer and I find myself getting on to my knees and thanking God.

Thanking him for finally giving me back my big sister and my mum.

At the end we file out into the sunshine and I leave Mum with Angie while I go and have a word with Parker, who's standing awkwardly by a clump of daffodils, looking repeatedly at me and then back at the ground.

He smiles slightly nervously as he sees me approach.

"Thanks for coming," I say.

"How are you doing?" he asks. "Really?"

"I'm OK," I say. "At least I will be."

"Good. That's good."

My eyes sweep the group. There are good people on the force too. As for the others, the bad ones, Mum's words from nearly thirty years ago echo in my head. *Nobody ever changed anything from the outside.*

In my periphery I see Angie beckon me over. She needs help with Mum. I turn to go.

"Oh, and Parker," I call over my shoulder, "I'll see you Monday."

And with that I walk away.

ACKNOWLEDGMENTS

If it takes a village to raise a child, it takes a small town to produce a book. I'm enormously grateful to all the people who helped shape this story and make it the best it could possibly be. Huge thanks first to Rowland White, my brilliant editor, for really championing this book and for your insights which are second to none. Thanks also to Grace Long for your energy and expertise. I feel honoured to work with the whole Penguin Michael Joseph team including Lee Motley, Ellie Morley, Sriya Varadharajan, Emma Henderson, Riana Dixon, Serena Nazareth, Christina Ellicott, Kelly Mason, Eleanor Rhodes Davies, Bronwen Davies and Hannah Padgham. Thanks also to my eagle-eyed copy editor Sarah Day. My US editor, Marcia Markland, and her team at Crooked Lane Books have been equally enthusiastic and supportive—thank you.

I am so lucky to have the wonderful Jane Finigan as my agent—thanks so much for taking me on and making my dreams of becoming an adult thriller writer come true. Thank you also to Prema Raj and the foreign rights team at Lutyens Rubinstein, Mark Casarotto, my film agent, for selling the TV rights and David Forrer at InkWell Management for securing my US deal.

Thanks so much to my early readers—Sarah Harris, Nina Duckworth and Helen Ballard—for your really helpful feedback and encouragement and to my author friends for letting me moan on and on at you—you know who you are!

Thanks to my parents, sisters and all my family, to Earl—my not-so-secret weapon—and to Noa, Alba and Ned, for being generally awesome and for staying out of the attic long enough to let me write this book.

Finally, thanks to you, the reader, for picking this book up and giving it a go. I hope you enjoyed it and that it will be the first of many!